summer
at firefly
beach

BOOKS BY JENNY HALE

The Summer Hideaway
The Summer House
Summer at Oyster Bay
Summer by the Sea
A Barefoot Summer
We'll Always Have Christmas
All I Want for Christmas
Christmas Wishes and Mistletoe Kisses
A Christmas to Remember
Coming Home for Christmas
It Started with Christmas

summer
at firefly
beach

JENNY HALE

bookouture

Published by Bookouture in 2019

An imprint of StoryFire Ltd.

Carmelite House
50 Victoria Embankment
London EC4Y 0DZ

www.bookouture.com

ISBN: 978-1-78681-734-1
eBook ISBN: 978-1-78681-733-4

For Mary, who I truly believe has been
a silent creative force in our family.

Chapter One

If there was anything Hallie Flynn should have learned over the years, it was to listen to her best friend Ben Murray. But she never did. And today was no different.

At fourteen, she hadn't listened when he'd advised against her eating the entire triple-decker strawberry sundae at Milly's Ice Cream. She'd insisted she could eat it all, but spent the rest of the evening lying on the sofa, unable to move, shooing away her mother's dinner offers. Or the time he'd promised her that she looked better as a natural brunette rather than a platinum blonde, but she'd bleached her hair anyway.

And now, in the face of grief, he was by her side again, and she knew she needed to listen to his advice even though she wasn't sure she would.

The news article her mother had kept on the counter for the last few months was burned in her memory: *Firefly Beach resident, locally loved and nationally known designer Clara Abigail Flynn-Eubanks, of the much-admired Starlight Cottage, passed away after battling a heart tumor, surrounded by family, at 9:07 p.m. Tuesday…*

Ben had been a strong emotional support for her through Aunt Clara's funeral six months ago, and today he was there to do the same.

"Let me take a look at the list again," Ben said, stepping over from the edge of her mama's driveway, his blue eyes just as concerned now as they had been when she'd first told him about Aunt Clara's final and very personal letter to her, and the list she'd included within it.

A prolific letter-writer, Aunt Clara had started writing to everyone she knew the moment she'd heard that she wasn't going to beat the tumor. Her family had all gotten hand-written words from her, with her wishes for them and what she was leaving behind as a gift to each one of them, but only Hallie's had a stipulation to go along with it.

Hallie retrieved her great aunt's crumpled letter from her pocket and held it in her fist. She'd carried it around since she'd gotten it, trying to make sense of it. Aunt Clara had given her a list to complete before she could receive her inheritance, but the list was one Hallie had written herself when she was only twelve years old. And if that wasn't perplexing enough, the additional piece of the puzzle was the fact that her inheritance was a mystery, sealed in a second envelope and locked away in the family safe.

She held it out to Ben and then leaned over his shoulder as he read it.

Things I want to do before I die:
1. *Build a three-foot sandcastle like Uncle Hank can.*
2. *Become a photographer.*
3. *Live somewhere new.*
4. *Kiss a boy I love.*
5. *Make a wish and have it come true.*

"I agree with you; it does sound crazy," he said, scanning the list again. He passed it back to Hallie and she stuffed it into her pocket. "But what if the answer for why Clara asked you to do these things is so simple that you can't see it?"

"Okay. Then what is it?"

He chuckled. "It's so simple I can't see it either." But then he sobered, that familiar look of fondness washing over him. "That doesn't mean you shouldn't try to complete it. I think you should."

Of course Ben thought she should. Hallie closed her eyes and filled her lungs with humid, sun-soaked air, aching to hear the gulls overhead and feel the rush of turquoise water around her ankles like she had so many summers. But even that wouldn't soothe her this time.

Ben was suggesting that she could actually do this. Nothing she'd done in the last year had been a success, and this, she feared, would be no different.

"Remember when I was sixteen years old and you caught me dressing up in Mama's wedding dress?" Hallie asked him, squinting to focus on him through the blazing Tennessee sunlight that only June could bring, Ben's presence causing memories of her childhood to roll in like a gust of coastal wind.

"Yeah," Ben said quietly as he stood in front of her, a calming presence in the midst of a chaotic day. He had his hands in his pockets, so relaxed that she was actually envious of the steadiness in his breath, the lack of tension in his shoulders. She wanted to know the feeling of it again, to have that kind of peace soak into her bones and heal her aching heart.

"As a girl, I never imagined *not* wearing that dress one day or having a family of my own." She pinched the bridge of her nose, tears welling up as they did so often these days, and like a flash, Ben was at her side, rubbing the tops of her arms to comfort her. She squeezed her eyes shut until the wetness in them dissolved.

The hurrying around, and the noise from her family buzzing back and forth to the car all morning, had given Hallie a headache. The car was parked in front of Ben's jeep, both vehicles packed to the brim with beach chairs, suitcases, bags of food... To anyone else, it would seem they were all going on a summer vacation full of laughs and long days in the salty spray of the ocean.

But that was far from the truth.

A memory of happier times at Starlight Cottage slipped into her consciousness despite her diligence to avoid thinking of it at all: Hallie and Ben were teenagers. Ben had chased her down the beach with a giant water-launcher as she dodged the pelting spray, her laughing slowing her down, Ben gaining on her while Aunt Clara and Uncle Hank hooted from the dock.

The recollection, however, was too difficult to manage now, after Aunt Clara's death. Even as she pushed it out of her mind, snippets of other memories found their way through. Like the crunch of crushed shells under her feet as she ran down the seashell path, sketchpad in hand, to draw the sunset before it disappeared. Or the walkway leading to the grand front porch; the place she sat with Aunt Clara for hours talking about design, Hallie showing her the pictures she'd drawn of ideas for how to rearrange her bedroom.

If Hallie closed her eyes she could see the old ship's rope that wrapped around the large posts lining the winding drive, or the lattice of the gazebo out back, painted white to match the other buildings on the grounds, the place she'd dreamed of getting married as a girl...

She ran her thumb around her now bare ring finger, its nakedness a glaring reminder of everything that had gone wrong over the last few months—the painful days, the even more excruciating discussions, the counselors... She was the third Flynn to have gambled on love and lost. But that was only the side of things that she'd shared with her family. She dared not say the rest out loud for fear nothing would ever be normal again.

"I still remember what you said about the dress."

"What was that?" Ben asked, his gaze on her.

"You told me to take it off, that it didn't look like me."

The corner of Ben's mouth twitched upward and she knew now that he remembered that day. Their shared moment was a welcome diversion from the life she'd been living recently. Just that tiny smile filled her with hope that things could get better, as if the whole ordeal was some sort of nightmare she could wake up from if she just stayed locked in Ben's eyes. Yesterday, when he'd come over to help them pack, was the first time in four months that she'd seen him or even so much as gotten a text. Even when they'd moved away and attended different colleges, they'd called each other nearly every day. But recently, their lives had moved in different directions, and when they had, she'd felt disoriented.

"You also said that it's impossible to have any fun in a dress like that. And after I changed, you took me by the hand and dragged me into the woods and made me climb that big oak tree that scared me to death, remember?"

Ben broke into a laugh then, and a content grin settled upon his lips. "Yep."

"When we got to the top, we sat there on that thick branch we'd found, looking out over the hillside. We were up so high that I was shaking like a leaf, but you were totally relaxed. You pointed to the sky and that hot air balloon swung right over us. It felt like I could've reached up and touched the basket. It was so beautiful that it took my breath away."

By the look on Ben's face, the memory was clear. There was an undeniable fondness in his expression. She could always count on Ben when she was scared. He was that calm force in the storm inside her head. When he'd arrived this morning, she wanted to cling to him, to feel his arms around her to keep her safe from her troubling thoughts. But they'd had work to do to get ready for their trip, so instead, she'd simply stayed by his side, allowing the feeling of being with him, his composure and peaceful demeanor, to wash over her and cleanse her of the misery that plagued her.

"You said," she continued, "'See? You can have lots more fun when you aren't in that old dress.'"

He'd been so right. And the last month, when things had gotten substantially worse, she felt like she couldn't breathe without Ben's support. It had been so long since she'd held his reassuring hand… When faced with her biggest fear, even her fiancé Jeff couldn't fill the void, and by that point she and Jeff had lost most of the love they'd had for one another anyway. She'd wanted to hear Ben tell her it would all be okay, despite the fact that she knew it wouldn't, because she trusted him with her life, and even if he was the only one who believed it, that would be enough.

"I should've listened to you way back then," she admitted, swallowing to keep her emotions in check. She'd stopped the counselor appointments earlier than recommended, and she'd been struggling, but now she had even more to deal with. "It was true. And Jeff and I rushed into things. It's as if we both noticed something wasn't right as soon as he asked me to marry him." She didn't dare tell Ben the rest.

"What happened to finally end it?"

Her breath sped up and she felt lightheaded, scrambling to come up with something that wasn't a lie but also hid the real truth. "I think the finality of an engagement made us take a hard look at one another, you know?"

Ben nodded.

"I realize now that I didn't love Jeff the way I should love someone before jumping into a marriage, but in the early days of our relationship it felt so good to have that person there every day to rely on, you know?" She kicked at a stone on the pavement. "And now when I'm faced with this…" Hallie surveyed the packed car, its engine running on all cylinders to cool off the interior in the summer heat before they headed out. "I feel exposed, like I don't have anyone to lean on," she confessed.

"You can always lean on me," Ben said.

After so much time away from her, his words almost brought her to tears again. She was so happy to hear him say that.

"Hallie?" Mama's voice sailed between them.

Ben offered a knowing look. "I'll help her," he said, and headed inside the house to get the last few things when Hallie's mother called again, like she had all morning.

"Thanks."

To clear her heavy thoughts, Hallie closed her eyes and listened to the rustle of the trees against a single uncharacteristically strong breeze that blew through, cooling her skin briefly before disappearing to wherever all the air went during the summer months in Nashville. The stagnant warmth fell upon her once more. It was this feeling of dead heat that used to fill her with excitement when they packed for Firefly Beach, as she yearned for soft white sand under her bare feet, the continuous wind that rippled the light, gauzy sundress she liked to wear over her bikini, and the scent that only came from her family's unique mixture of home cooking and coconut cocktails.

"I don't know if we've packed the wine," Mama said, rushing past Ben as he entered the house, her arms full. "Hallie?" She maneuvered around Hallie, threw it all in the backseat, and shut the car door again.

"Did you get the wine from the fridge and put it in the cooler? I didn't see anyone bring it out." Mama thrust the paper with the article about Aunt Clara into Hallie's hands. "Let's take this to show Uncle Hank. I don't know if he has a copy, and he might want to read these kind words."

Hallie clutched the folded newspaper to her body. With the final preparations for their journey nearly complete, the weight in Hallie's chest felt even more cumbersome than it had before.

"Oh, Ben! You're a doll!" Mama hurried over to Ben and planted a kiss on his cheek after he returned with her two bottles of chardonnay. He handed them over. "Hallie, where's your sister?" Grasping the wine, her mother wiped the perspiration from her forehead with her wrist, and then placed the bottles into the cooler wedged between two suitcases in the open trunk. Then she ran back inside without waiting for an answer.

She'd been going a hundred miles an hour all morning—Hallie knew it was her way of handling her emotions. When she was more herself, Mama had a lively personality with a laugh that could make anyone happy.

"You've got this," Ben whispered into her ear, standing behind Hallie, his gentle but strong hands on her shoulders, pulling her in tentatively, as if he wasn't sure if he was allowed to embrace her like he used to. Things had changed so much over the last four months, but that shouldn't have changed at all. He was her best friend. She leaned in to him to let him know that.

Ben could always assess the situation and offer kind, caring suggestions that never failed her. But even *his* words couldn't break through the grief that kept ebbing and flowing since she'd heard about Aunt Clara. She tucked the paper under her arm, her palms sweaty from nerves, her hands shaking.

Mustering strength from the bottom of her empty shell of a body, Hallie turned around to face him. "*Do* I have this?" She noticed then that her voice sounded withered and exhausted, the tears just waiting to spill over like they had the other times she'd allowed herself to think about life without Aunt Clara. Her favorite aunt, who was known for her impeccable timing, had left Hallie at her very lowest and because of that, there were times when Hallie wasn't sure if her shattered heart could make it through this.

Ben wrapped his arms around her and let Hallie bury her head in his chest. The familiar scent of clean cotton and the mix of mint, sandalwood, and vanilla had filled her lungs more times than she could count. She closed her eyes to keep from sobbing. As if he could detect her swell of sadness, he squeezed her tighter like he was holding her together. And in a sense, he was.

"Thank you for being here," she said into his shirt, her words broken but his embrace making her feel a little better for the moment. Hallie pulled back. "I hate that it was this situation that brought us back together, but I'm glad it did. We haven't seen each other in months. That's not like us." She'd wanted to hear his voice so many times over those months, but in every instance that she'd considered calling him she hadn't, because she thought she should be strong enough to deal with her own problems. But even when she'd decided not to tell him what was going on, she ached to have her best friend there to talk to. She'd think about it in the middle of the night, but couldn't call then... "Why did we let time get away from us?"

Ben took a step back, and she let go of him.

He looked over the car, to somewhere in the distance. "Life, you know?" he said, his face full of thoughts.

"Yeah..."

Suddenly, the words tumbled out like they'd been waiting to erupt from her heart this whole time. "I wish we could spend time together with nothing hanging over us." She longed for the days when they were young, when they had their whole lives ahead of them. "I love being with you because you don't want anything more than what we have, and it makes me feel safe."

Ben held her gaze. He didn't have to say anything because after all their years together, she knew he understood.

"Hey, baby girl. You doin' okay?" Hallie's older sister Sydney said from behind them. She stepped up next to Hallie and rubbed her back, her consoling eyes having met a few tears this morning as well.

Hallie took in a jagged breath and gave her sister a sympathetic half-smile. They would get through this, she told herself, although she wasn't sure she believed it. Hallie piled her long hair onto her head to combat the sweltering weather. The heat was so strong today that she could see it as it danced off the long winding asphalt drive, rising into the sky in hazy waves and disappearing amidst the view of the surrounding hills.

"Ben! I want to ride with you!"

Sydney's seven-year-old son Robby came running out, hopping excitedly in front of Ben. Like Hallie, he'd been by Ben's side all day, until Sydney had made him sit down for breakfast before they got on the road. Ben took him by the hands and spun him around, Robby's feet flying, his laughter floating into the air, the sound like angels singing in the hollows of Hallie's mind. When Ben set him down again, Robby wrapped his arms around his waist.

"I think you're gonna go with your mom," Ben told him. "But we're all heading to the same place."

Robby pulled away and pretended to pout, but his face brightened right up involuntarily around Ben. "Will you show me the new fishing pole you bought?"

"Of course I will! I was planning to have *you* fish with it." He lunged toward him with his fingers in the Tickle Monster position, the way he always did with Robby, making Robby dart out of the way with a giggle, the boy's light brown hair fanning across his forehead with the movement.

"And can we play football?" Robby asked, still snickering as he ducked Ben's arm.

"Absolutely."

Robby maneuvered around them and climbed through the last open door of Mama's car, wriggling into a comfortable position in the backseat next to a blow-up donut and a bag of sand toys. He pulled the seatbelt out and attempted to fasten it, his little hands sweaty in the heat, causing him to struggle to secure it. Ben walked over and helped him.

"Will you ride with us, Ben? *Please?*" Robby asked.

"If I ride with you, then that means Hallie will have to drive my jeep, and you remember what it was like when she tried to take it to the store that one night?"

"That was a whole year ago," Hallie said, having nothing better to retort, glad for the lighter conversation, the pain shifting to the back of her mind for just a moment, giving her much-needed relief.

"And how many stick shifts have you driven since then? You need me!" He winked at her.

Yes. She certainly did.

"If you want me to get there, Robby, I have to drive."

Hallie made a face at him, but she knew he was only teasing her to make Robby smile.

"Honey, did Nana seem like she was about finished inside?" Sydney asked.

Robby shrugged.

"I'll go check on her," Sydney said.

They'd all finished packing, but Mama had kept going back in, announcing things they "needed," but sooner or later, Mama too would have to face the road ahead. They were all just letting her prepare herself to do that in her own way.

Sydney went into the house and brought Mama outside onto the porch. Beau barked from Ben's jeep. Ben had taken the top off of his vehicle, and the lab-spaniel mix had been waiting patiently in the back most of the time. Ben walked over to him and petted the top of his head.

"Almost time, boy," he said, checking that the bowl of water he'd set in the backseat was still full.

Beau looked at Ben with those big trusting brown eyes, his tongue hanging out the side of his mouth. Hallie could almost swear she could make out a smile on the dog's face. A faithful companion, Beau never left Ben, trusting Ben's every move. Hallie could understand that kind of devotion completely because, growing up, Ben had been that type of person for her too.

"Anything else we need?" Mama asked from the open front door. She tried to fluff her short, disheveled hair, the few graying strands she had nestled in the crop of dark brown catching the light, making her look older than her face would suggest.

There was nothing more they could possibly pack. When no one spoke, she locked up behind her.

"I guess we're as ready as we'll ever be," Sydney said.

"Has anyone texted Uncle Hank?" Mama worried aloud.

Ben raised his phone. "I did. I told him we'll see him in about nine hours."

Robby leaned out of the car, oblivious to the emotions they'd all been keeping from the seven-year-old for his benefit. He'd put on his sunglasses. With a grin, he said, "Firefly Beach, here we come!"

Chapter Two

"How many have we found so far?" Ben asked, tapping his fingers against the steering wheel as he counted. "I've got three, right?"

Hallie rode beside Ben in the metallic sierra blue vintage jeep he'd treated himself to, using the first earnings he'd made after opening his own production company on Music Row in Nashville. One of his newest bands, Sylvan Park, was playing loudly over the jeep's speakers and had been since they'd emerged off of Interstate 65, heading south, the melody as carefree as any summer day should be.

Hallie looked down at the sheet of paper that had been waiting for her in the passenger seat along with an ink pen when she got in. It was one of their road-trip games: every time they took the nine-hour drive to Firefly Beach, Ben made a list of things they had to find on the way down, and the person who found the most bought the other their first drink when they got there. Hallie was always amazed at how they'd played this every trip and he managed never to repeat the items from year to year. This list had been the most challenging of them all.

"You've got a Virginia license plate, a baseball cap…" Hallie ran her finger down the long list of items in search of the third spot where she'd put his initials. "And—"

"Teddy bear!" he cut her off, pointing to the car next to them.

Hallie looked inside the vehicle beside them to find a little girl clutching an oversized pink bear. "How can you even see that when you're driving?" she asked with a laugh.

"No idea. That's four."

"Hang on. I think you have three."

"No, I have four. And you have two. Check the list. You're goin' down!"

"Then what was number three?" she asked, taunting him.

Ben glanced between the paper and the road. "You're covering it up with your thumb!" he said, pawing at the sheet.

Hallie playfully held it out of his reach.

With his eyes on the highway, Ben reached over and tickled her side, causing her to collapse in on herself with a squeal, her arm moving inward enough that he could grab the paper. "Sofa!" Ben called out, handing it back to her. "Ha! I'll start thinking of my drink order now. I want to have a really good one in mind by the time we get there. One of those fifteen-dollar beauties…"

Hallie rolled her eyes, but it was all in jest because she knew he'd never make her pay—he never had. She'd always had to surprise him with a drink on the years she'd won, so he wouldn't offer to take care of the bill.

They settled into an easy silence after that.

The sun warmed Hallie's bare feet resting on the dashboard, her dark chestnut hair pulled into a ponytail to keep the wind from having its way with it. The summer humidity cried out for the cool breeze that could only be found on the coast. She turned toward the passing landscape. A runaway strand of hair blew into her face and she tucked it behind her ear.

She straightened her knees and stretched out her legs along the dash, the sun casting flickering spots of light through the trees onto her skin as they sped down the road. But Hallie hardly noticed, her mind quickly returning to thoughts of everything she'd been holding in and how she'd be able to manage once they reached their impending destination. She glanced down at the news article she was bringing to Uncle Hank, folded between them in the console.

Hallie lowered her feet to the floor, reached over, and turned down the music, the twang of guitars fading into the wind. Beau shifted behind her.

"What if I'm not strong enough to support Uncle Hank?" she said, feeling the fear in her words rising in her throat as signs for the little fishing village turned creative haven for the arts came into view.

Firefly Beach: one mile.

"I might break down completely when I see him like I did at the funeral, and I'd feel awful if that happened."

Aunt Clara was the glue that held their family together. Uncle Hank had had his moments when she'd gotten sick, and they weren't sure how he was going to cope when the end came. His friends had told Mama that he'd isolated himself at Starlight Cottage since Aunt Clara's death, and he was hardly taking any visitors, which wasn't like him.

Hallie picked up the article and spread it over her lap, peering down at it, her gaze sweeping over the paragraph that read: *Born April 3, 1933 to Howard and Willa Flynn, Clara married Hank Russell Eubanks on the grounds of the Starlight Estate in 1968, in a small but formal ceremony designed entirely by her—she wouldn't have had it any other way. Her wedding dress, also her own creation, is currently on display in the Harlow Museum of Fashion in New York City.*

Hallie ran her hands along the back of her neck, and closed her eyes to relieve the pinch.

"I don't think he expects you to be strong, Hallie. But I also believe that you're stronger than you think you are."

If he only knew that it wasn't that she couldn't muster the strength, but rather the fact that she'd used it all up over the last few months and now she had nothing more left in her. Hallie had called Ben the Friday before last when she'd found out she'd be visiting Uncle Hank, still unsure about whether or not she could handle going to Firefly Beach. When Mama heard that Uncle Hank had completely isolated himself and people were worried, she went straight to Hallie and asked her to go to Firefly Beach. Concerned that he was still reclusive six months after Aunt Clara had passed, Mama didn't want to waste any time.

Ben had convinced Hallie to go, and she'd asked him to come to Aunt Clara's cottage with her because she couldn't do it without his support. He'd immediately cleared his schedule. Now they were almost there. Uncle Hank was waiting for them… She *had* to go through with this. But all she really wanted to do was jump from the moving jeep and run as fast as she could in the other direction. Maybe that way she could pretend none of this was real.

"I can't face that place." She rubbed her eyes, the numbing ache that had been in her head since Aunt Clara's death returning. "It'll bring all the memories back like a flood, and I might not survive it." She turned around to Beau and scratched his neck as he inched his head between her and Ben. "Mama's better at taking care of people than I am. She always knows just what to say. I don't think I should be there. And I feel guilty because, deep down, I'm hoping I can convince Uncle Hank to give me the second envelope."

Beau put his paw up on the console between the two of them and Ben snapped his fingers lightly, pointing toward the back. Beau kissed his hand before returning to his spot, hanging his snout out the side of the jeep. He looked so content. Hallie guessed that if Beau could've talked to them, he had leaned forward to tell them that if they wanted to relax, all they had to do was to inhale the sweet smell of honeysuckle that always penetrated the air right before the welcome sign for Firefly Beach.

They passed Berkley's Farm, the place where Aunt Clara had driven every June to load up on preserves for her cherry cobbler. Ben used to chase Hallie around the fields, playing Hide and Seek in the old barns.

"You know he won't just give you the second envelope," Ben said. "Not when Clara advised otherwise."

Ben was right every time, and if this time was no different, then why was she making this trip at all? Her frustration bubbled up as anger. "Mama and Sydney were both given their inheritance. They didn't have to do anything for it. Why is Aunt Clara making this so hard on me? I don't even want her money. I just want *her*. And none of this ridiculousness is going to fix that."

Ben put on his blinker and changed lanes, coming to a stop at the only light before town. "Have faith, Hallie," he said, his gaze lingering on her face until she nodded toward the light that had changed. He turned his focus back to the road and they were off again.

"*Why* did she want me to do this?" Hallie asked, looking over at him as if he had the answer.

Hallie had no idea Aunt Clara had even kept the list, and now, her request was simply baffling. When Hallie first read it, she said to herself, "This is ridiculous. She can't be serious. I don't even want these things anymore." Everyone else had been gifted large sums of money or coveted pieces of jewelry from her designer collection, rare china, or even items she'd collected from her travels around the world, but Hallie had gotten this. After everything Hallie had been through, her list seemed trivial at best.

"The last one about making a wish come true might take me years, my whole life, even," she said, knowing none of her previous wishes—and she'd had so many—had come to fruition. "It's absurd."

"She was a wise woman, Hallie. You know her: until her final breath, everything she did had purpose. You have to trust her direction and take a few chances. Just relax into it and see what happens."

Ben was right. Not only was she wise; she was the very picture of love. Everything she did was out of affection for others. Hallie opened up the paper in her lap to view the article one more time, as if the words on the page would give her some clarity. She smoothed the folds, the edges fighting against the wind, flapping madly.

A renowned designer, Clara traveled as far as London and Paris, decorating for many well-known figures with her design firm Morgan and Flynn, leaving her business partner Sasha Morgan to manage the affairs of the multimillion-dollar company…

Hallie wondered what Sasha felt, taking it all on herself at her age. Being the same age as Aunt Clara, she had to be thinking about retirement. Hallie hoped she would. If anyone deserved to rest, it was Sasha. She and Aunt Clara had worked so hard and built so much over the years. Hallie hoped that Sasha wasn't still trying to keep up that pace on her own. At the funeral, she'd been kind and courteous, not divulging any feelings of her own apart from the sadness of losing Aunt Clara. But she'd looked as energetic as ever. Rest was probably foreign to her.

It was Aunt Clara who was the expert in rest. Hallie continued reading:

But it was the sprawling, unfussy cottage of Starlight that held Clara's heart, where she chose to spend her days writing what she referred to as "love letters" to everyone she knew, visiting with friends, or "recharging her creative voice," as she put it, on the beachside porch of her home.

Hallie folded the paper and turned her head toward the passing landscape, to the palm trees lining the edge of the road and the little multicolored cottages perched between them. Formally named Lauk Beach, a Choctaw word meaning "fire," the town was nicknamed Firefly Beach in the nineteen-twenties because, at certain times of the year, the coastline was full of them, like little stars that had fallen from the heavens.

Hallie fell back into her thoughts as the Firefly Beach welcome sign slid into view.

Chapter Three

The first thing Hallie noticed was that Aunt Clara wasn't standing on the porch of the sprawling Starlight Cottage, which sat like a pearl on the grounds of the estate. This house had been her refuge, her place of comfort nearly her entire life. It was a symbol of the love that was shared within its walls, a beacon for her, a grounding point to which she could always return when life got difficult. But without Aunt Clara, it suddenly looked different to Hallie, and she feared that it had lost what it once had.

The house stood in front of her, and in an odd way, Hallie felt betrayed by it. Because Aunt Clara wasn't there to greet her when Hallie pulled up this time. Hallie had been to the cottage to see her aunt when she was ill, and again for the funeral, but it was this visit that the house itself stood out. Even though Aunt Clara had always returned to this house to recharge and breathe in life again after a hectic work schedule, it couldn't save her this time. It had failed her.

Those last visits had been a blur. Hallie had been so preoccupied that she hadn't felt the void until this trip. She sharpened her hearing to see if she could pinpoint conversation anywhere, while simultaneously feeling the rise of emotion at the colossal emptiness of the cottage and grounds.

The hedges had grown out of their usual boxy shape, the branches pointing upward resembling haphazard, leafy fingers, as if even the foliage were reaching for Aunt Clara—nothing like the way her aunt would've kept them. The whitewashed exterior was in need of touch-up painting, and the driveway had become slightly overgrown with weeds. The last year, while Aunt Clara had fought for her health, had clearly taken its toll on the property. Where was the staff that usually took care of the grounds?

The peeling bottom step was now obscured by thistles and weeds that had pushed their way through the crack between the wood and the seashell walk. Hallie moved past the sight to realize the front door was open, and in the entryway she could see just a corner of the old black-and-white photo of Aunt Clara and Uncle Hank standing beside the clapboard Starlight sign, holding a glass of champagne. The cottage had been in the family for generations, but they were the first to give it a name. The photo captured her memory of them perfectly. Aunt Clara's heart-shaped lips were smiling, the gesture reaching her eyes. Beside her, Uncle Hank had an undeniable sophistication. Hallie had always admired him in that photo. He looked like Cary Grant.

They'd named the cottage Starlight because of the lighthouse that sat on its own private peninsula, jutting out into the sea, behind the main building on the Eubanks' expansive property. For years, the lighthouse illuminated the water with a breadth of nearly twenty miles, assisting the usually dazzling stars when cloud cover hid them. With the increased use of electronic navigational systems, it wasn't a working lighthouse anymore, but Aunt Clara had always maintained it, and on Christmas, she lit it. She said that, on that night in particular, she wanted just one more opportunity to get sailors home to their families where they belonged. Hallie used to play in its echoing staircase, facing the gulf, pretending she was alone, shipwrecked on a deserted island. The lighthouse seemed isolated now, abandoned and showing wear like the main house, giving her an eerie feeling that her childhood musings had foreshadowed future events. It made her shiver.

Suitcases dotted the long country porch that wrapped around the enormous dwelling. Hallie and Ben had been quite a distance behind Mama on the way there, so she wondered why her mother hadn't finished unpacking. Mama's car doors were still ajar, the trunk open. Sydney would've gotten Robby's things, certainly…

Beau jumped out of the jeep, landing beside her, his tail wagging furiously, while Ben pulled two bags from the back and set them onto the drive. Hallie focused on the hissing of the small gulf waves as they broke onto the shore behind the cottage, and the tinkling of the wind chime on the corner of the front porch, which was missing one of its sea-glass pieces.

Ben offered a wide glance of the property, but his appraisal didn't show any judgment. It was clear, when he turned his attention back to the jeep, that he didn't want to linger on the disrepair or the fact that things were amiss with her family. He was clearly trying to keep her spirits up, not knowing what they would find inside. "I'll get everyone's things into the house," he said. He pulled a duffel bag from the back and dropped it onto the driveway, the bag making a smack as it hit the pavement. "I'm guessing your mama's gonna have her same room in the main house. Want me to put our things out back?"

By "out back," Ben meant the guesthouse. Hallie had always stayed in the guesthouse. It was her own little retreat, nestled on the edge of the property, a stone-walk away from the main dwelling. As a teenager, she'd liked the independence; in college, she'd savored the solitude; and now, it was a safe distance from the grief she knew would wash over her completely the minute she set foot in Aunt Clara's house without her. She couldn't shake the feeling that this moment in her life was the most important time to have Aunt Clara to help her, but she'd left them all, and if Hallie allowed herself to think about the permanence of everything that had happened, panic would set in.

"That'll be good," she managed. "But let me help you."

"Don't worry yourself with it. You need to find your family. Check on your uncle." He lifted another bag from the backseat and slid it onto his shoulder, then took one of the suitcases by the handle. When she didn't respond, Ben moved in front of her. "You can do this, Hallie."

She knew she should listen to her best friend—she'd learned how important that skill was—but this wasn't like anything she'd faced before.

"Hey," Ben said, bringing her attention back to his face. "The minute you need me, I'll be right in the guesthouse."

"You won't come with me?"

His face softened, an affectionate look in his eyes. "I will if you want me to, but I think facing this is something you need to do with your family. I'll hang back and get some work done. And I also think once you realize you have the strength to do this, everything will seem easier."

"Okay." She didn't believe him. He didn't know what he was saying with the word *everything*.

Ben whistled and Beau trotted over from the edge of the yard, standing at attention beside him. "Let's get all these bags in, boy," he said, patting Beau's side with his free hand. Then they headed to the guesthouse, and when he left Hallie in the drive, it felt like he'd taken all her oxygen with him.

Hallie slowly moved down the seashell walkway leading to the house and climbed the wide steps to the front door, the boards creaking under her feet. She stopped in the entryway, Aunt Clara's familiar scent of lilac and cinnamon taking her breath away again momentarily. She longed to nestle down into her aunt's loving embrace, under the spell of Aunt Clara's soft words telling her it would all be just fine. She held her breath briefly and closed the front door behind her, shutting out the coastal breeze.

Hallie steadied herself, fighting off the feeling of loss before it swallowed her. She counted her breaths to refocus until her inhalations were shallow but manageable. She called, "Mama? Sydney?"

No one answered.

She passed Uncle Hank's old Steinway piano in the corner of the grand formal living room just off the entryway. It sat empty, dust having dulled its usually shiny black surface over the long year he'd had, nursing Aunt Clara and mourning her death. The ghostly tune of his rendition of Franz Liszt's "La Campanella," the *tink tink tink* of Uncle Hank's fingers against the keys, his head down, his arm stretching to the furthest end of the piano—it played in her mind, making the hair stand up on her arms.

Hallie moved down the hallway toward the back of the house, pausing at the antique table against the stairs to find Aunt Clara's car keys, presumably still placed where she'd put them last. Her chest constricted with an unbearable force. She reached into her pocket and wrapped her fingers around the list, as if it would summon her favorite aunt back into her life.

"Mama?" she called again, her voice breaking. "Where is everyone?"

In the silence, her flip-flops slapped the hardwoods leading to the family's preferred gathering place, facing the southern side of the property and the glistening gulf. The kitchen stretched along the entire back of the house, with a farm table that could easily seat sixteen, a vase she remembered someone sending in condolence after the funeral, now containing only withered stems and remnants of baby's breath, in its center, the rest of the flower arrangement long gone.

The back was open just like the front had been, and the screened porch door outside rattled against its frame in the coastal wind, the heat sailing inside and enveloping her as she neared it. Hallie stepped out, facing the backyard, closing the door, and slipped on the sunglasses that were on top of her head. The sun was relentless, beating down on the coastline, which snaked around the peninsula like a soft sandy pearl-colored ribbon. Robby was down on the beach, playing in the sand, and Hallie made out the rest of them just past the lighthouse, in the gazebo at the end of the dock that sat in a tiny alcove of calm water, where Hallie had learned to swim.

"Oh, Hallie! You're here!" Mama called, waving to her from the gazebo across the huge stretch of property. "Come help us with Uncle Hank!"

Mama's voice was strained, worried—Hallie could hear the alarm in her tone even from that distance. Picking up her pace, she pushed any thoughts she'd been having out of her mind, her total focus on the present situation. Her strides swallowed the massive yard as she ran through the grass toward the shore, where Mama and Sydney were struggling with Uncle Hank on the dock.

Dismay and uncertainty pelted her while she ran. Uncle Hank was like a father to her, since her own father had left them when she was only three. No Flynn had been successful in love except Aunt Clara. She'd managed to find happiness with Uncle Hank. Because he was a good seed. Uncle Hank was different from the others. He was always there, as reliable as the morning sun. When Hallie arrived, she'd hoped to come through the door with him quietly sitting at his piano or reading the paper on the back porch like he used to, but she found herself in the reality she'd feared instead.

She reached the dock that had seemed to stretch into eternity when she was a child, but was now much shorter. Hallie rushed down to her uncle, careful not to wobble in her flip-flops as they slid around her feet with perspiration and the humid air.

When Hallie got to the gazebo and to Uncle Hank, Mama was leaning over him and Sydney was at his side, holding his hand as he sat, slumped, on the bench.

"What's wrong?" she asked, out of breath.

Hallie was immediately overcome with her uncle's appearance. He was frail, thin, nothing like the towering man who had been her family's protector growing up. His shoulders hunched forward as he tipped his head up to her, his skin almost translucent, and she wondered when he'd been outside last. She choked back a sob, the great loss they all had suffered overwhelming her. She pressed her lips together and pushed her shoulders back so as not to crumple into tears.

"I've just been dizzy, that's all," Uncle Hank said. His voice was gruff and lifeless, not the voice that had cheered her on as she took off down the pavement on her first bicycle after he'd let go of the back of the seat. Sydney gave her a worried look out of his line of sight.

"He lost his balance when he tried to greet us," Mama said, her face no softer than it had been when she was packing the car. "I'm calling the doctor as soon as we get him inside."

"You don't have to talk about me like I'm not here," Uncle Hank barked.

"I'm sorry," Mama said, whipping around to face him.

Uncle Hank showed remorse before he peered over the railing at the water that ceaselessly lapped under them. He looked older, more tired than he had at the funeral. The rims of his eyes were red.

Hallie bit her lip to keep from breaking down. The tidal wave of emotion that had plagued her in the last weeks was washing over her, filling her up again, and she didn't want to fall apart here. She'd been right to be scared to come. She felt empty, no tears left, but they still managed to prick her eyes. She wasn't in any shape to help Uncle Hank, and he looked like he needed a lot of help. He deserved to have family around him to lift him up—and she couldn't. She tried to think of what Aunt Clara would do in a situation like this, but she was so emotionally spent that her mind was blank.

Clara was the sister of Hallie's grandfather, but Hallie had never met him. Being considerably older than Aunt Clara, he'd passed away before Hallie was born, and her grandmother a few years later. With no other family to help Mama when her husband left, Uncle Hank and Aunt Clara had taken in her, Sydney, and Hallie until Mama could get on her feet financially.

Aunt Clara and Uncle Hank had never had children of their own, and when Aunt Clara wasn't consumed with her company, she took great care to rest at Firefly Beach. She was a firm believer that one should work and relax in equal amounts, so Hallie guessed that, given how hard she worked on the business, there was no room for children if she wanted to have the down time she needed. But her love was enormous and all encompassing, and if anyone would've been a wonderful mother, it was Aunt Clara. Without her, it was as if they were all floundering around, unable to take care of one another.

"I'll get Ben," Hallie said, her voice breathy, taut with the sadness that had welled up in her throat. "He can help us get you to the house."

Uncle Hank wobbled as he tried to stand, his twitching hand clutching the railing, the other pressing into Sydney's grasp, causing her sister to scramble to support him. "I'm fine. I got myself out here; I can get myself back inside."

"I panicked when he wasn't in the house when we arrived," Mama said. "We found him sitting by himself out here. Where are the groundskeepers and your cleaning staff?" Mama clipped, her concern for him making her edgy.

"I let them all go." Uncle Hank grappled again for the railing, but he couldn't get a hold on it and collapsed back down on one knee. Mama helped him up. "Someone keeps prowling around near the windows in the evenings, and I'm not in any shape to ward anyone off, so, since I couldn't tell who it was, I gave everyone their notice."

Mama's eyes widened as she put her arm around his waist, Hallie and Sydney supporting his other side. "Someone's been lurking on the property?"

Sydney tipped her head up and scanned the beach frantically, exhaling loudly when she caught sight of Robby.

"I haven't been able to sleep well," he said, once he was securely standing with their help. "It's a lone figure in the night, a male. Lumbering, not in any hurry. I don't know what he wants."

"Have you called the police? At the very least, that's trespassing," Sydney offered, her forehead creased with concern. Her head continued to swivel, her maternal instincts on overdrive.

"No. It was only a few times. And to be honest, what is there that he can take from me that isn't already gone?" He became unsteady again, grabbing on to them.

"We'll get someone to look into this," Mama said.

"I thought the fresh air would do me some good. I'm suffocating in that house…"

"Robby!" Sydney called. "Let's go inside for a little while."

Robby ran toward them as they labored to hold Uncle Hank. Despite his deterioration, he was still a big man, and it was taking all their might to keep him steady. With nothing but water on either side of the dock, Hallie didn't even want to think about what might have happened if he'd lost his balance getting out to the gazebo.

They all stopped for a second to catch their breath, and Hallie took stock of her surroundings. The breeze blew in, carrying with it the briny air and salty residue that settled on her skin whenever she was there. The sky was a perfect shade of blue against the emerald sea that pawed at the powdery sand the same way it had when she was a girl. The lighthouse cast a long shadow across the once pristine yard, in need of work now. Other than the yard requiring a little sprucing, nothing had changed on the edge of the water she knew so well, yet at the same time, nothing was the same. She squeezed Uncle Hank tighter, stepping along beside him as they began to move again, wondering what the weeks ahead would bring.

Chapter Four

Hallie was shaken to the core, unable to understand how anything could ever be okay from this point forward. Once they'd gotten Uncle Hank into the kitchen, she went back outside, around the side of the house where no one could see her, and cried until that familiar feeling of emptiness took over and her tears stopped. The wind blew against her, tunneling from the sea, past the boathouse and up to Starlight Cottage. She caught sight of a sailboat on the horizon, and focused on it to try to get herself together.

"Oh, sorry." A voice startled her, making her yelp.

She wasn't prepared to see anyone. And the man standing in front of her was someone she didn't recognize. She looked around carefully to find a clear path in case she needed to run, her hands beginning to tremble. Once she had a well-defined line of exit, she made eye contact with him. He didn't seem dangerous, but she didn't trust her intuition these days. He was wearing paint-splattered clothes with a clearly unintentional streak of blue in his hair, and he had kind green eyes. "Are you okay?"

"Yes," she sniffled, squaring her shoulders and blinking rapidly to clear her vision.

Compassion washed over his face. "I wasn't trying to sneak up on you. I'm so sorry—I know your uncle has been careful about who he lets onto the property." Cautiously, he leaned around her. "My paint cans are behind you." He nodded toward a stack of silver containers by the spigot. "I'm Gavin Wilson. Hank Eubanks hired me to redo the trim on Starlight Cottage. The storm last winter really put a hurting on it." He held out his hand in greeting.

"I'm Hallie Flynn, his great niece." She shook the man's hand.

"Nice to meet you." He had a gentle smile, as if he were treading lightly, given her obviously emotional state. "Hank and I had a long talk when we first met a couple of months ago, and I know he prefers to be alone out here, but when he's on an up-day, as we call it, he gives me a ring and I come out to see him. He's still very particular about when I'm to come. I can't get here too early and I have to leave before dark. He sits in the front living room and watches me go from the window. He said he's concerned about my safety. I'm not sure why…" Gavin huffed out a little chuckle. "Shouldn't it be the other way around?"

"I'm surprised he's painting the trim when there's so much more that needs to be done," she said, still a little suspicious, taking stock of every twitch or movement Gavin made.

"Well, he didn't seem interested in aesthetics. He noticed an area that was rotting and causing a leak inside because the wood was bare and open to the elements. He only wanted to seal it up, but I replaced it with weather-resistant wood. Painting it all with a good water-repellent paint and then the sealer helps to keep it in good shape during storms."

"Oh," she said, figuring he seemed to be genuine. She wiped her sweaty hands on her shorts, her nerves getting the best of her.

"Hope I didn't get paint on you," he said, inspecting her fingers. There was an awkward pause. "So… I'm sorry. I've been going on and on but… You might need to be left alone."

"We had a tough moment with my uncle just now and it shook me up."

"If you don't mind me asking, what happened?"

Hallie recounted the events, every word sounding like someone else's life.

"I just got here; I wish I'd come sooner. Is there anything I can do to help?"

"Thank you, but he's okay for now, I think. We got him inside and settled."

"I worry about him, being out here alone. Sometimes I break up my painting into different days just so I can come more often to check on him. The people I've met in town are all really concerned about him. They say he's never been like this. They all miss him, but I know he's hurting." He took a step to the side, and she felt her shoulders momentarily tense, but Gavin had a trustworthy quality about him that made her remind herself to relax.

"That's really kind of you."

"Well, I'll get back to work, but let me know if you need anything." His words were friendly, and he spoke with a familiarity as if they'd known each other for some time.

"Thank you."

"You're welcome." His gaze lingered on her for a moment, as if he could sense all her pain, and see through her counterfeit smile. But he picked up the paint cans and said goodbye over his shoulder, before disappearing around the side of the house.

The house was so isolated that no one would hear if they needed help, so it was good to know Gavin was around at least sometimes. What had it been like for Uncle Hank to spend every night here alone? She'd been selfish not to have come before now, and her heart ached with that reality. She was glad they were all there. She couldn't believe Uncle Hank had lived here on his own in the shape he was in, and without Aunt Clara.

Mama had been able to get some time off to visit a few months ago, but Uncle Hank hadn't been as frail as he was now. As far as Hallie knew he'd been fine then, and he also hadn't mentioned anything amiss about the property. With Aunt Clara gone, people around Firefly Beach had tried to look out for Uncle Hank, but amidst his grief, he'd shut everyone out. He hadn't seen any of his friends since the funeral. When their good friend Maggie had called Mama to say no one had seen Hank in weeks, they all knew that they had to go down to be with him.

It had taken them quite a while to get Hank inside from the dock, his steps awkward and small. He kept creating excuses—he was just tired; they were making more of it than it was—but he'd been struggling to catch his breath by the time they'd made it into the house and to a chair. Hallie noticed he hadn't gotten up after that.

Hallie headed back inside to check on Mama and her sister. She found them both outside Mama's bedroom. Mama was grateful to have her bags in her room, thanks to Ben. By her downturned features, the day had clearly taken its toll on her, and she told Hallie that after she called the police station about the prowler, she wanted to lie down for a little while.

"This is a big house," Sydney said quietly, as the two of them walked outside so Robby could play on the beach again. "How will he continue to live here if every day is like this? His room is upstairs. He could hardly find his balance to get up the three steps to the back porch. And what if he's in danger?" Sydney pulled her eyes from Robby and cast a troubled look over to Hallie, her auburn curls fuzzing up with the humidity and the effort she'd exerted to bring Uncle Hank inside.

"Maybe he'll get better with all of us here. And maybe our presence will keep whoever it is away from the house," Hallie said, grasping for hope. If she didn't hope, she'd start sobbing right there in the yard. Her head pounded and she felt exhausted. All she wanted to do was to get into a cool shower, let the water run over her until she was numb, put on her pajamas, and crawl into her crisp sheets, drifting off to give her mind a break from all this.

"You look really beat," Sydney said. "I'm gonna sit on the beach with Robby for a little while. Why don't you go find Ben and fill him in on everything? We can take a break and then regroup once we've all rested. Let's have dinner together."

Hallie inhaled the salty air and let it out. "That sounds great."

"Tell Ben thank you for bringing in our bags."

Hallie was so lucky that Ben had been able to come with them, and she needed him now more than ever. Her limbs shook with the events of the day, and she wanted to curl up next to him and bury her head in his chest. "I'll tell him," she said. Hallie turned around and headed toward the guesthouse.

When she entered, Ben had papers full of lyrics, sheet music, and timetables spread out on the island and music playing—there was always music playing when he was around. The air carried a sweet scent of blackberry and alcohol, and she knew immediately what it was. Two small glasses, filled with her favorite dessert wine, sat on the kitchen counter.

The sun streamed through the large windows that overlooked the gulf, giving a glow to the whitewashed walls and painted floors. Aunt Clara had decorated the guesthouse in whites and nautical blues, and Hallie had always loved the rustic, beachy feel of it. When Aunt Clara was drawing the design, Hallie had sat beside her, madly scratching her own sketches in her drawing book, trying to copy what Aunt Clara had done.

She took one of the glasses and walked through the open room to the sofa, sinking down into it.

"I heard you heading up the walk," Ben said, coming in from the small hallway that led to the single bedroom. He grabbed his glass and lowered himself onto the sofa next to her. Their eyes met before he took a sip of wine. "How tough was it?" he asked, placing the glass on the coffee table, which was made from an old rowing oar. "From the look on your face, I'd say it was pretty hard."

Hallie leaned forward, positioned her wine next to his, and put her face in her hands, totally drained. "Uncle Hank isn't well," she said through her fingers. Her eyes ached with the threat of tears, which made her whole body feel weak. "And there's more than that." She told him about the prowler and Uncle Hank's lack of strength, the dizziness, how worried she was…

Ben pulled her in for a hug. Hallie nestled against his chest. His calming presence would keep her afloat. It had only taken one call to let him know she needed him and he'd packed, and driven straight over to be with Hallie and her family. But suddenly, something hit her. She'd been so wrapped up in her own emotions that she hadn't even stopped to consider what Ben was giving up by being there.

"Weren't you going to cut that record with the band you'd heard at The Bluebird?" she worried aloud. He'd texted her before things had gotten so bad with Aunt Clara, so excited to have found this group—only now had she remembered through the fog of everything going on. She tilted her head to look up at him.

"I pushed it to the end of summer."

Her eyes grew wide, knowing how long he'd already had to wait to get them into the studio, given his busy schedule.

"It's fine. It's music festival season; everyone's focused on that. I told them it would be wise to hold off until the fall. September's really the best time for new bands. They said they could use a little more writing time anyway. They have a slightly different direction they're thinking about, and they want to run it by me, but they need more time to get their songs down."

"That seems awfully easy. Are you just trying to make me feel better for dragging you away?"

He chuckled and then his face became humorless, his entire focus on her. "I wouldn't have missed this for anything." Then he gave her a big squeeze, leaned forward, and handed her the glass of wine.

She was still apprehensive, realizing that not only had she not thought about his work commitments, she hadn't asked about Ben's girlfriend either. Ashley was three years younger than Hallie, kind and soft-spoken, and Hallie could relate to her quiet nature. She and Hallie had hit it off right away when Ben introduced them at a Christmas party, after Ben had first met her. Hallie and Ashley had all kinds of things in common: they shared the same taste in music, they'd read the same books, they'd even both volunteered at the same homeless shelter. But more noteworthy was the fact that Ashley had also spent summers at Firefly Beach since she was a girl. Her family had a cottage just down the road. It was a wonder, with all that, that they hadn't met sooner.

"Was Ashley okay with you coming?"

Ben nodded. "Yeah."

"She's so great. She's just the kind of girl you should be with. You deserve someone fantastic like her."

He smiled, and then shifted away from Hallie again to reach his wine. He took a long swig. "What's the plan for the rest of the evening?" he asked, changing the subject. That was just like Ben: always giving her his full attention, worrying more about her wellbeing than his own.

She yawned, the day's events catching up with her. "I think we're all going to try to have dinner together."

"Everyone's too tired to cook, I'm sure. How about if I order some food for everybody and run into town to pick it up? Maybe Wes and Maggie's?"

"That sounds amazing."

"Perfect. Find out what everybody wants, and I'll put in an order."

Hallie pulled out her phone and texted Sydney to let her know the plan. "I'll go with you," she said, happy to have a reason to go into town and let the magic of Firefly Beach seep into her soul, like it always could.

Chapter Five

The red and blue bungalow known as Wes and Maggie's was surrounded by palm trees and sat right on the water in a strip of sand. The restaurant's glow of outdoor lighting made it shine against the streaks of aqua and deep blue of the Gulf of Mexico behind it. Matching red and blue flags, fighting madly against the coastal wind, lined the outdoor seating, which was full of vacationers, their faces all flushed from too much sun and the cocktails they were being served under the evening sky. The intense heat had subsided to a bearable balminess with the sunset.

"It's been a while," Ben said, opening Hallie's door of the jeep.

Next to Wes and Maggie's was Cup of Sunshine, the local coffee shop. It was quiet this evening, but in the mornings, year-round, every seat was full. Locals and visitors alike couldn't get enough of their signature butter pecan latte or their homemade pumpkin pie breakfast bread, and the owner Melissa even prepared delicious French toast served with a drizzle of cream cheese syrup. Every patron, no matter how small the purchase, went home with a complimentary dark chocolate truffle that had an icing-piped chocolate sunshine on the top. As they walked past, Melissa caught her eye through the window of the shop and waved.

"Should we get a drink at the bar before we pick up the food?" Ben said, pulling Hallie's focus back to him.

"I owe you one anyway," she said, playfully knocking into him with her shoulder. "We were tied the whole trip! And you found golf clubs at the last minute before the game was over—I can't believe you found golf clubs." He'd spotted them hanging out of the back of someone's car, filled to the brim with vacation paraphernalia.

It felt good to be in town with Ben. It made Hallie feel more normal, since they'd spent so many years here together. Before everything had happened with Jeff and Aunt Clara, Hallie had been full of life. She loved to laugh—Ben could make her laugh without even trying and sometimes, when he *did* try, they'd get to laughing so hard that her sides hurt and her jaw felt like it would cramp up and freeze into a smile if she didn't offer it relief. She yearned to feel it again.

"Nah, my treat."

"You won, fair and square."

"You can get me one later," he said. They reached the restaurant, and Ben allowed Hallie to enter first, the interior taking her back to better times.

The small bistro tables with starfish and seashells floating from the ceiling, suspended by fishing lines, were just as they had been the last time she'd visited; the bar had the same driftwood stools, and Wes was serving drinks. He greeted them across the room with an excited wave and a warm smile.

Simon Petty, a local landscaper, was at his post at the end of the bar, next to the dartboard. As long as Hallie could remember, that's where he'd always sat. In return for taking care of the grounds and surrounding beach, Wes and Maggie paid him not only his fee but in drinks and meals as well, since Simon was a lifelong bachelor.

Maggie had told Hallie once, "That poor man has never known the delights of having a woman cook for him—probably not since his mama—and that's a tragedy." So Maggie made sure he had a good meal once a day.

"Oh, am I glad to see you two," Wes said when they got over to him. Hallie pulled out a stool and sat beside Ben. "Guess what I got in the other day."

"Dare I ask?" Hallie said, already feeling better.

Wes had a big personality. He was always making friends with visitors to Firefly Beach, and he was famous for doing lavish things at the restaurant. No one knew when they were going to happen. He'd been known to set off fireworks, give away surfboards he'd painted himself in a spontaneous restaurant raffle, or even offer everyone free dessert.

"Well, I was going to have the staff dress up one night…" Wes leaned down below the bar and when he came up, Hallie snorted with laughter.

Ben let out a loud "Ha!"

"You didn't," Hallie said. "No way."

"Way." Wes was wearing an enormous Elvis wig.

"Where did you get that?" Hallie said, her amusement seeping through her words. She cupped her hand over her mouth, remembering the night as clearly as if it had happened yesterday.

Wes had set up an impromptu karaoke stage. Hallie and Ben had had a little too much to drink—just enough to make her uncontrollably giggly. Ben had chosen "Don't Be Cruel," and he was belting it out, off key, while pretending to profess his love to Hallie on his knee, his arm stretched out as if he were beckoning her over. The crowd had started to chant for her to go on stage, but she couldn't stop laughing. Apparently, their performance was such a hit people requested it the whole week after.

"Online!" Wes took off the wig and put it back under the bar. "Ben, you let me know when you're ready for an encore. All you have to do is say the word."

Ben chuckled, and Hallie could see the effect of the memory of that night in his eyes.

"Are we feeling rum or wine this evening, Miss Flynn?" Wes asked.

"Rum," she said, a little life buzzing inside her again.

Wes slid Ben's favorite local beer across the bar with a grin. "I've missed you two!" he said to them, grabbing a shaker and filling it with all Hallie's favorite ingredients. "It's been too long. Maggie's off tonight or she'd have pulled a seat up beside you. She's dying to pick your brain about what to put in that corner over there. It's too small for a table, but after we moved things around, we can't figure out what would go well there."

Hallie leaned across the bar and grabbed a white paper napkin and a pen. She marked out the two wall lines and studied them. "I'd do something like this." She sketched a little table with a plant that had some height to it. Then she drew a frame on the wall above it and turned the napkin around for Wes to see.

"I'll save this for her," he said, opening the register and placing the napkin under the cash tray. "She'll love it."

Hallie had known Wes and Maggie since she was a kid. A lifelong dream, they'd finally opened this place the same year she'd entered high school, and it was the most popular spot at Firefly Beach. Wes didn't just make drinks; he built creations. An artist in his off time, he was locally famous for putting together just the right concoctions to match each person he met. He'd labeled Hallie as "rum, coconut milk, heavy cream, pineapple juice, and mint" when she turned twenty-one and she'd never deviated. It was divine.

"What brings you into town?" he asked over the rattle of the ice, as he shook the shaker back and forth.

"Uncle Hank," Hallie said, not wanting to let on that there was any more than that, but aware that he probably knew better. The truth was, even without Uncle Hank's issues, she had plenty of reasons of her own to want to escape to the beautiful coast at Firefly Beach. She hadn't shared the whole of it with anyone, and she definitely wasn't prepared to divulge anything tonight.

"How's he holding up?"

"Not too well. I think he needs to get out of the cottage, but his health is failing him."

His hands stilled. "If there's anything I can do…"

"Thanks, Wes."

"Ben, you doing all right?"

Ben held up his drink and nodded. "Doing great, thanks. How's Maggie's knee?"

"She can't play tennis like she wants to, but it's been fine. The joys of old age… We've been getting walks in, though. She likes to stroll through town and have a look around in the shops. There's a new art gallery that just opened—owned by some famous photographer. I'd never heard of him." Wes pointed to a frame on the wall leading to the dining area: an incredible shot of the sun coming up on the gulf, with a historical home in front. "I got that at the gallery. He does work for national magazines, apparently."

Hallie got up to have a closer look. "Wow." It was exactly the kind of angle she'd have used. She loved to make the corner of an object the center line of the shot—it made the photo take on a linear quality. But this was absolutely incredible. The background was blurred in an unusual way that she'd never seen before, making it resemble watercolor, and she wondered how the photographer had achieved it.

When she walked back over to her bar stool, Ben had perked up, and Hallie knew exactly what he was thinking. How convenient that there was a photographer in town to help her with Aunt Clara's request… Well, if he worked for national magazines, he was out of her league. Her low-end camera shots would never stand up to that.

Wes poured Hallie's drink into a large glass and topped it with a hand-painted paper umbrella—his signature.

"Let me know if you two need anything. I'll be at the end of the bar."

Hallie thanked him and then answered Ben's quizzical look, trying to be positive, relishing the fizzle of happiness Wes had provided them. "We can check out the gallery, but later, okay?" She took a long drink from her glass, the smell and taste of summer filling her. "I need more moments like these," she said, turning to Ben. "If I'm going to have to face all this, I'll need you to help me balance it with a little sunshine."

Ben offered an understanding nod.

"You always know how to make me feel better." Hallie remembered when, at the age of fifteen, Ben had said he'd marry her one day. They'd had a long discussion about it. He wanted to have a big family with at least two boys who were just like him, because he could take them fishing. He'd also teased that three was a good number because they could hold their own as a backyard football team, which had made her laugh. He'd promised Hallie that as soon as they were old enough, he'd ask her, and he assured her they'd never break up. When she questioned him about how he was so certain, he'd said, "Because whenever you're upset, I'll just make you feel better." Life had moved along, and their lives had gone in different directions, but they'd always remained best friends. She was glad she hadn't ruined what they had by trying to have a relationship.

"It's nice being with someone who has no agenda, no pressure." She peered down at her empty ring finger once more. "Jeff was a good friend, you know? And we muddled it up with dating each other," she said, her introspection making its way out. Ben was always there to listen, though, and she liked telling him things, so she didn't mind. She swirled the little umbrella in her glass, the ice clinking against the side with the movement, and set it onto the bar.

"Jeff wasn't a friend," Ben said, picking at the corner of the label on his bottle. He smoothed it back out and looked at her.

"We went to work functions together for a year before he asked me out. I'd call that a friendship."

Ben stared at her silently, as if her line of conversation was frustrating him.

"Why are you looking at me like that?" she asked.

Wes went to the back to get their dinners, leaving them sitting together at the empty bar.

"You didn't notice that Jeff was trying to get you to go out with him the entire year? I could see it plain as day."

"None of it matters anyway," she declared, meeting Ben's stare. Even through his slight frustration, those blue eyes of his were so comforting and familiar. "I'm only thirty. I've got loads of time to settle down. I'm not dating anyone else for a good while." She dared not allow the dark thoughts to come back in right now. Best to stick to the lighter reasons she and Jeff hadn't worked out. "He made me feel like I wasn't good enough. He actually told me once that I'm not grounded. What does that even mean?"

"Never change that about yourself," Ben said emphatically.

"So you think I'm not grounded too?"

"I didn't say that." Ben tipped his beer up and took a swig before setting it down and returning his attention to Hallie. "You're plenty grounded. You're just overly optimistic. I understand the difference because I know you so well."

Hallie considered this, but was distracted by the grin that spread across Ben's face, his earlier irritation gone.

"What?"

"For example, you actually believe you'll win when you buy a lottery ticket and you're genuinely disappointed when you don't." He shared a warm look with her, their common experiences from years of being side by side giving her life again. "I love that about you."

In the face of a difficult day, Ben had made her smile. It was his gift, a talent that had been perfected over years of practice.

She'd originally only sought out one drink, not wanting to have too much and end up crying on Ben's shoulder when the heavy thoughts set in like she knew they would, but he was making her feel so much better, reminding her of the good times. It was as if being with him had erased the awful things that had happened—even if only for a little while—and she changed her mind about that one drink.

"Ben, I'm thinking… After dinner, let's find a quiet spot on the beach, where we can talk until we forget what drink we have in our hands. I don't want to go back to the guesthouse until I'm racked with exhaustion and I can just fall into bed and not have to think about everything."

He looked thoughtful. Then, with a wink, he said, "Your wish is my command."

"My knight in shining armor," she teased.

He laughed, his gaze lingering on her in that way it did when they got to talking. She'd rattle on and on about whatever was on her mind, and just when she realized she'd been dominating the conversation, she'd notice how he was looking at her like he was right now, and it always seemed like he didn't mind at all.

Wes handed Ben the receipt and his card. Ben signed the slip of paper and grabbed the bags. "But dinner first! Let's see if we can bring some Firefly Beach cheerfulness back to the cottage, shall we?"

She hoped they could.

Chapter Six

"I haven't seen Hank yet," Ben said, as he sipped another beer while they sat in the sand, the waves rushing up to their bare feet. It was pitch black outside and Hallie couldn't get the idea out of her mind that someone could be hiding down the beach, walking past her window tonight. She rolled her head on her shoulders, trying to feel as calm as Ben looked sitting beside her.

"Sydney said Uncle Hank was asleep before we'd even left to get dinner. He had a pretty traumatic day with the fall, and she didn't want to wake him."

Their plans to lift everyone's spirits over a nice meal had been dashed. Mama said she would have her dinner later. After spending the afternoon calling the local police department and then speaking to a few home-alarm companies to get installation quotes, she didn't have much of an appetite. So Sydney and Robby ate with Ben and Hallie, and the four of them spent most of the meal talking about fixing the old tree swing for Robby. Ben told Robby he'd work on it tomorrow.

They'd eaten rather quickly, and afterwards, Sydney had thought it best if she and Robby locked up and stayed inside, so they'd opted to watch a movie, but Ben insisted on taking Hallie to the beach, since she'd asked him to at Wes and Maggie's. They'd stopped off at the guesthouse and grabbed a few things. In a flash, Ben filled his cooler with ice, bottled beer, and the rest of the wine to bring with them, Hallie following him inside since she was a little spooked by the trespasser that Uncle Hank had said he'd seen. Then they went down to the water.

The stars were like diamonds in the inky sky as Hallie lay back on the quilt Ben had set out for them, causing Beau to shift positions. The dog sniffed her empty wine bottle and then stretched out along the blanket.

"I hope Uncle Hank is in better spirits tomorrow. I'm really worried about him."

Beau let out a snort and moved, curling up next to them. The dog's sudden change in position caused Hallie to jump, her senses on high alert, but Ben had assured her that he could flail around and make it look like he knew ju-jitsu—it was a great party trick he'd learned—and he'd scare off anyone who came into view. Hallie resolved that she needed more wine, but Ben lay down next to her and twisted to face her so she stayed put.

Hallie looked him in the eyes.

"You're tense," he said.

She nodded.

"Seeing your uncle struggling has to be tough when you're already dealing with your own grief."

Grief. That word had so many dimensions for her. "Maybe you can work your magic and make Uncle Hank smile," she said, giving him her total attention, losing herself in his face, in an effort to relax.

"Ah, I don't have any magic," Ben said, turning his face toward the stars. "I wish I did."

There was an unusual vulnerability in his voice just then that Hallie had never heard before. What she loved so much about Ben was the fact that he always seemed to have everything under control. It centered her and gave her a sense of safety she couldn't get with anyone else. So his slight falter caught her attention.

"You okay?" she asked.

"Yeah, I'm fine," he said, his tone lifting just a little.

Hallie rolled over and propped her chin up on her hands, wondering what could possibly be bothering him. Something clearly was. "Everything all right with work?"

"Yeah."

"Ashley?"

Ben smiled, putting her at ease. "Ashley's just fine. You're worrying for no reason. Standing, he reached down for her hands, pulling her up with him. "We're supposed to be forgetting about everything tonight, remember? Time to make you laugh again." Without warning, he scooped Hallie into his arms. Then, out of nowhere, he started toward the waves, swinging her as if he were going to toss her in.

Beau jumped to his feet, letting out a playful bark.

"Ben! Put me down! I've got my favorite shirt on—it's gonna get wet!"

He pretended to throw her, making her squeal while she tried to get free, Beau running into the crashing waves and then back up onto the sand. Just as the tide rushed in, Ben set her down, the salty water washing around their ankles, playing games with her balance. She held on to him to keep steady. In that moment, with Ben holding her, the familiar scent of honeysuckle and salt, and the tiny flashes from the few fireflies that had emerged, Hallie felt like her younger self. If only she could unlearn the things that she now knew to be true, if only they could go back to the times where their ice cream flavor was the biggest decision they had that day…

"Thank you for tonight," she said. "Being with you makes everything better. I don't know how you do it…"

Ben grinned and shook his head, clearly a little baffled himself at how he could make her smile so easily.

Another wave crashed around them and she held on to him more tightly. "Actually, I *do* know how you do it. It's just you being you."

His gaze lingered on her face, nearly swallowing her, as if he wanted to say something. He licked his lips ever so subtly, and she found her fingers intertwined with his. All her fears and sorrows slid out to sea with the tide, and the warmth of his touch made her feel like everything would work out. As they stood there, the rush of wind struggling to get between them, he pressed his lips together like he wanted to tell her something important. She willed him to say it, but he didn't.

"This looks fun," Sydney said, walking over the dune. "Much better atmosphere than in the house." She reached down to pat Beau's side as he greeted her, his wagging tail rippling the blanket he was sitting on. "Robby fell asleep before the movie even got started, so I locked up and came out to find you." The ring of keys for the property dangled from Sydney's finger. "I need a break," she said, her honesty evident in her tone. "I'm exhausted too, except if I try to sleep…" Sydney shook her head, but her thought was derailed, something sheeting over her face as she noticed Ben and Hallie's hands. Sydney shared a silent moment with Ben, an odd look on both their faces, before Ben let go of Hallie and turned toward the water.

Snapping out of whatever it was, Sydney lifted the lid of the cooler and sunk her hands into the ice. "Anything left in here? I need a drink." She pulled out a bottle of beer and twisted off the cap. While tipping it up to her lips, she shut the cooler, dropped the large keyring on top, and slumped down onto the blanket, crossing her legs.

Hallie turned to Ben for an explanation but he had his back to her, looking out over the water.

"What are the others doing inside?" Hallie asked, her curiosity still hanging in the air. She sat down next to Sydney and took the beer out of her sister's hands, drinking from the bottle and then handing it back.

"They're all asleep now. Mama got up for a while and rushed around the house, trying to clean up for Uncle Hank, but I think she wore herself out and she turned in for the night. I spent most of the time with Robby, trying to entertain him."

"I'll get that swing up for him tomorrow," Ben said, turning around. He grabbed Beau's ball from beside the blanket and chucked it down the beach, the moonlight illuminating the yellow enough to see it splash into the surf. Beau galloped through the sand after it.

"Thanks, Ben. I think he'll really like that."

Beau returned, dropping the ball at Ben's feet, his tongue hanging out the side of his mouth as he panted in heaving breaths, his tail swishing back and forth incessantly. Ben threw the ball again and off he went, kicking up sand behind him.

"Y'all want anything else from the cooler before I take it up to the guesthouse?" he asked. "I think I'm heading back." He gave Hallie a fluttering glance, making her wonder what had caused the change in atmosphere. Just moments ago, he looked like he had the world to tell her, and now he was leaving them.

"Stay," Hallie urged him, grabbing one more beer.

"I'm beat," he said with an uplifting look. "And you and your sister could probably use the time to talk." He opened the cooler and set a row of beers in the sand.

"Maybe she can help me figure out how to complete Aunt Clara's list." Hallie nudged her sister playfully, trying to keep things light.

Ben grinned and then whistled for Beau, who'd been distracted by something on the edge of the sea grass. Beau raced toward him. "I'll be up at the guesthouse, Hallie," he said. "See you in a bit."

Hallie and Sydney lay on the blanket, their faces to the stars, the swish of the gulf waves lulling Hallie and quieting the remnants of her thoughts, already hazy from the beer. She'd forgotten all about the things that were weighing on her, or the fact that someone could be lurking on the property.

"I keep thinking about how Aunt Clara used to make us picnic breakfasts out here," Sydney said. Her knees were bent, and she was wriggling her toes and kicking up sand onto Hallie's ankles. The gentle sensation of it was relaxing.

"I'd hardly call them picnics." Hallie laughed through her words. "She made Uncle Hank put the old porch table and chairs in the sand for us, and she had full-on serving dishes and tablecloths." The memory settled like a light feather in her mind—gentle and soft. "It made me feel like a princess."

"Me too. She baked cookies just for us and let us eat them at the crack of dawn, remember? I miss that." Sydney rolled onto her side. "I made sugar snaps for Robby last week and gave them to him for breakfast, but I just couldn't pull it off like Aunt Clara. She made everything seem dreamlike."

"Speaking of dreams!" Hallie laughed before she could even share the memory. "Were you awake that night I had the really bad nightmare and Aunt Clara made Monster Dust?"

Sydney smirked. "No. What happened?"

"I think you were sleeping in the sewing room… I was probably six years old. I had a bad dream in the middle of the night, and Aunt Clara made a place for me to sleep with all kinds of pillows and blankets on the floor by her bed. Then she sprinkled Monster Dust all over the room. I think it must have been glitter. It worked, and I got to sleep, but the next morning, Uncle Hank dropped his wedding ring—remember, he always took it off to sleep—and it rolled away from him. He looked everywhere, crouching down, peering under furniture. He found it eventually, but it woke me up and I nearly screamed at first, thinking he was the monster because he was covered in glitter! It was on his cheek, in his hair…" Hallie burst out laughing, savoring the feeling of it. "He'd been all over the floor looking for his ring, picking up that glitter as he went. When I started to giggle, he couldn't figure out what was so funny, but his face looked like a giant disco ball."

Sydney laughed out loud.

"Aunt Clara couldn't get it off him. Even after he had his shower that day, we still found little shimmers on his skin."

Hallie and Sydney both continued chuckling until the silence took over, and they settled into a quiet calm. They hadn't talked about anything of real importance since Ben had gone in, both of them reminiscing and clearly trying to find a respite for the day's events. But, even under the spell of the night and the alcohol, something else had been bugging Hallie. She'd pushed it out of her mind this whole time, but it kept surfacing, so she figured she should ask.

"Syd? I've been wondering what that look was that you and Ben had?"

"What look?" Sydney kept her eyes to the stars.

"When you first came out. There was a look."

"I don't know what you're talking about…" Sydney folded her hands and put them behind her head.

"You didn't deny it. You're just playing dumb the way you do when you don't want to tell me something."

Her sister took in a large breath and let it out. "I think we were both just… Trying to make sure that you don't fall apart, as you say. I'm sure you probably could with all this going on. You were the closest with Aunt Clara. And it's all coming on the heels of the Jeff situation."

Hallie didn't believe her sister's response entirely, but with her emotions surfacing again at the mention of Aunt Clara and Jeff, she'd already moved on from whatever Ben and Sydney had been communicating to each other. Despite her grief over things she hadn't even uttered, the idea of the list was bothering her more than she'd let on. Hallie couldn't fight the niggling feeling that Aunt Clara didn't feel like she deserved her inheritance, that Hallie somehow needed to work for it. Perhaps it was just because Hallie didn't feel terribly secure with her decisions lately. She felt pretty inadequate about most things at the moment.

"What are you thinking about?" Sydney asked.

Hallie deliberated. "I…" She started to let out her secret, the alcohol giving her courage, the words bubbling up more easily than usual, but then she stopped short. She couldn't do it.

Sydney turned to hear the rest of the sentence.

"I… did the right thing, calling off the wedding," she said instead, choosing to mention the easier one of her burdens. It came out as if she were still trying to convince herself. The truth was, she knew she'd been right. She didn't miss Jeff, just the security of a relationship, so her decision had to be the correct one.

"Of course you did. Take it from me, you don't want to have to go through all that *after* the wedding. It's so much harder."

Sydney had no idea… "I believe we're cursed." The Flynn women could never seem to find that happiness that lasted a lifetime. Not a single Flynn since Aunt Clara had managed it.

"Maybe."

"You never really talked about the day Christian walked out."

"There's nothing to say, really. He'd found someone else—what could I do?" Sydney sat up, wrapping her arms around her knees. "And I think the purpose of it all was to give me Robby."

Robby was Sydney's whole world, the last remnant of the life she'd worked so hard for which had come crashing down around her a few years ago when Robby's father Christian had left. Just like that. Sydney and Christian had known each other since his family had moved down the road from them when he was fifteen. They'd been really close friends until he and Sydney had gone off to college. They'd lost touch for a few years, but after graduation found each other again, and they'd fallen quickly in love. They were married a year after returning home, their degrees in hand. But their marriage was short, and out of nowhere Christian had disappeared, leaving Sydney's life—and heart—shattered.

The one thing about Sydney was that she didn't often share her feelings, even when Hallie wished she would. Hallie was always right there, waiting for the moment when Sydney would finally let down that protective wall she'd put up around herself. But now, with the kind of contemplations Hallie was holding on to, she understood a little.

"I never asked because I didn't want to upset you, but for some reason, everything with Aunt Clara has put things into perspective for me. I feel like I should know what you went through—as your sister." Perhaps if she heard Sydney's deepest feelings, it would give her the strength to divulge her own.

"I haven't talked about it to anyone. It was too hard."

"Can you tell me now? What happened the night that he left?" Hallie urged her.

Sydney's eyes dropped to the blanket. And then, suddenly, she started to talk. "I could tell the moment he got to the door." She ran her hands over her arms, and it looked as though she could still feel the emptiness caused by that moment. "Something had shifted in his face, something wasn't right—I could tell. He had a look I'd never seen before. He was distant. And I immediately started to shake all over—like my body already knew and began to react before my brain."

The tiny line that formed between her eyes when she cried started to show, and Hallie reached out and grabbed her hand.

"He came in, but said he couldn't stay, and that was when I knew for sure. He didn't have to say anything else. Our whole relationship flipped through my mind like a deck of cards, and I scrambled for any reason that this could've happened, but I came up empty. All I asked him was, 'Why?' He broke eye contact then, and his voice was oddly soft, like he was trying not to upset me further. And then he told me he'd found someone else." Sydney blinked away tears, the pain still very present even three years later.

"You can't prepare for something like that," Hallie said, clutching her sister's hand.

Sydney turned toward her. "In an instant, things can change. Our world can change. We have to be so careful with our choices, you know?"

"Yeah." Now, more than ever, she understood how important her choices were. Hallie opened her mouth to let out this terrible thing she was hiding, but she didn't have the courage. "Who needs guys when we have each other," she said, holding out her arms to her sister.

Sydney embraced her, and the two of them held on to one another. Sydney squeezed her tightly in solidarity. "Nothing can ever change between *us*. So we don't need them," Sydney said. "Plus, you're way cleaner than Christian was. I'd much rather live with you."

Hallie laughed. "Let's just live out our days as the two old Flynn women: men-less but darn clean."

"That sounds like the best plan I've heard."

Then something rustled in the sea grass, making them both nervous.

Sydney grabbed the keyring and stood up, looking around. "What are we still doing out here? We should get inside."

Hallie wadded the blanket and kicked the bottles far enough toward the house that they wouldn't wash away. She'd get them in the morning. "Let's go." She linked her arm with Sydney, the way they used to do as girls, and together, they headed up to the path leading to the house.

Chapter Seven

"Whatcha doing?" Ben said the next morning, his bare feet sinking into the sand as he neared Hallie on the beach, holding two cups of coffee as he stopped next to the piled empty beer bottles from last night. He lifted one of her plastic buckets just slightly with his foot, and inspected it.

"I'm trying to make a sandcastle—the first item on Aunt Clara's list." She dipped her hands into one of the buckets she'd filled with water, and patted the small lump of sand.

Beau ran past them after a seagull.

The gulf was translucent this morning, the white sand stretching endlessly under the water as it lapped quietly onto the shore, its sound the hymn of their childhood. Maybe it was the fact that she'd finally had a restful night's sleep, or perhaps it was having Ben around after so long without him, but this morning, as the sunshine hit her face through the window, Hallie had felt a little more like herself. She lay in bed and made a promise to focus on the present, right now, not the past. None of the bad things that had happened could be changed. There was nothing left to do but move forward.

Ben yawned, and only then did she notice that his hair looked untouched. His T-shirt was wrinkled, presumably from the night's sleep.

He'd been under his blankets on the pullout sofa when she'd come in from the beach last night, and she'd made her way to the bedroom through the dark. Beau had greeted her and then resumed his post at the end of the sofa. She'd fallen into bed, losing her battle with consciousness without a moment to consider her thoughts, which hadn't happened in a long time.

Ben set one of the mugs in the sand next to her. "Glad to see you're trying." He gave her a supportive nod. Perhaps he could sense her change in mood.

Aunt Clara had always liked Ben. It was as if the two of them existed on the same plane of consciousness sometimes. When Hallie faced challenges, Ben would give his advice, and then if Hallie shared the same questions with Aunt Clara, she'd offer a carbon copy of what Ben had told her. Hallie wished he could decipher Aunt Clara's motivation for all this.

She rinsed the sand off her hands and picked up the coffee, taking in the warm liquid. She'd risen with the sun this morning, the conversation with Sydney running through her mind. She was going to be intentional about her choices from here on out.

"I think what you told me on the way here is right," she said. "If Aunt Clara wants me to do the things on the list, there has to be some reason. I just can't see it yet."

"That's my girl."

She inhaled the earthy, nutty smell of the coffee and peered over at the small lump of sand beside her. She'd been trying for quite a while and still had no idea how Uncle Hank could get the sand to pack down like he had.

"I'm not doing very well, though," she admitted.

"I think your uncle needs to show you." Ben lowered himself down next to her, his eyes as vibrant as the water.

Hallie caught the familiar scent of him on the breeze, and it was as down-home as Aunt Clara's cherry cobbler. She'd missed this.

"I don't think Uncle Hank is in any shape to build a sandcastle."

Ben frowned sympathetically. "Have you been up to the house yet this morning?"

She shook her head. "I needed some time to get myself together first. Sydney texted that breakfast will be ready at around eight, and for us to come over then. What time is it now?"

"It was seven thirty when I came out, so I guess I should jump in the shower. I can be ready in ten."

"I'll clean up my mess here and join you for breakfast."

Hallie picked up the buckets, stacking them unsteadily and filling the top one with the empty bottles as she held on to her coffee with her other hand. Ben reached down and picked up the last pail for her, dumping the water onto the sand.

"I've got it," she said. "Go get ready and I'll take care of all this."

"Hello." A tentative voice came from behind Hallie as she washed out the last bucket with the hose by the porch, startling her, the remaining coffee in her mug sloshing dark brown liquid onto the white siding before she clutched it to her chest.

She whirled around to find Gavin. This time he wasn't covered in paint, but spruced up and clean-shaven, and without the fear that he was a trespasser, she could actually pay attention. She realized just then that he was rather handsome. His dark brown hair fell across his forehead just a little, the tan on his face showing off those green eyes framed by tiny laugh lines that made him seem friendly before he'd even spoken.

"I keep making you jump," he said with an apologetic smile. "Am I that scary?"

She laughed softly. "No. I'm just generally on edge." She took in his casual but neat clothes—not a single blue smear on them. "No painting today?"

"Not until later. Your uncle lets me come down and use his beach. I live just outside of town and you know how the Firefly Beach public access is—so busy."

Thankfully, Hallie had never had to use it, but she remembered how hectic the small public beach could get in the summer months. She and Aunt Clara had waited for droves of vacationers to lug their beach umbrellas, chairs, towels, and rolling carts of beach toys over the crosswalk, the only stoplight in the town turning green and then yellow and red over again, no one able to move, until a stream of cars snaked down the road behind them. "Yes, I stay away at all costs."

He grinned, putting his hands in his pockets. "I like the light out here in the mornings. And if you can catch a glimpse of them, there's a pod of dolphins that play in this area. They're so lighthearted, bumping each other and jumping out of the water. It's amazing to watch."

"I know those dolphins! I've seen them." Until he mentioned it, she'd forgotten about them. It had been a long time since she'd sat on the beach to observe them, without a care in the world.

"Were you making a sandcastle?" He pointed to the lump of wet sand down the beach.

"Trying." She stacked the buckets next to the house and sprayed the coffee off the siding, then wrapped the hose around its holder, freeing her hands.

"I could never make them either…" He stopped talking and took a step closer to her, into her personal space.

She looked up at him, surprised.

Gavin's chest filled with air and she thought he was about to speak but then didn't, and he smiled instead.

"Were you going to tell me something?" she asked.

For a second he seemed stunned that she could read him, but it only intensified the interest in his eyes. "I thought about asking you... but I didn't want to seem forward, and then I ran into you now and..." He looked out at the water and back at her. Then he just spat it out: "I was wondering if you'd like to get a drink sometime."

Her eyebrows shot up. "Oh! You're asking me out?" His flirting game was clearly rusty, but she didn't mind. Hallie wasn't exactly great at it herself.

Gavin let out a nervous chuckle. "Well, I was attempting to. Very badly. I'm not good at this sort of thing, but after meeting you yesterday, I just thought that if I wanted to ask someone to get a drink then it would be someone like you. You seemed... nice."

"Is that your line?" she said, feeling heat in her cheeks. His honesty, while bumpy in its delivery, was actually quite sweet.

"No," he said, looking a bit embarrassed. "Believe me. I have no lines."

Gavin's timing couldn't have been worse. It was just too soon after Jeff and what she was dealing with. And then there was Uncle Hank and trying to get Aunt Clara's wishes taken care of...

"It's okay," he said quickly, his face falling into a gentle smile that didn't quite hide his disappointment. "I just thought..."

"It's not you," she said. "I'm not in a dating kind of place right now."

"Well, we could get a drink as friends then."

Yes. Friends was good. She'd promised herself never to date a friend so he'd be way off limits, and it couldn't hurt to have another friend. "I'd be happy to get a drink as friends."

"Okay," he said, excitement swelling in his features. "I'll pick you up at seven o'clock tomorrow night."

"I look forward to it. Now, I have to get inside for breakfast. My family's probably waiting on me." She picked up the sandcastle buckets, snagging the handle of the coffee mug with her last free finger.

"Will you tell your uncle that I'm here?" Gavin asked. "He and I had gotten to talking the other day, and he mentioned that he was looking for his bucktail lure. He couldn't locate it, which is a real shame since it's one of the most productive fishing lures on the market. I found him another one. Maybe you can convince him to let me help him out to the shore at some point to use it."

"I hope I can," she said, moved by Gavin's generosity. This went beyond his painting duties. "I'll tell him."

The kitchen was bustling when Hallie entered. Bacon snapped in the frying pan on the stove, Sydney buzzed around Robby, buttering his biscuit—the flaky, hand-rolled look of them making Hallie wonder how long her mother had been up this morning—and Mama was whisking eggs in a bowl like her life depended on it. Uncle Hank sat quietly at the end of the table. He was staring out the window.

The spectacle in front of Hallie was a far cry from the days when Uncle Hank played piano while Aunt Clara cooked, or the late afternoons when early supper was nearly ready, and he lingered around the counter telling jokes just so he could dip his finger in the cookie batter, Aunt Clara swatting his hand away with a loving scold. Seeing him now, it was clear that that version of Uncle Hank had left with Aunt Clara. Hallie's aunt was noticeably absent, the melody of her humming silenced, the air thicker, heavier without her. Ben walked up behind her. Uncle Hank didn't even seem to notice they'd come in.

Hallie didn't move. She wanted to turn around and walk right back out the door, forgetting all about the renewed sense of duty she'd felt this morning. Her appetite was suddenly nonexistent, anguish crawling up her face and pricking her eyes. As if Ben could decipher her body language, she felt his protective hands supportively settle on her shoulders, the steady rise and fall of his chest at her back.

"Can we help with anything?" he asked, to no one in particular. He'd comfort any of them if he could.

Mama's head whipped up from her bowl and she blinked rapidly, as if she needed help understanding for a second. "We're just fine, dear," she said, whisking harder. "Go on and have a seat and I'll bring it to the table."

Ben walked over and pulled out a chair, motioning for Hallie to sit. Then he put his arm around Uncle Hank. "How ya doin'?" he asked.

Uncle Hank finally acknowledged Ben, his eyebrows rising in silent contemplation. He shrugged, but his attention remained on Ben instead of the view out the window.

Ben sank into the chair next to him, between Uncle Hank and Robby. "After breakfast, I was going to hang the old swing back up for Robby." He held up his fist and Robby gave him a fist bump. "Pow," they both said, opening their fingers. Then he turned back to Uncle Hank. "I'll put a chair out there if you'd like to guide me. I know it's been a while since you hung it, but maybe you can teach me how to do the knots in the rope like you do."

"You need double running bowline knots," Uncle Hank returned, his voice gruff. It must have been the first thing he'd said all morning, because both Sydney and Mama stopped and looked at him before glancing at each other.

"I knew you still had it in ya. I'll get that chair out for you," Ben said with a smile. "How high are we going to swing, Robby?"

"As high as we can!"

"That's going to be pretty high. Uncle Hank's swing is really fast. Think you can handle it?"

"Yes," Robby said, excited.

Uncle Hank's expression softened just a little.

Mama set a plate of bacon down. "How many pieces would you like, Uncle Hank?"

"I reckon two or three," he said, his words surfacing a little quicker now. "Where's that old dog of yours, Ben?" The question came out cautiously, almost as if he was afraid to think about anything other than his current state, like he was testing his own waters to see if he could exist in the regular world again.

It was a surprising change in mood, but then again, that was what happened when Ben was around. Just as Hallie had noticed Ben's similarity to Aunt Clara in temperament and opinions over the years, so had Uncle Hank, and the two of them had become fast friends. They'd changed the oil in Uncle Hank's old farm truck together, fished off the dock most Sundays, and of course in the fall there was football.

"Beau's in the guesthouse."

Uncle Hank grunted and scooped an overflowing serving spoon full of eggs, dropping them onto his plate. "Better leave a piece of bacon for him then."

Ben grinned.

Uncle Hank's attention moved to the empty chair where Aunt Clara used to sit and have her coffee every morning, and all the noise fell silent for a moment.

"Robby, what would you like to do today other than swinging?" Mama asked, forcing a smile. "We could go into town and get some ice cream." She tousled his hair.

By the look on Robby's face, he could sense something was amiss with the situation, his eyes now unsure. His gaze moved around the table as he shifted up onto his knees. "Maybe we could take Uncle Hank with us to get ice cream."

Uncle Hank tore his eyes away from Aunt Clara's chair.

"What kind of ice cream do you like, Uncle Hank?" Robby asked.

"Oh, I don't know, son. I like a lot of flavors. I suppose if I had to choose, though, it would be chocolate."

"Everywhere has chocolate, so you should come with us."

Ben piped up, "We should all go. Robby, you and I can hang the swing and then maybe go fishing. By then, you'll be ready for some ice cream."

"Fishing?" Robby's face lit up.

"Yeah. The ladies can do lady-stuff and you, Uncle Hank, and I can fish."

Hallie thought it might be a good time to mention the lure Gavin had gotten for Uncle Hank, which might lift his spirits a bit, but before she could, he cut in.

"All that sounds exhausting," Uncle Hank said, his focus returning to the chair. He filled his fork with eggs and took a bite. When he'd finished he said, "Jacqueline is taking me to see the doctor, and after that, I think I'll just stay in my room."

"I got him an appointment at one," Mama said. She turned to Uncle Hank. "But we'll be right back after, and the fresh air will do you some good. Why don't you help Ben?"

"No," Uncle Hank snapped.

Ben looked thoughtful. "I'll at least bring Beau over to get his bacon," he said. "He'd be happy to see you. And he needs a good walk anyway."

Uncle Hank didn't argue.

"Mama told me that the police department is going to patrol the main road leading to the house," Sydney said to Hallie as the two of them sat side by side in rocking chairs on the expansive porch that stretched along the back of Starlight Cottage, overlooking the gulf. The unceasing coastal breeze sent the paddles of the porch fans above them in soft circles.

With Uncle Hank retreating to his room after breakfast, Ben decided to give him some time before they hung the swing, and he'd enticed Robby to go fishing first. Robby seemed happy to do anything with Ben, and they'd been out there on the shore together the rest of the morning.

"I don't know how policing the road will help," Sydney added, "if the guy's on foot."

"From what Uncle Hank told Mama," Hallie said, "it's always a silhouette of a man, and he walks with a leisurely pace until he's seen. But he doesn't run. He just hides. That's creepy." Hallie looked down the beach at the empty shoreline. "We haven't had any evidence of an intruder since we've been here. Do you think he's real? Or is Uncle Hank imagining things?"

Sydney shrugged, clearly worried. "The officer who spoke with Mama *did* say it's possible that someone could be parking on the main road and walking in. They found some footprints near the property line, but that could be anyone. I'm not so sure. People would notice his car."

"If he is real, what do you think he wants?"

Sydney pressed her toes against the floorboards of the porch to rock backwards. "I have no idea. Everything of any value is in the safe, and only Uncle Hank knows the combination."

Hallie wondered if the prowler was someone wanting to get a look at the property. At least she hoped that was what it was. Because any other reason would make her freeze with fear. "I'm so glad Ben's here," she said. She felt protected when he was around.

Sydney didn't say anything, the silence between them palpable suddenly. It was enough to make Hallie pull her eyes from Ben and Robby to look at her sister.

"What will we do, Hallie?" Sydney asked, her question not clearing things up very much.

Hallie waited for Sydney to help her understand.

"Ben." Sydney nodded toward the water, where Ben and Robby stood together with their fishing poles, Ben patiently showing him how to cast his rod.

"One day, Ben's going to have his own family and we're going to have to let him go."

Sydney's comment stung Hallie. She sat there for a second, trying to imagine life without her best friend. Fear slithered through her and she struggled to maintain her composure—just the thought made her want to cry, given her state. An indescribable feeling came over her, but she couldn't figure out what it was. Incomprehension? "What do you mean?"

"I worry about you."

Hallie stared at her sister, unable to say anything.

"You lean on him a lot. I think it could be unhealthy for you, that's all."

If Sydney only knew that Ben was the *healthiest* thing for Hallie's mental state. He was the only one who could reach her, the only one who could make all the pain leave her mind. And she couldn't believe she'd wasted so much time away from him when she was with Jeff. "It's unhealthy to have a best friend?"

"What if he were to choose to spend time with Ashley when you needed him? Could you handle that?" Sydney ran her fingers along the armrests of the rocker as if she needed something to do with her hands, and it occurred to Hallie that she may have been thinking this for some time. She hadn't relied on Ben through the worst of the last few months, and look at where that got her. But the minute they were together again, they were nearly inseparable.

Ben had always been such a constant in Hallie's life that it hadn't really occurred to her that she might be monopolizing his time. At some point, Ashley may have a problem with it, and one day he might stop coming around. Then she considered how Ben had become mysteriously absent during her engagement to Jeff. Had he been giving her space?

Sydney watched Ben and Robby for quite a while and then said, "I fear Robby will be just as heartbroken when Ben leaves us. He's the only solid male influence in Robby's life. How will we cope without him when he starts his own family?"

Every time Sydney said the word "family," it sliced Hallie like a knife. The day would certainly come when Ben would have a wife and children of his own, and Hallie didn't even want to think about that for fear that it might rip her heart out. "You're getting ahead of yourself." Hallie stopped rocking and turned toward her sister. "You act like he's walking down the aisle."

"Mama said when she was at the jewelry shop getting her watch fixed a few weeks ago, she ran into Ashley. She found her at the ring counter... What if it's closer than you think?"

Apart from the last four months, Ben had always been there for her. And now, as she pondered the idea of Ben entering into a committed relationship, an unexpected feeling of insecurity and unease slinked through her. "You're just speculating."

"I am. But he's a handsome, caring, thoughtful man. You said yourself that Ashley was a great person. You really liked her." Sydney took a band from her wrist and pulled her hair into a ponytail to allow the breeze to cool her neck. "I guess, on the heels of our last talk about choices, I just want to make sure that you have a clear distinction of what the two of you are. It's important. While you're comfortable spending all kinds of time together and being affectionate toward one another like you've always been, the people you both date might not be."

"We have a family-like affection for one another," she said, feeling defensive, put off by the whole conversation. "Being loving toward him wouldn't be weird if he were my brother." She scrambled for some sort of rationalization for all this.

"But he's not," Sydney said gently.

Hallie didn't like what she was hearing at all. It made her anxious. "You're acting really weird. What's bringing this on?"

Sydney's emerald eyes landed on Hallie with purpose. "He *is* like family. To all of us. I want him to be in Robby's life. If Ashley or anyone else he dates doesn't feel comfortable with the way you two are, then I'm worried he'll stay away… Like what happened with Jeff."

That last remark floated in the space between them, stopping Hallie in her tracks.

"What?"

Sydney's brow furrowed. "I wondered if Ben would tell you."

"Tell me what?"

Sydney chewed the inside of her lip, as if she were deciding at that very moment whether to divulge more than she had. Finally, she relented. "Jeff asked him to back off."

Hallie's mouth flew open, her eyes nearly bulging from their sockets. "What?" she said mid-gasp. A firestorm of irritation shot through her veins. All that time she'd needed Ben, at her very lowest, when she didn't know how she'd go on, and he'd stayed away—that was Jeff's doing? "Why would Jeff do that?"

"He got nervous something might be developing between you two."

Four whole months… "How do you know all this?"

"Ben told me." Sydney looked back out at Robby. He cast the line into the water and then said something to Ben that made him chuckle. "After Jeff had told him to stay away, Robby barely saw Ben. I know it's not Ben's job to be with my kid, but Robby adores him. Ben's been there his whole life…"

Hallie had to work to focus on her sister, her mind going a hundred miles an hour. She still didn't know what to say. She couldn't believe it.

"I just wonder if you should be more careful around him. Out of consideration for Ashley and, indirectly, Robby."

The last thing Hallie wanted was to ruin Robby's only chance right now to have a positive male influence. He needed that. "I guess you're right." The idea of being anything other than the way she'd always been with Ben seemed foreign to her. Just when her world had been totally shaken, she now had yet another blow. Life as she knew it was changing…

Chapter Eight

"Let me help you," Ben said, taking Uncle Hank by the arm and gently guiding him to the lawn chair that had been set up for him. Ben made sure to hang the swing before the doctor's appointment so that Uncle Hank could be a part of things.

Flashes of Uncle Hank teaching a young Ben how to bait a fishing hook filtered into Hallie's mind, and she couldn't help but acknowledge that the roles were reversed. Uncle Hank now required caring for when he'd always been the person who cared for everyone else. Ben helped him get settled, and then popped the top off a bottle of beer from the cooler beside Uncle Hank and handed it to him. It was a good thing Mama was out running errands or she would've snatched it right back out of Uncle Hank's hands, claiming he didn't need alcohol in his system.

Hallie made out the hint of a smile at Ben's gesture. Uncle Hank hadn't been thrilled about going outside after his last attempt at the gazebo, but Ben and Robby had convinced him. He'd grumbled all the way out there and hadn't stopped.

"You're perfectly capable of doing this on your own," he said to Ben.

"If I tie the wrong kind of knot," Ben said, opening the cooler again to get himself a bottle of water, "Robby's safety could be at stake. I need you to show me how to do it."

But Uncle Hank continued his pouting. "I don't buy that for a minute." He tipped his beer up and took a drink. "I know you too well, Ben Murray. You'd never do anything to put that boy in harm's way. And you can just as easily search for the answer on that phone of yours. I know you've got it on ya because it keeps ringing off the hook."

Ben didn't offer an explanation, leaving Hallie to wonder who'd been calling. He was terribly busy at work. So many bands came in and out of the studio that he should have installed a revolving door. Hallie wasn't certain at all how they were managing without him. Ben acted as the creative director for many of the artists. He was the magic-maker.

The old tire swing sat in a lump on the front lawn. One solid oak tree, with a trunk bigger than Hallie could wrap her arms around, stood in the middle of the yard, a ladder perched under its lowest branch. She'd sat under that tree to read books as a girl, and she and Ben had hidden behind it when they played Hide and Seek. A storm had knocked the original branch that held the swing down, and no one had ever replaced the swing after. Not until now.

Hallie took a seat on the cool grass next to Sydney.

"What do I need to do?" Robby asked, the width of the heavy rope barely allowing him to grasp it in his little hand. He lifted it, throwing a section of it over his shoulder, the task making him winded.

"Hold that end just like you are, and I'll reach down for it," Ben said, stepping his way up the ladder. "Okay, hand it to me," he said once he was up a few rungs.

Robby dutifully gave the end of the rope to Ben, looking on as he threw the rope over the branch and climbed the extra rung to reach the other side.

"How are those muscles, Robby? Think you can hold that tire?" he called down.

Robby worked to lift the tire, his face serious as he tried his best to help Ben, his thin frame working overtime. He dropped it with a thud and picked it back up, then rolled it over to the ladder and put his hand on it to keep it from falling onto the grass. At last Ben took it from his hands and threaded the rope through it.

"Just hold it steady now," he told Robby. Robby wobbled the tire again and batted Sydney away when she tried to help him stabilize it.

"I've got it, Mama," he said with pride.

"Uncle Hank, this is where I need you," Ben called down, his voice slightly strained from holding the massive ropes in place.

"Make yourself a double loop first," he called up to Ben. "Remember how we did it on that climb in the mountains when you were younger? Do it like that."

"Oh yeah," he said, making two loops and threading the working piece through them.

"That's right. Yep. Wrap it around. Now, tuck it in the hole you've made," Uncle Hank said.

"Right here?" Ben held the wad of rope with one hand and pointed to a small opening in the folds of cord.

"You've got it." Uncle Hank took another sip of his beer.

With the knot secure, Ben came down the ladder. "You can let go now," he told Robby. He put his foot in the tire and stood up on it, testing the safety of the knot under his weight.

"Put your legs through it and I'll push you," he said to Robby.

"Will you push me really high?" Robby asked, threading his legs inside the hole and hanging on to the tire like he was giving it a big bear hug. "Like I said at breakfast. Super high!"

"Want me to?"

Robby nodded excitedly.

"Okay, get ready!" Ben grabbed on to the tire and pulled it back toward him. Then he ran, thrusting the swing forward with all his might.

With a squeal of laughter, Robby sailed through the air, his feet dangling above the grass. "Uncle Hank! Look at meeee!" he cried, before bursting into a fit of giggles as the tire twirled while swinging like an enormous pendulum.

Then the most wonderful thing happened. Uncle Hank laughed— really laughed; a loud guffaw, his earlier scowl softening. Hallie wished Mama had been there to see it, but she'd been out all morning, probably getting the groceries they'd need for the week. She'd been gone since just after breakfast.

"Push me again!" Robby said as the swing slowed.

Sydney got up to play with Robby, allowing Ben to come over to Hallie and Uncle Hank. He plopped down beside Hallie and draped an arm around her shoulders. The gesture felt strange now, after the talk she'd had with Sydney. His phone rang again. He pulled away from Hallie and reached into his pocket to silence it, without even checking to see who it was.

"Who keeps calling you?"

"No one important," he said. "Uncle Hank, you got Hallie worried with your comment. My phone's only rung twice."

Uncle Hank set his empty beer on the cooler beside him. "Three times if you count just now. That's more than I get all week."

"Is it work?" she asked.

Ben gave her a content look. "Work is fine." Then he got up and helped Sydney push Robby on the swing.

As Hallie watched them, it occurred to her that she'd missed out on a lot of family time when she was with Jeff. It hadn't been intentional, but they'd just done things together rather than with everyone. Watching Sydney and Ben playing with Robby, spinning him on the tire swing, Hallie had an overwhelming feeling that it had been a close call with Jeff. She'd gotten so wrapped up in her life and everything she'd gone through that she'd forgotten what it was like to be a Flynn.

She wondered if Uncle Hank had forgotten too. He was smiling, with a tiny glint in his eyes that showed her the old Uncle Hank was still in there. If they could just have more moments like these… She looked at the house. It had seen its share of tragedy when it was taken over as a hospital by Northern troops during the Civil War; it had weathered countless storms, but it stood proudly and firmly in its spot, despite it all. The Flynns were like that too. They could get battered, feel empty, but they were strong. It was how they were built.

"I'll be right back," Hallie said, and without any further explanation, she ran to the guesthouse.

She pushed open the screen door, the familiar scent of gardenia from the nearby bushes wafting toward her with the movement. She progressed quickly down the hallway to the bedroom and opened her suitcase, squatting down next to it. Carefully, she moved her clothes until she got to the box she'd packed, not understanding why she'd packed it until now. She opened it up and retrieved her camera. It wasn't anything fancy—an old Canon that she'd had for years—but it took beautiful photos and she did have her list to consider…

With the camera in hand, Hallie headed back out to the yard. But as she neared the others, Uncle Hank stood up and lost his balance. Ben and Sydney had their backs to him, Robby's laughing like an eerie echo in the silence of motion as Hallie started to run. She dropped her camera, pushing her muscles as far as they'd go. "Ben!" she called, just as Uncle Hank hit the ground.

Ben rushed over to him and started to help him up. Hallie reached them and put her hands on her knees, gasping to catch her breath.

"I lost my balance," Uncle Hank said, clearly stunned by his fall. He stumbled toward the chair that had turned over, the empty beer bottle in the grass, but Ben stopped him.

"I'll get it," he said. "Just hold on to me for a second."

Sydney hurried over and righted the chair.

"Does anything hurt? Are you in pain anywhere?" Ben asked.

"I can't live without her," Uncle Hank said without warning, ignoring Ben's efforts to assess the situation. Uncle Hank looked at all of them, his eyes pleading, but there was nothing they could do to help him with this. "I'm falling apart now that she's gone. What's the purpose in me staying behind? So I can just exist in a chair somewhere?" His eyes filled with tears. "I'm trying, but I just don't see the point in sticking around."

Hallie's moment of hope slid away from her. Uncle Hank didn't see the point in living. That was a horrible thought.

"If you're still here," Sydney said frankly, "then you're needed. We need you. We couldn't cope with both of you gone. You have to help us all."

"I can't help you," he said, dejected.

The man who could always fix everything couldn't fix this. He was broken himself. And Hallie knew that if they all allowed themselves to think too much about Aunt Clara, they'd be just as broken. How does a family move on after someone so important leaves it?

"You doing okay?" Ben said, peeking out onto the screened porch of the guesthouse.

Hallie held her phone in her hand, the rippling gulf only calming her slightly. She'd texted Mama after she'd returned from the doctor with Uncle Hank, but hadn't heard back. Uncle Hank wanted to be alone, and Sydney had taken Robby to get some lunch in town. So, while Ben made a few work calls, Hallie had gotten her book and settled on the porch.

"I'm okay," she said.

"You sure?"

"Yeah."

He was in fresh clothes, his hair combed, his face clean-shaven. "I have to go out for a little bit. I wanted to make sure you didn't need anything."

"Is it something I can help with?"

"No. You just sit back and enjoy the sunshine. You can read your book—what are you reading?"

Hallie held it up and he broke out into a huge smile. "*The Art of Photography*."

She allowed the small moment of amusement to pass between them. She'd packed the book with an eye roll but now it seemed to be calling her. "I go back and forth with that list, but in a weird way, I feel like it brings me closer to Aunt Clara whenever I consider it again. I just wish I could've talked to her about it. I'd have done anything she wanted me to do—but it would've been nice if she'd told me why."

"Perhaps the why isn't as important as the journey."

"Maybe you're right."

"I can feel it, Hallie." Then, with that grin she'd seen so many times, the one that he seemed to save just for her, he said, "Back in a bit."

Not wanting to pry, she wondered where he was going, but didn't press him any further. "Okay. See ya," she said.

With a wave, Ben shut the door and Hallie texted her mother again. No answer.

She opened her photography book and tried to focus on the pages in front of her, but her mind was on a million other things. She closed it and decided to head into the cottage to see if she could talk to Uncle Hank. She was worried about him after his fall, and wanted to see if he was all right. And maybe, if she could get him talking, he could offer some direction in all this. The two of them thinking together might just crack Aunt Clara's code and help Hallie to understand what Aunt Clara really wanted from her. Hallie was hopeful they could.

Chapter Nine

Hallie picked up her camera and her sketchbook and took them with her as she walked to the main house. A gull flew overhead, and instinctively, she pulled the camera up to her eye, the feeling of it in her hands like tangible nostalgia. As a girl, she was rarely without it, catching so many shots of her childhood that if she ever organized all the photos, she could have her entire autobiography in vivid color.

She pointed it at the bird and clicked, then held it out to view the digital picture. Capturing an image and freezing it in time, the light coming in just right, the angles perfect—it was as uniquely satisfying as it had been for her so long ago.

She couldn't remember the day she'd set her camera down for the last time, or when she'd boxed it up with her drawings and shoved them in the top of her closet, but just this one image made her wonder why she had. She pointed it at the restless gulf and snapped another shot. When she'd reached the porch, the sight of Aunt Clara's rocking chair caught her eye, that familiar void coming back. She turned her camera toward it and took a photo. The image was hauntingly clear on her screen. Hallie crouched down on the top of the porch steps and opened her sketchpad, drawing the chair in the same light she'd just found in her photo. She imagined the chair with the birds she'd seen carved into the back of it. Her pencil moving effortlessly, she dug the lead into the page, carving the birds out on the back of the rocker.

Hallie remembered sitting on these steps doing the same thing when Aunt Clara was alive. The two of them would sketch out designs, and while Aunt Clara was actually working, Hallie would pretend she was too. "Make sure you find a job that doesn't feel like work," Aunt Clara would tell her. "That's how you know you're where you belong." Hallie looked down at the chair she'd drawn, thinking about her job right now at the advertising agency.

With a deep breath, she closed her sketchpad and went inside.

"Uncle Hank!" she called into the quiet.

His voice sailed in from the kitchen. "I'm in here."

He was sitting at the table, facing the window with the view of the water outside. How long had he been sitting there alone? Hallie set her drawing pad on the counter and took a seat beside him. He looked down at the camera in her lap.

"The old thing still works?"

Hallie turned it around and clicked through the digital images she'd captured on her way in, so he could see them.

"Looks like *you* still work too," he said, allowing himself a smile.

"Would this qualify me as a photographer?" she teased.

He chuckled. "I believe it does. But your Aunt Clara and I had long talks about your talent, and she was always baffled as to why you never put it to use. I think that might have been what she was hoping for."

"I miss her," Hallie admitted.

Uncle Hank looked back out the window, his expression contemplative.

"I notice the emptiness without her."

Uncle Hank didn't speak for a couple of breaths and he wiped a tear that had escaped from his eye. "I reached for her hand last night in bed, and it wasn't there. I've reached for her hand every night, for fifty years." His lips wobbled and he cleared his throat.

Hallie got up and wrapped her arms around his neck, embracing him tightly. "Aunt Clara told me that you used to steal the covers," she said, in hopes that sharing their feelings might help them both.

Uncle Hank rolled his eyes, his playful side taking over. "She claimed I stole the covers as a reason to yank them all to her side, so I suppose that I did steal the covers, in her mind, since apparently they *all* belonged to her."

Hallie laughed. When she did, Uncle Hank laughed too and she quickly picked up her camera and snapped a shot. Uncle Hank didn't seem to mind.

She showed it to him.

"You could work for magazines with shots like that. You need to be doing something creative. Why are you working as a receptionist at that advertising agency?"

"I'm not a receptionist. I'm a project manager and it's a creative job. I've had a hand in some very large projects," she said, her defensiveness coming through when she hadn't meant it to.

She liked her job. It was interesting, and the people were great. She actually had a few projects that had piled up that she was excited about. Her boss really believed in her creative vision, and sometimes she was able to offer sketches and ideas in the design meetings. He'd even let her manage a few large-scale displays around Nashville. She had a nice little set of ideas started for a new venture with Crystal Water, a bottled water company and one of their biggest clients, even though she was leaving them behind unfinished at the moment, her coworker Stacy taking care of what she could for the next two weeks in Hallie's absence.

Having work made her feel needed, and it squashed the guilt she'd always felt for dropping her great aunt's name into the conversation during the interview. Aunt Clara, a well-known figure in the design world, would never allow any of her family members to use her as a reference. Aunt Clara had started her company from ground zero, using her own hard-earned money, and she didn't believe in raising her family in privilege. While she'd never let them fall, she wouldn't allow them to take the easy road either.

"Life is what *you* make it," she'd say, "not what *I* make it. Your life is a blank slate. Dream it up just the way you want it, and then go get it. It's your own masterpiece to create."

Working at Willis Advertising wasn't what Hallie would call a masterpiece-move, but did anyone really have a job like Aunt Clara's? Not many. It was just like her to romanticize life, because that was how she lived it. They should all be that lucky.

In the end, Hallie had settled for the life of a regular person, a nine-to-five of mediocrity that gave her enough money to enjoy herself and let off steam on the weekends. But there was a tiny piece of her that always wondered what else was out there, and being near Aunt Clara made her hope that some of that magic her aunt had would penetrate the air around Hallie and send something special her way. When Aunt Clara died, any likelihood of magic had dried up right on the spot.

"It never even occurred to me to be a photographer."

"Clearly it did. It was on your list."

"I made that list one Saturday when I was bored. And I was twelve! My interests had changed completely by the next day. I probably wanted to be an astronaut after that. Good thing I didn't write the list *that* day."

That made him laugh.

"That's what makes this so frustrating. Aunt Clara is holding me to something I never even intended to be a permanent thought. Being a photographer was just a schoolgirl whim."

"Or the tiny seed of a dream that had yet to be dreamt."

Hallie looked back down at the image on her camera, and it was as if someone else had taken it. She didn't want to admit that Uncle Hank might be right. She scrolled through the others she'd taken on the way over. She didn't have technical skills. She hadn't even taken a photography class. How was she to know if she was any good? What if she put herself out there and everyone could see her inexperience right away?

"I'm an amateur," she said.

"That's how everyone begins, Hallie." He leaned into her view. "Aunt Clara was a designer. She knows design when she sees it, and she was adamant that you have talent, but not just in photography. You're a creative just like her. That's why the two of you were inseparable—you had a different way of seeing things, an unspoken understanding of one another."

Hallie knew he was right. "Will you teach me how to build a sandcastle?" she asked.

It was then that Uncle Hank grinned just like he used to, a wide, endearing smile that spread across his face. "Of course."

"Where have you been?" Hallie asked Mama when she finally emerged on the back porch of Starlight. She was holding an envelope. "I was starting to worry."

"I was…" Mama's attention was on Uncle Hank, who had spent the last hour on the porch with Hallie. He'd opened up a little, and talking to Hallie seemed to lift his spirits, but Mama coming in had changed his demeanor. "May I speak to you for a second?"

Hallie stood up and followed her mom into the kitchen, shutting the door behind them. "Is something wrong?"

Her mother set the envelope on the table, and cut the plastic wrapping off a bouquet of flowers she must have picked up at the market. She dumped the old baby's breath from the table's centerpiece, rinsed out the vase, and started arranging the new blooms into it. "I never said anything to you growing up, but remember how Aunt Clara always left an empty seat and place setting at the table at Thanksgiving? Did you ever notice that? Even when we had so many people we had to push tables together, there was always an empty seat." She snipped the end off of a daisy and threaded it through the other greenery in the vase.

It hadn't occurred to Hallie before, but now that Mama mentioned it, she did remember that.

"Uncle Hank gave me another letter addressed to me when we got here. Inside were directions to pass this along." Mama slid the envelope across the table to Hallie before she started searching the cabinets, eventually pulling out a second vase.

Hallie opened the letter inside and read Aunt Clara's script, addressed to Lewis Eubanks. "Who is Lewis Eubanks?"

"I asked Uncle Hank and he wouldn't say anything, but I could tell he knew exactly who it was, and he got really angry. In my whole life, I've never seen him like that. I was glad when Ben came to ask him to hang the swing because it cut the tension in the room. I left right away and stayed out of his way until I felt like I'd given him enough time to get over it." She plunged a few small flowers into the second vase.

"I don't understand."

"In the letter accompanying this one, Aunt Clara told me she saved a seat for him every Thanksgiving and that we have to find him. He must have meant a lot to her. She's left him a hundred thousand dollars and a second letter that's locked in the safe."

"Oh my gosh." That was a lot of money. This Lewis had to be family—he and Hank shared a last name. And he must be close family or Aunt Clara wouldn't have expected him to come to Thanksgiving. "Why wouldn't Uncle Hank tell you who he was?" Hallie placed the letter back on the table.

"I don't know. He clammed right up and just kept shaking his head with his jaw clamped shut." Mama looked back down at the envelope. "He seemed so bothered by it that I didn't press him any further. But you know that Aunt Clara only left letters and inheritance payouts to her immediate family."

That was true. Hallie's mother had been renting a farmhouse outside of Nashville; the lease had the option to purchase. She'd rented with the intention of saving up her money and buying it one day. With the inheritance, she'd be able to do that now. She dreamed of filling the front porch, overlooking a neighbor's horse farm, with a large family. Hallie couldn't understand it. Robby's father had left Sydney, surprising them all, and plans for Hallie's impending nuptials had fallen apart, so the outlook of big family gatherings on the old porch wasn't very promising. But it was just like her mother to plan for the best-case scenario.

Sydney had been left a large sum of money as well, and while Hallie hadn't read what was in her sister's letter from Aunt Clara, she did know that her aunt had left some pretty inspirational words—Sydney gave her two weeks' notice at the law firm where she worked as a paralegal without anything else lined up.

Robby was given funds with explicit instructions for Sydney on how to create an account and when to invest through a college savings plan.

Which left Hallie, and she was still waiting to find out what Clara had left for her once she completed her list.

"I've been in town, seeing if anyone knew Lewis Eubanks, but I couldn't find anyone who did."

"Wes doesn't know?"

"Nope."

"That's so strange… Do you think he's a long-lost cousin or something? I've never even heard Uncle Hank mention him."

"No idea. I wondered the same… It's probably best that we let it go for now because it only seems to upset Uncle Hank, and he has enough already to make him emotional. Maybe we can find this Lewis quietly and just pass along the money. I'll call the lawyer tomorrow and find out the best way to do that."

"Yeah, that's a good idea."

She handed the smaller vase to Hallie. "You can put this in the guesthouse," she said. "How is Uncle Hank?" Mama nodded toward the door.

"I made him smile."

The tension in Mama's face melted and happiness washed over it. "That's great, Hallie. If anyone can lift his mood, it's you. I'm so glad you decided to come."

"Me too." And she meant it.

Chapter Ten

Hallie lay on the sofa in the guesthouse. The sun had almost completely disappeared behind the horizon, but she hadn't turned the lights on just yet. She rotated her camera toward the bay window and snapped a picture, Mama's vase of flowers she'd put on the counter shadowed against the purple sky. Happy with the outcome, she set the camera on the coffee table.

But then she narrowed her eyes and picked it back up, a tingle of worry sliding down her spine. Squinting at the screen, she saw the dark image of a person, way out by the beach. Hallie got up and ran to the window, comparing her photo with the view. It was definitely the outline of a person, but now whoever it was had gone. *Could it have been Ben?* she wondered. But he wouldn't be coming home via the beach at the back of the property, unless he'd decided to walk in from town, taking the path that ran along the coast.

She was just about to turn on the lamp, her fingers trembling over her phone keyboard to text Ben, when he came in, causing her to scream.

Beau, who'd been curled up at the door waiting for Ben, jumped to his feet.

Ben stumbled over Beau and clicked on the kitchen light, momentarily blinding Hallie.

"What's the matter? Did you have a nightmare?" He squatted down and gently wrestled with Beau for a second.

"No, I was just resting and I saw this." She held out her camera with a shaky hand. "Did you come in through the beach?"

Ben shook his head, clearly confused by her question. Before she could even explain, she was on the phone with her mother, recounting what she'd seen through the lens. Mama told her she'd call the police right away.

Ben peered out the window, the camera still in his hand, along with a brown bag that he'd come in with. "Could it just be someone taking a walk?"

"On a private beach?" She ran to the door and locked the bolt.

"The little shadow of a person doesn't seem menacing. If it's even a person. It could be just a glitch in the photography." Ben tried to zoom in on the image but it got blurry.

"Uncle Hank lets Gavin, the painter, use the beach. Could it be him?" Hallie prayed it was.

"Maybe."

"It scared me to death."

"Well, I'm here now to protect you." Ben threw himself into an energetic ju-jitsu move, making her laugh despite how scared she was.

"You're making jokes and this person could be anyone... He could be a killer!"

"A killer who is casually strolling away from the house, nothing is stolen, and he's now gone. And that's *if* it was even a person at all."

"It was a person! And they shouldn't be on the property."

"You said yourself that it might be the painter. And there isn't anyone there now, that I can see." He set the camera down and held up the brown bag he had in his other hand. "Let me distract you... Sorry I took so long." He paused dramatically, shaking the brown bag, getting Beau excited. "I got pie to apologize."

Hallie perked up. "Is it...?"

"Yes. It is."

Hallie gasped.

Neither of them had to actually say "Sally Ann's Bakery" to know that inside the bag was one of Sally Ann's homemade peach cobblers. The whole town knew about her famous cobbler, and in the summer months they had to be ordered specially, because they sold out faster than she could say "pie."

"How did you get one?"

"I promised her a pre-release Sylvan Park CD and she got one from the back. She said she saves them for emergencies. I told her that leaving you without a word all day was definitely an emergency." He set the bag on the table. "It'll go great with the wine we have."

"Yes. It will." Hallie got up and retrieved two plates from the cabinet, while Ben grabbed napkins and the wine glasses.

He filled their glasses and pulled out a kitchen chair for her.

"So what were you doing all day?" she asked, setting the plates down and opening the bag, sinking her hand into it and removing the plastic cobbler box.

"Ashley's in town."

"Oh! I'm glad you were able to see her," Hallie said over her shoulder, as she opened the drawer to get the pie server. She cut them each a slice and placed one on each plate.

"Yeah." Ben took his plate and sat down across the table.

"Feel free to have her over."

There was an odd pause. It was so subtle Hallie almost missed it. "I don't want you to feel like you have to entertain her," Ben said. "You have enough going on."

"I love her, though! She and I have so much to talk about. We seem to like all the same things; we can chat for hours."

He stared at her, his face unreadable. And then he snapped out of whatever thought he had. "I know." He scraped the point off his slice of cobbler and took a quiet bite, looking tired all of a sudden.

"Is there something you aren't telling me?"

Their eyes met and he held her gaze, his lips parting just slightly as if he wanted to tell her, but he shook his head. "Nothing new. How's Uncle Hank?"

"Sad. But he's going to show me how he makes his sandcastles."

"Ah, that's awesome. How did you manage that?"

"We were reminiscing about Aunt Clara and it just seemed like a good time to ask. He looked happy to show me."

"I'm so glad to hear it. And I want to see that. We should get him to show us tomorrow morning. I have no plans."

Beau sighed and switched positions loudly under the table.

"I know, boy. You need a walk. Maybe Hallie will go with us after we finish our pie."

"I'd love to."

Ben smiled. "I'll refill our wine before we go. We can take it with us."

The police had been out to the house to investigate what Hallie had seen, but they couldn't find anything amiss. No one else in the area had reported seeing anyone, and their patrols had been relatively quiet, which was typical of Firefly Beach. It was so secluded from the other villages that, unless it was tourist season, people left their doors unlocked because they all knew one another. But even at its busiest, if some stranger were to show up around town, people would talk, and that person wouldn't be a stranger for long.

Without a solid description, locating the individual once they'd gotten off the property was like finding a needle in a haystack. The police officers filed the report and said they'd send around a couple of guys to monitor the property, and as one of the officer's fathers was a good friend of Uncle Hank's, he promised to drive past every day, even when he was off duty. Once they had the all-clear from the officers that the property was free of intruders, Ben and Hallie walked Beau and finished off the wine. Their empty glasses sat beside them on the dock, their sandy bare feet dangling above the moonlit water.

Hallie kept looking down the beach in both directions, but the only thing she saw was sand and surf, the lighthouse towering over them as if it were keeping watch.

"Don't worry," Ben told her.

"How can you say that?"

"Because all we have is a grainy photo of something that might or might not be a person. There are pictures of Big Foot that are clearer than that, and we still don't know if Big Foot exists." Ben threw a ball into the surf and Beau loped off the dock, diving in to retrieve it. He swam to shore and ran onto the beach, shaking the water from his fur. "And the police didn't find a thing. So let's enjoy ourselves."

"If it was the same person Uncle Hank has seen," Hallie said, a wave rippling up under her toes, "I'd think if he were trying to steal something of value, he'd drop in when no one was here. But there's no evidence to suggest that's happening. In the past, Uncle Hank said he saw him at the window, but, if that was him tonight, he's staying out on the beach now, further from the house. It doesn't make any sense. What does he want?"

"The only way we can answer that is by catching him. *If* he comes around again. Maybe he's just a curious wanderer."

"I wish we knew."

Ben put his arm around Hallie and she let him keep it there. He made her feel safe.

As the night went on, Hallie and Ben talked about all kinds of things. She'd told him about Lewis and Aunt Clara's letters. He'd shared stories about a few of the singers he'd been working with and one of the songwriters he really liked. It had taken all evening, but she'd finally gotten up the nerve to ask him about those four months…

"Why didn't you say something to me?"

"I didn't want to get in the way of your happiness," he said.

"You think I'd be happy with someone who wouldn't want me to see you?"

Ben looked thoughtful. He squeezed her tighter and she laid her head on his shoulder. However, she thought about what Sydney had said and wriggled away from him, grabbing the ball that Beau had set beside them. "Beau!" she called, standing up on the dock and tossing it with a *plop* into the water. Beau happily followed it in. The briny air rushed over her skin. She took in a deep breath and let it out.

When Hallie turned back, Ben was watching her. Whenever he looked at her, it was as if she could see whole thoughts in his eyes. She could never read those thoughts, but they were ever present in his gaze. He approached everything with such passion; so different from her other friends, different from Jeff—anyone really.

There was no one like him, and she was so glad she was lucky enough to have him in her life. Sydney was right. Hallie didn't want to ever lose him.

But she needed to be adult about things, despite her grief. She had to find her own strength and try not to rely on Ben so much. She'd make sure she didn't mess this up.

"I might sleep in the main house tonight," she offered, despite wanting to continue their evening together. "You know, stay in the empty room next to Uncle Hank."

Those indistinguishable thoughts behind his eyes seemed to multiply right in front of her. "Why?"

"I really got somewhere with him today. I think I should be close by."

Ben's eyebrows rose in contemplation. "I can move us into the main house."

"I was thinking just me. I wouldn't want you to feel squeezed in there. The bed's small and you'd end up on the sofa in the living room. You'll sleep better in the guesthouse bedroom with Beau, and the quiet will give you an opportunity to work on your music. I'd feel guilty if I didn't give you time to get it done."

He smiled but it didn't reach his eyes, and she hoped she hadn't offended him. But then he got up and grabbed their glasses. "I'll help you get your things into the house."

"Thank you."

Ben called for Beau and they started back to the guesthouse.

The eleven o'clock news had finished, and a barrage of commercials blared on the screen in Hallie's new bedroom, so she muted the television, preferring silence while still requiring the light from the screen.

She didn't want to be alone in there in the dark. She'd be left with only her other senses and the sounds of the waves outside. The smells all around her, and the feel of the extra soft bedding Aunt Clara used, took her back to her childhood.

The space doubled as a sewing room, so one wall was full of shelving with Aunt Clara's fabrics and spools of thread. Her lilac scent still lingered everywhere, and her reading glasses sat untouched on the sewing table. Hallie lay on the bed and closed her eyes, wishing for those days when her heart was young and her burdens were light. What happened to them when they got older? Why did the innocence of youth have to fade?

Her phone buzzed with a text: *Whatcha doing?*

It was Ben.

She rolled over and texted back: *Nothing. Just lying here. Everything okay?*

Yeah, I only wanted to say hi. I saw the light from your TV through the window so I knew you were up. I'm bored out here by myself. Even Beau left me for the comfort of your bed.

She smiled at her screen as if he could see her now, and typed, *Uncle Hank has vanilla ice cream in the freezer…* Hallie waited for him to come back, the three little dots pulsating under her text. They disappeared and her phone screen sat empty. Maybe Beau got up… When Ben didn't answer, she turned over and stared at the ceiling, everything racing back through her mind again.

A quiet knock on the bedroom door pulled her from her thoughts.

When she answered it, Ben was standing in the hallway, holding up the bottle of her favorite blackberry wine. He whispered, "I've heard this is divine over vanilla ice cream."

She laughed softly, and his eyes swallowed her, that ever-present fondness that she loved so much showing in them.

"And," he said, "we really need to get Uncle Hank to move the hide-a-key. Everyone knows the first place to look is under the front mat." He held it up and put it in his pocket.

Hallie took him by the arm and they walked soundlessly to the kitchen, careful not to put too much weight in each step to creak the floorboards.

"Where does Uncle Hank keep the ice cream scoop?" Ben whispered, as he reached into the cabinet and pulled out two bowls.

Hallie pointed toward the drawer by the sink, and Ben slid it open while she clicked on the small lamp in the corner of the counter so they could see, even if only a bit. He ran his fingers along the contents of the drawer, making them clink softly. Hallie went over to help. She moved in over his hand, feeling for the rounded edge of the scoop until she got it without a sound, and held it out to him.

When he reached out to take it, they fumbled the exchange in the dim light and the scoop fell to the floor with a clang. Hallie threw her hand to her mouth to stifle her giggle.

"Always when you're trying to be quiet," he said faintly, bending down to pick it up. He took it to the sink and washed it off. Even the running water sounded loud in the darkness.

"We're gonna wake the whole house up," she said with another snicker.

"Nah. We're fine." He got out the tub of ice cream and scooped a large helping for both of them. Then, with a hollow pop, he uncorked the bottle and poured the sugary-sweet blackberry wine over the top.

"How much wine did you bring?" she teased him.

"Clearly not enough. This is the last bottle, apart from your mama's chardonnay. We're definitely going to need to run in to town tomorrow. Unless you want ice cream with beer on top. Which might not be terrible…"

She laughed, her heart so light at their banter that she wished they could stay in this moment forever.

Ben put his finger to his lips to remind her to keep it down, and placed her bowl on the table. Then he sat across from her, the soft light filtering around them like a warm hug. Ben was the only person she could have wine and ice cream with at midnight and consider it normal behavior.

"Remember that night when we were nine, and we both crawled out of our windows and met each other in your tree house to eat chocolate bars at two in the morning?" She laughed into her fist to suppress the sound.

"Yes. We fell asleep out there and our mothers nearly killed us."

"Mama called Sheriff Jones! They thought we were missing."

"We tortured our poor parents over the years." He scooped up a spoonful of ice cream. "But we never meant to. I just wanted to offer you chocolate because I knew it was your favorite. That's all it was."

Hallie couldn't take her eyes off him, and in that instant, she realized how insignificant her relationship with Jeff had been compared to this. Her conversations with Ben were more intimate than even a kiss. In those moments, he had all of her, everything she could give. It was a feeling she'd never had with anyone else, and defining it was too difficult to get her head around. While Jeff had been romantic at first—and sweet—he didn't hold a candle to Ben. How had she not seen it? Her years with Ben were worth more than anything else in her world. But what did this realization mean?

They both shared their moment of nostalgia before the harsh kitchen light clicked on above them, making them squint.

"What are y'all doing up?" Mama said, standing in her summer bathrobe, rubbing her eyes.

"Having ice cream," Ben said, teasing as if it were totally normal to have ice cream at that hour.

"Y'all scared me half to death. You're lucky I found you earlier and not later. I was coming in to get a frying pan to defend myself. I could've clubbed you one." She went over to the counter and tipped the tub toward her with her finger to peer down into it. "I hope you have enough for me." Mama turned around and walked over toward them, her nose in the air, following the scent of something. "Is that alcohol I smell?"

"Blackberry wine." Hallie held up a spoonful.

Mama leaned in and took a bite of it. "Oh my! That's wonderful."

Ben had already gone to the counter and retrieved another bowl, scooping more ice cream and drizzling the wine on top. He handed it to Mama. "I feel like I haven't seen you," he said, before pulling out a chair at the table for her beside Hallie.

"I've been busy," she said. "I followed a noise down here, but then hearing your giggling took me back to old times and I just had to be a part of it. I hope it's okay if I join you two."

"Of course," Hallie said, putting her arm around Mama and giving her side a squeeze. "I've missed you. I feel like we've had so much going on that we haven't had time to just be, you know?"

"Yes." Mama shook her head but then smiled as she looked between Hallie and Ben. "It doesn't feel like it, I'm sure, but I'm so glad you two are here. It makes everything better." She swirled her spoon around in her ice cream. "I recall when Aunt Clara used to get up in the night and make coffee. I would tell her the caffeine wasn't good for her at that hour and she'd always say, 'Well, I'm up anyway, so it can't hurt.'"

Hallie grinned. "She was so calm and collected, but at the same time, restless."

"Yes. It was her creative soul. She always wanted to be doing something, filling her minutes to their fullest. You know what she said about sleep? She said, 'I can sleep when I'm gone from this earth.'" Mama took a bite of ice cream and swallowed, clearly pondering that statement. "She'd be happy to see us all together, up in the middle of the night."

"I'll bet she's here with us. She's still not sleeping," Ben ventured.

"You're probably right." Mama said.

Hallie let her gaze fall on the empty chair and this time, it didn't feel as empty as it had the first time she'd seen it. She caught Mama looking at it too, and they both smiled at each other knowingly.

"Uncle Hank is going to show me how to make a sandcastle tomorrow."

"Oh?" Mama continued swirling her ice cream around in her bowl, the wine coloring it a light shade of lavender. "I was wondering if we should hire someone to stay with him during the day when we aren't here, to make sure he can get out to the gazebo when he wants to, and to keep an eye out for anyone who comes onto the property."

"That's a good idea," Ben said. "I know Wes had someone helping Maggie when she had her knee surgery. We could go into town and ask tomorrow."

Hallie scraped the melting ice cream in her bowl to get a mouthful onto her spoon. "Let's go in together. I wanted to take a look at that gallery." She finished her bite and then turned to Mama. "Would you like to go with us, Mama?"

"I'd love to. It would be nice to get out again and talk to people. Aunt Clara would've wanted that for us. She was a people person.

Her love of being around others was what made her such an excellent designer. She could read people really well, and she was a great judge of what they'd want."

Hallie had to wonder if it was that judgment that had made Aunt Clara give her the list. Her aunt might have known what Hallie wanted before she did. But only time would tell…

Chapter Eleven

"The key is water," Uncle Hank said from the chair that Ben had set up for him under a nautical-striped beach umbrella in the sand this morning, so he could help Hallie build a sandcastle. Ben had taken everything out to the shore for them, but then Ashley had called and asked him if he'd go into town to have coffee. Hallie had encouraged him to go, even though Ben had wanted to be with them for this.

"Even when you think you've got too much," Uncle Hank continued, "you dump more on. It won't hurt at all. It just soaks in." The umbrella flapped wildly against the wind, rippling above them, but Ben had secured it well.

Hallie tipped a bucket over, the salty water splashing onto the sand.

"Get one more bucketful."

She turned another over, the white sand becoming a pale shade of tan, the umbrella casting a long shadow over it.

"Now, start to shape your sand. Pack it into that plastic castle mold you have there."

Hallie did as she was told, and what had seemed nearly impossible was now so easy. She was building it high, each section staying in place perfectly. All she'd needed was a little help from Uncle Hank.

For years, he'd held his secret in. No one knew how he was able to do it, and surprisingly none of them had figured it out.

She stacked another castle on top of the other, using her hand to mold it gently. "This is so easy. When I was growing up, why didn't you tell me how to do this?"

"You never asked."

Hallie tucked a strand of hair behind her ear, thinking about his statement. They'd had lots of conversations and he'd offered so much about himself in them, but he was right: *she'd* never asked *him* about things. What had he felt over those years? What did he miss the most about them? Perhaps she should start now.

"What's your favorite memory of this place, Uncle Hank?"

His focus landed on the bending sea oats before turning back to her. "It's too hard to choose one in particular. That would be awfully unfair to all the other memories, and there are so many."

"What would you take away from Starlight if you ever had to leave?" she asked, as she packed sand around the base of the tower, smoothing it with her fingers.

"Mmm. The soul of it."

"Which is?" She rinsed her hands in the bucket of water and flicked off the excess.

He ran his fingers over his knees, thinking. "Love. There was a lot of love here. More than I've ever seen anywhere else in my life."

Hallie stood up, her entire attention on him. Uncle Hank was the lucky one. Hallie's father had run off when she was little, Sydney had met the same fate with Christian, and now Hallie had broken off her own engagement. Yet Uncle Hank's first thought was of love. It had to be his and Aunt Clara's. "How did you and Aunt Clara do it?"

"What do you mean?"

"How did you and Aunt Clara manage that level of happiness for so long?"

"There's not just one answer to that question, but I suppose if I had to choose the most important thing, I'd say it's just showing up. During the good times, the bad ones, the moments you can't believe you'd ever be as busy as you are, just be there for each other. Show up."

"How do you know when you've found that one person you want to show up for?"

"Because you can't go through an entire day without thinking about them."

Hallie considered this. The only person like that for her was Ben. "I hope I'm lucky enough to find someone like that one day," she said.

"Sometimes, it's when you stop looking that you find what you're searching for. You have so many good years ahead of you. Don't rush it. He's out there. It's just not quite time for the two of you yet." He cleared his throat. "But when it *is* time, pay attention to every single moment because it flies…" He looked back out to the sea oats.

"I will, I promise," she said quietly. "Look!"

He peered down at her castle. "You did it."

"I did!" She laughed, delighted to have finished it so easily.

"Number one on your list is done!"

Hallie didn't want to mention that number one was the easiest on the list. "Was I supposed to learn something from this? I feel like Aunt Clara is trying to tell me something."

"Oh, I suppose you could learn a lot of things: patience… perseverance… that you should spend time talking to an old man because he enjoys that…" He grinned. "Thank you for taking my mind off the hard stuff for a while."

She soaked up the delight she found in seeing his happiness. "Any time."

*

"Are you ever planning to bring Ashley to Starlight?" Hallie asked Ben as he got out of the jeep. She would be a breath of fresh air to have around.

Beau, who'd been running in the water all morning, raced over to greet him, and Ben reached down and scratched behind his ears. Beau pressed his forehead to Ben's leg while his tail whipped back and forth.

"You really don't have to spend all morning in town. Have her over. We can make her breakfast. It would be fun."

"I think you all need to have family time." Ben shut the door to the jeep. "I'd feel horrible imposing on the family with an outsider. Uncle Hank probably likes the solitude to grieve. It's bad enough I'm eating his ice cream…"

"You might as well be family, so don't think for one minute that you being here is an issue." She walked around the vehicle and stood in front of him in the shade of the palm tree, to avoid the blazing sun. "And Uncle Hank told me today that he was glad I pulled him outside and talked to him. It got him away from all the heavy thoughts he's been having for a while. I don't think he wants solitude." She walked along with Ben to the water hose. He cranked the rusty wheel and the water came on. "He really loves being around you. He wouldn't mind at all if you brought Ashley over, I'm sure."

"Maybe another time." Ben held the hose over Beau's water bowl and filled it up to the brim before turning the hose off. Beau ran over to it and lapped half of it up, the water sloshing back and forth, dropping spots onto the stoop.

"Nobody else would mind either. It would probably lighten the mood."

Beau ran back out to the beach.

"It might not be the best timing. I went into town to give her some closure… I broke things off with her."

"Oh my goodness, Ben. I'm so sorry. What happened?"

He stared into her eyes for a second before shaking his head. "I just didn't have the same feelings for her that she had for me."

"That's too bad. I really liked her."

Ben took in a long breath and nodded in understanding.

"What time are we taking your mama into town?" he asked, clearly wanting to change the subject.

Hallie let him. He seemed troubled by the situation with Ashley and she didn't want to make him rehash things. "I think she's ready whenever we are." Hallie grabbed Ben's arm. "But first, I want to show you something!"

"You do?" He gave her his complete attention, a loving grin on his face.

"Yep! Follow me." She pulled him toward the water, leading him until they reached the sand. "Look what I made."

"You built a sandcastle! That's great, Hallie—I'm so excited for you." He gave her a little squeeze. "Only four more things on the list. What's number two?"

Hallie frowned. "Become a photographer. Just up and change an entire profession—no big deal."

"Perfect. We're stopping by the gallery in town. Bring your camera. With your talent, we'll show the owner, he'll hire you immediately, and we'll be able to mark that off the list by dinner."

"I hear you," she said dryly, trying not to let on how much his upbeat teasing helped her through this.

"Let's go in and get your mama. We should ask Sydney and Robby to come too. The more the merrier."

"I'll round them up while you get Beau into the jeep."

Sydney offered to stay with Uncle Hank in case he needed anything, but Robby wanted to go, talking a mile a minute to Ben as they headed out to the guesthouse driveway. They all reached the jeep and climbed in.

"Should we go to Wes and Maggie's first? We can have lunch and see if Wes can give us the name of that caretaker," Mama said, holding back her hair as the warm summer wind whipped through the open jeep.

"Maybe I can have the drink I like with the whipped cream and cherry? The Orange Smash," Robby asked. "And their homemade caramel popcorn pie for dessert?" He reached over and rubbed Beau, who was sitting between him and Mama.

Wes and Maggie were friends with Sally Ann, and she delivered novelty pies daily for their dessert menu. The most popular was the caramel popcorn pie, exclusively baked for the restaurant. "I wouldn't dream of going to Wes and Maggie's without having the caramel popcorn pie," Ben said, as he made eye contact with Robby in his rearview mirror. "That's the real reason we're going, right? So we can all have the pie?"

Robby giggled.

They drove down the scenic route connecting all the villages, and dotted with restaurants and shops along Firefly Beach's little stretch of it. With the tourist season in full swing, the walk-up gelato and hot dog stands were full of vacationers, clad in their swimsuits, brightly colored beach towels thrown over their shoulders and wrapped around their bodies, their hair wet from a morning in the warm waters of the gulf. While Firefly Beach was known as Florida's best-kept secret, the little village was slowly gaining traction among artists and those seeking a quieter beach vacation than its neighboring towns could offer.

It was only a few minutes' drive into town and they pulled up at the restaurant. One whole wall of garage-style doors was open to the sea. The deck overlooking the gulf was crowded, the red umbrellas up on every table, with matching pots of geraniums lining the edges of the decking, which sat right in the sand. The brightness of it against the aquamarine background was the picture of summer.

"I texted Wes before we left, and he's holding us a table just inside near the opening to the deck," Ben said.

Beau jumped out with them and walked beside Ben. He was so well mannered that Wes allowed Ben to have him on the deck whenever they were in town. Their lunch table was the same one every time—right at the open doors so they could eat in the cool shade inside while Beau lay on the deck. Wes even had a water bowl for him. While Wes always joked that he was making special arrangements just for Ben, Hallie knew that he'd probably let anyone bring their dog if it was as good as Beau.

They all took their seats and Wes joined them from the other side of the bar.

"Glad to see my favorite family!" he said, assisting Robby with his chair. "Let me grab your drink order and then I'll get Maggie. She's in the back. She'd love to see you!"

"You know what drink I want!" Robby told him with a big grin.

"I've got you covered—one Orange Smash coming up!"

Wes took the rest of their orders and hurried into the kitchen to get Maggie. Hallie couldn't wait to see her. Maggie was one of Aunt

Clara's good friends. If Hallie tried to count the number of times she'd found the two of them in the rockers on the back porch, drinking sweet tea, she'd be there all day. They'd met when Maggie had first moved to Firefly Beach, and they'd become fast friends.

"Oh, my stars!" Maggie said, shuffling quickly from the kitchen, both hands on her heart, showing off a large silver and turquoise ring. Her long, graying hair was twisted up into a clip to combat the summer heat, completely exposing her smiling face. She'd made a name for herself nationally, singing jingles for commercials, but gave it all up to run the restaurant, and she made everyone there feel like family. "I have missed you!" She ran over to Hallie and gave her a hug, moving around the table and greeting each person the same way. "We're missing a few. Where's your mom?" she asked Robby.

"She stayed with Uncle Hank," he said.

Maggie offered a knowing smile toward Hallie. "Sydney is always the helper," she said. "I hope Hank is doing okay."

"He's up and down," Mama said.

"Is he able to come in sometime? I really miss him. And I know he could use a cup of his favorite coffee! I've always got a pot on for him."

"We haven't gotten that far yet. He's still grieving pretty badly. It might do him some good to come in though."

Wes maneuvered around Maggie and set Robby's drink down in front of him. He'd put a dollop of whipped cream on top and two cherries instead of one. Clearly he remembered how much Robby liked them.

"We're looking for someone to take care of him when we aren't there," Mama said. "Didn't you have a woman who helped you while you recuperated from your knee surgery, Maggie?"

"I did, but she left town to be a songwriter. Moved to Nashville—I should've called *you*, Ben. You might have been able to show her the ropes."

Ben smiled.

"I wanna be a music producer when I grow up," Robby said, attempting to join the conversation. "I wanna be just like Ben."

"You do?" Ben said, clearly amused. "What makes you think so?"

"I like hearing different instruments."

"That's a big part of it. The fun bit is when you get to put all the sounds together. It's like that big puzzle we did last year: the whole picture isn't there until all the pieces are in the right order."

Robby moved up onto his knees and took a drink from his straw. Then he said to Ben, "Do you ever get tired of doing your job?"

"Nope. It's one of my favorite things to do."

Robby sucked down a little more of his drink, never taking his eyes off Ben. "What's something else you like to do as much as making music?"

Ben glanced over at Hallie. "Hanging out with this family." Ben's parents had been older when he was born, and by the time he was old enough to travel around, they weren't able to keep up, so he'd spent most of his days with Hallie and her family. His parents had been grateful to Mama for taking him in and allowing him to travel with them.

Maggie put her hand to her heart. "Ben, the family is lucky to have you in it."

"Oh my goodness!" A familiar sugar-sweet voice sailed over to their table. Ashley walked toward them, smiling, her white and red floral sundress showing off her tan. Her blonde hair was pulled loosely into a ponytail with little wisps falling around her face, complementing her blue eyes, which seemed sad today, despite her pleasant demeanor. She was one of those people who seemed to have no idea how pretty she was; her beauty was effortless. And she was as nice inside as she was out. She looked over at Ben with unsaid words, but she didn't break that welcoming smile of hers. "Hi Hallie!"

Hallie was genuinely happy to run into Ashley. She'd been able to spend time with Ashley on a few different occasions, and the more they got to know each other, the more they realized their similarities.

"Hi, I'm glad we saw you!" Hallie said. "We should have coffee sometime. How long are you here?"

"A couple of weeks." She looked unsure. Her gaze fluttered back over to Ben.

Ben was silent, but his expression was kind. He had one arm propped up on the back of his chair, his concentration on Ashley.

"You can eat with us now, if you'd like, Ashley," Mama offered. "I'm sure Ben would appreciate having you join us for lunch. He's too polite to ask since he's here with all of us, so we'll do it for him."

"Oh, I can't. I'm sorry. I'm here picking up a to-go order for my grandparents. Mimi's bridge club is playing today and they've ordered everyone lunch. But maybe another time."

"I'll get Wes to bring it out for you," Maggie said. "Follow me up to the bar."

"She's such a nice girl, Ben," Mama said when Ashley was out of earshot.

"Yes, she is," Ben said. He was quieter than usual in Ashley's presence. His lightheartedness and fondness didn't come through the way they did when he and Hallie were together, and Hallie realized that she hadn't *ever* seen that level of affection between Ben and Ashley. They seemed like the best couple on paper, but sometimes things just weren't meant to be.

Wes came out with carrier bags full of food, and handed them to Ashley.

Ben stood up immediately, going over to them. "Let me help you," he said, taking the bags.

When he'd left, Mama addressed the rest of them. "I feel bad that he's setting his own life aside to help us. Please make sure Ashley comes over. It's the least we can do after everything he's done."

"I will," Hallie said. Why did everything feel like it was changing all at once?

Chapter Twelve

The water was restless today, crashing as angrily as the small gulf waves could muster, the red warning flags flapping wildly on the public beaches. There was the possibility of a thunderstorm, according to the weather report, but so far the sun was still shining. Ben and Hallie walked ahead of the others as they made their way to Coastal Lens Gallery, the sunshine glaring off its shiny new sign.

"I'm excited to see what they have," Hallie said. "If there's more work like the photograph in Wes and Maggie's, I might have to break out my wallet."

Ben seemed to enjoy her excitement. "Is your camera in your handbag?"

"No," she said. "Wes said the owner is a trained photographer, an artist like him. The last thing they would want to see is my unskilled photography."

"You don't give yourself enough credit."

"I'm self-taught."

"So was van Gogh."

Hallie laughed.

"What's so funny up there?" Mama called from behind.

"Ben's comparing me to van Gogh," Hallie said over her shoulder. Mama laughed, and Hallie was glad someone had sense enough to find it funny.

They reached a thick maple door with beveled glass panes.

The gallery was in an old house that had been converted into a business. Against its blue clapboard siding, an "Open" sign hung beside a small emblem to the right of the door, with the name of the gallery in bright red and yellow streaks of paint. Ben opened the door and let Hallie enter as her mother and Robby caught up, meeting them on the porch.

The timeworn wooden floors creaked underneath their feet as they entered the space. There were vacationers browsing inside, talking quietly about the different pieces. The walls had a fresh coat of white paint to showcase the modest black frames that allowed the photography to speak for itself.

It was like walking into heaven for Hallie, every single shot evoking emotion and a barrage of questions as to the technique. She'd never seen angles like those, or the way the colors of ordinary things blended to make a brand-new, almost abstract image. It was right up her alley—an alley she never realized she had. She'd always liked to take photographs, but until she'd seen these pictures, her technique had been a shot in the dark. Hallie twisted her head to the side to determine how the photographer had captured one photo in particular. Not only did she see the photography itself, but she had a million ideas of where to put each piece, what to place around it; she imagined different locations that would highlight the colors.

"I'm going to take Robby to the shop next door for a look around at the toys," Mama said into Hallie's ear. "He might be a bit too restless in here. They all look expensive…" Then she waved to Ben and Hallie and went back through the front door.

Ben stood beside Hallie, curious and interested himself by the photos. While he wasn't a photographer, he'd always appreciated Hallie's work and he'd been supportive of it. Hallie was so taken with the images, as she moved from one to the next, that she barely noticed the fact that someone new was standing in the entryway with them.

"Do you like what you see?"

She tore her eyes away from a shot of a mint-flavored ice cream cone that almost took on the same quality as the sand and water outside. It was incredible. But what was even more surprising than that was the person who was standing before her.

"Gavin?"

"Hi." He was drinking her in, clear delight on his face at seeing her. "I took that one right outside." He pointed to the ice cream cone.

"These are yours?" She gestured toward the shot on the wall.

"Yep."

"Do you two know each other?" Ben asked, his curiosity clearly growing to astronomical levels as he looked between the two of them.

"Ah, yes," Gavin said, "we met at Starlight Cottage. I'm doing some trim painting for Hank Eubanks."

"Why are you painting houses?" Hallie asked, completely floored that someone with this amount of talent would be slapping blue paint onto the trim at the cottage.

"Funny story." Gavin led the way into the house, each room's artwork designed to have its own personality—some were more masculine, while others were lighter and softer in tone and color. "Your uncle called here because apparently I'm the only one in town that comes up on an online search for the word 'painter', and he specifically wanted someone new to the area."

"New to the area?"

"I moved here just a few months ago."

Then it hit Hallie. She knew how Uncle Hank thought, and she was willing to bet that he would only let someone onto the property who couldn't possibly be the trespasser. While she'd already decided that Gavin was too kind to be lurking in bushes, this made her feel considerably better. Although, when she looked at Ben, he was eyeing Gavin suspiciously.

Gavin pointed her toward a room to the right and Hallie gasped.

"You paint too?" she asked.

"Yes."

Large canvases covered the walls, all of them abstract but with actual images hidden in them, just like his photographs.

"These are absolutely stunning."

"Thanks."

"The photos you take look like they're shot in natural light. You play with that same color in these paintings."

"That's right," he said, smiling at her, those green eyes on her.

"I'd like to have a long conversation about the lighting and your use of angles, but I don't want to monopolize all your time. I know you're working."

"We can chat about it tonight then."

A new interest washed over Ben's face. "Tonight?" he asked.

Gavin explained, "We're going out tonight." Just then, a woman asked him a question and he politely moved toward her to answer.

Ben's attention turned entirely to Hallie, all those thoughts filling his eyes, and she knew that he was getting overprotective like he did whenever she dated someone new. He didn't have to. She was a grown woman, fully capable of taking care of herself. But she could understand his concern, given the fact that they still hadn't found who was peeking in on the Starlight Estate.

"We're going out as friends," she added in a whisper. But it didn't seem to change anything in the expression on Ben's face. He swiveled around to look at one of the paintings, and she wondered what he wasn't saying.

When Gavin returned, he was clearly trying to figure out the dynamic between Hallie and Ben, and she knew that she'd have to explain their relationship to him sooner rather than later.

One thing was for sure: she'd learned from Jeff that anyone who didn't like Ben wasn't worth her time.

Hallie stood in the bathroom at Starlight Cottage, wearing her favorite baby blue sundress, the strappy sandals with the wedge heels, and her silver teardrop earrings as she combed her hair in the mirror. The summer sun had laced tiny gold strands through her chestnut hair.

"Where is he taking you?" Ben asked. He was sitting on the edge of the tub with a bag of chips in his hand while she finished her hair. He popped one of the chips into his mouth and crunched on it.

"I'm not sure." She applied her barely there lip gloss. When Ben didn't say anything, she looked over at him and saw he was staring at her. "What?"

"You don't even know him. And you're going somewhere with him by yourself. With everything going on with strangers on the property, shouldn't he at least tell you where you're going? How do you know he's a good guy?"

"You're worrying unnecessarily. I have my cell phone, it's fully charged. *And* everyone knows who Gavin is—he owns a gallery in town. He's not some guy I picked up off the street."

Ben was quiet.

His behavior was upsetting her, and now she had a strange feeling about going out with Gavin, even just as friends. She suddenly wanted to change into her pajamas and curl up on the sofa with Ben. Maybe it was because her emotions were right on the surface with everything going on, or perhaps it was her own insecurities after her breakup. But she had to be strong and move forward. Nothing would change if she stayed in with Ben tonight.

"I'm a grown woman and it's just an evening out," she said, her voice breaking, causing him to focus on her, his hand stilling in the bag of chips. He pulled his fingers out of the bag and set the chips on the tub. "It's going to be a perfectly wonderful night—it's something positive, which has rarely happened to me in the last few months. I'll be just fine."

He stood up, those eyes flooded with unsaid thoughts. "I didn't mean to upset you. It's just a natural reaction."

"Why is it natural to make me feel like I have to be afraid?"

"*You* don't have to be afraid of them." He looked as though the words had come out against his will, intensity engulfing his face. He turned away quickly and picked up the bag of chips.

What did he mean by that? Now he wasn't making any sense.

"Hallie?" Sydney came to the door. She peered over Hallie's head at Ben, probably wondering what they were talking about. "Gavin just drove up. I'll let him in."

Ben ran his hands through his hair, frustrated.

"Ben," she started, but he stopped her.

"It's fine," he said calmly. "Enjoy your night." He kissed her on the cheek and headed out. Hallie followed him.

Ben walked past Gavin and greeted him politely before leaving through the door. She watched him make his way to the guesthouse, wishing she could've had more time to discuss what was bothering him before going out.

"You okay?" Gavin asked. He slipped his hands into the pockets of his jeans. He was casual, but it looked as though he'd put a little work into his appearance, his hair combed, his face clean-shaven.

"Yes. Sorry," she said, putting on a happy face.

"You look nice."

"Thank you."

"You're forgetting something," he said, his eyes on her hands.

"What's that?"

"Your camera. You'll definitely need it tonight. When I called a few minutes ago, your uncle suggested I look at some of your photos."

"Oh my goodness, he told you?" she said, embarrassed.

Sydney ran off down the hallway and returned with the camera, passing it to Hallie.

"You don't have to let me see your photos if you don't want to," he said. "But you do have to bring your camera. I've got a few things in mind to show you tonight that look best through its lens." He ushered her forward and waved to Sydney, who handed Hallie her handbag on their way out of the cottage.

"What else did my uncle tell you?" she asked as he opened the door to his truck, the cool leather on her legs an immediate relief from the heat outside. She held her camera and her handbag in her lap.

"Not much. Why? Is there more to know?"

"I don't think so. How about you? There's more to know, for sure. Where you're from. Why you moved here. Why you decided to open the gallery…"

He took in a deep breath, his eyebrows rising. "Wow. Each one of those might take me all night to explain. How long have you got?"

Even though it seemed, by his reaction, to be a range of heavy topics for him, it was as if he wanted to tell her, and she was interested. "I've got as long as it takes."

With a grin, Gavin started the truck and headed down the long drive to the street.

Chapter Thirteen

Hallie couldn't help but consider Ben's concern as Gavin drove them out of town, down a winding road lined with trees. It had started to get dark and she had no idea where she was. She sneaked a peek at her cell phone and there was no service, making her suddenly nervous. "Where are we going?" she asked.

"To dinner." Gavin looked over at her, and seemed to guess her slight apprehension. He added, "At my house. It's outside of town because I like to have the quiet to paint and edit my photographs. I'm most creative in the silence."

He pulled up a long gravel drive and came to a stop in front of a fully restored two-story colonial home. It had white siding and midnight black wooden shutters, large iron hinges holding them in place. A front porch wrapped around three sides of it, shaded by towering oak trees with limbs covered in moss.

"All this for just you?" she asked.

"Not originally, but now it is." Gavin got out of the truck and walked around to open her door. "Watch your step." He held out his hand to steady her as she trod on the uneven stones of the drive.

"This is incredible." Hallie tilted her head up to view the three brick chimneys that protruded from the slate roof.

"Thank you," he said, as he let go of her.

"Do you own this?"

"I've had it for a while but just now finished it. The renovations got…
delayed." He offered a shaky smile and then opened the front door.

The outside was traditional but the inside was filled with modern
amenities. Gavin clicked on the lights, illuminating the room with
recessed lighting nestled in the raised ceilings. It gave off a warm
glow against the white interior. He turned on a few more rustic light
fixtures that offered a laid back, traditional feel. They walked toward
the kitchen along soft maple-glazed hardwoods as wide as the planks
of a ship, leading to a stone fireplace that took up the entire wall of
the living area, which, along with the kitchen, was open to where they
were standing. None of that compared, however, to the smell of dinner
wafting toward her.

"What are you cooking?" she asked.

"I'm not cooking anything," he said. "I have a housekeeper named
Geraldine. She's the best cook I've ever met—simply amazing. And she
has this way of drawing me in and making me talk. I let it slip that I'd
asked you out, and before I could explain that we'd decided to simply
meet as friends, she insisted she cook this romantic feast for us. She
put it in the oven before she left."

"That's sweet."

Gavin went over to a wine fridge and opened the glass door. "I
have several types of wine…" He pulled the bottles from inside and
set them on the counter, shutting the door. "And of course, I also have
the typical: lemonade, water, iced tea…"

"I'll have a glass of white, thank you," she said, setting her handbag
and camera down on one of the bar stools. "You just moved here?"
she asked.

"Yep. I'm originally from North Carolina, but I wanted a new start and less snow…" He popped the cork out of the bottle and poured two glasses.

"Is the lack of snow the only thing that brought you here?"

He handed her a glass. "For me, I'm most creative when I'm around light, and North Carolina had become a sort of dark place." He stared into her eyes kindly, as if he was hoping she'd ask him to elaborate, but at the same time he seemed nervous to say more. He turned away and checked the oven.

"How so?" Through the window, she caught sight of fireflies in the blue light that remained from the last strip of sun on the horizon behind all the trees, but she couldn't get a good view of them from where she was sitting. Gavin started to talk, pulling her focus back to him.

"I dated someone for a very long time. Her name was Gwen." The woman's name came out as if he'd had to work to actually say it. "She had a heart defect, and it went undetected until it was too late. She died two years ago. This was going to be our home, but Gwen never got to see it."

"Oh, I'm so sorry."

"Like I said earlier." He tried to smile, talking on an exhale. "I'm not practiced at this sort of thing. I didn't want to bring your spirits down with a sad story, but it's my story, so I figured that if I want to have any sort of friendship with you, I should get it out there. It might help you understand me a little more."

The oven timer went off, and he grabbed a potholder to pull a gloriously rich seafood casserole out of the oven. He set it on a trivet next to the stove.

"I've only told one other person in Firefly Beach my story, and that's your uncle. He and I related to each other on our shared experiences.

It's funny how it happened. He sounded so sad on the phone when he called for the quote to paint the trim that, even though I don't usually paint houses, I felt compelled to at least give him my time and go out to see the project. We spent hours on his porch. I told him I was new here and then it all just came out, and we both sat misty-eyed for a while. I took the job. I couldn't tell him no."

Hallie found herself leaning on the bar, her hand in her chin, listening to him. How incredibly moving that he and Uncle Hank were there to support each other. And what a sweet gesture to take on the job even though Gavin clearly had other responsibilities.

"When I first met your uncle, and explained that I was a different kind of painter than what he was looking for and I actually owned a gallery, we got to talking about the different media I use, and my photography. He told me that he thought you should be a photographer," Gavin said, leaving the dish to cool and returning to his glass of wine.

"My family seems to think I could be, but I've never pursued it." She felt less intimidated by him now, and found it easy to talk to him.

"Mm." Gavin picked up her glass, holding both of them. "Grab your camera and come with me."

He walked over to a small table where his own camera was sitting, and then opened the back door. As if the house wasn't magnificent enough, the back gardens were unquestionably the most beautiful southern gardens she'd ever seen, with rows of hedges, bright green grass, and flowers everywhere she looked, all under a canopy of trees. She could hardly see it all in the near dark, and could only imagine how expansive they were in the light of day. She turned around to find Gavin; he was at a stone fire pit in the center of the patio, throwing small logs into it. He grabbed some matches that were sitting on the ledge and lit the logs, a tiny blue flicker erupting into a dancing orange flame.

With a light tug, he pulled a chair over to the fire and moved Hallie's glass from the edge of the pit to the wide wooden arm of the chair.

"Let me know if it gets too hot for you," he said.

The coastal wind kept the intensity of the heat at bay enough to enjoy the fire.

"So have you always owned a gallery?" Hallie asked, taking a seat, the cool glass in her hand refreshing and light, helping her to relax.

"No. I was in medical sales before this." He leaned against the broad stones of the fire pit, the edge of it so far from the center of the fire that it could serve as a table. "I always took pictures, though. Even when I didn't have a camera. I remember things in moments and images, like the way your hand rested on your heart when I startled you the first time we met."

Hallie nodded happily, understanding exactly what he meant, delighted to know she wasn't the only one who did that. The idea of how she remembered things hadn't occurred to her before.

"You're so talented," she said. "I'm surprised you ever chose to do something other than take pictures for a living."

"I wanted a plan for my life. I wanted to know where the money would come from so that I could make a good living to raise a family one day. And then… everything went wrong. After Gwen…" He shifted a little, picking up his glass. "I stopped worrying so much." He took a long drink and then said, his face brightening, "I sent off a few of my photographs to some magazines and was surprised to find they showed interest in them. After that, I finished the renovations on the house, quit my job, left home, and opened the gallery."

"You were very brave to do all that," she said.

He chuckled. "Funny thing is that I did it all not out of bravery, but out of fear. Fear that I wouldn't be able to move forward if I didn't completely change my life, fear that I may never stop hurting if I had to wake up in the same house we shared, fear that I'd find myself an old man, wondering what I'd done with my life."

His comments made Hallie think of Aunt Clara's list. Could this be why she'd suggested it? Was she hoping for something different for Hallie, a new start to prevent Hallie from having regrets?

Gavin stood and brought his camera to his face, leaning over, tipping the lens up at an unusual angle. Hallie watched him, and she could see where he was going with it. He pointed it at the fire, twisted the focus, and snapped a photo.

"Let me see," she said, feeling more relaxed after he'd shared such a heartfelt story, almost eager to view his perspective.

"Wait." He kept his camera close to him. "You take a shot."

"What?"

"I want to see the technique you use."

Even though she felt comfortable talking to him about it, Hallie was frozen in place. She wasn't sure why, but she was afraid. She'd never had another person outside her family judge her abilities before. Regardless of how he'd got to this point, she was competing with a pro, and it was making her too nervous to think through how she wanted to take the picture.

Gavin took a step nearer to her, the skin between his eyes wrinkling with concern. "I only want to see your method out of curiosity. You see, the way we decipher light and angles is as unique as we are—no two photographers view it the same way."

"But how others perceive our view is what sets the best of the best apart from the average person," she challenged, not knowing where all of this feeling was coming from. She hadn't ever thought about any of this, but somehow she had opinions regarding photography methods, and her statement surprised her. Sure, she'd taken pictures growing up, but putting rules around it, creating a technique that was uniquely hers—she'd never considered it before.

"Ah, but what if the 'best of the best,' as you say, is simply an opinion as well? What if it's just a matter of people *connecting* with your interpretation of an image?" He took another step nearer, putting his face into her line of vision. "I'm not judging it. I just want to see what you see," he said gently. Gavin set his camera down on the chair and then came up behind her, leaving ample space between them. "Close your eyes."

Instead she turned her head to make eye contact, not sure of his motives.

He smiled hesitantly. "Hold your camera in both hands and close your eyes—go with me on this."

Hallie did as she was told, realizing he was just getting out of her view.

"Locate the heat from the fire on your skin," he said from behind her. "Take in the scent of the burning embers."

She inhaled deeply, the smell of summer and woods and fire... and Gavin's cologne—notes of lime and white pepper—consuming her.

"What do you want people to feel from this shot? Fear? Love? Fun? What?"

"Serenity."

He stepped away and she opened her eyes with his movement.

"Now look at the fire through your lens. Give me a serene shot of it."

Hallie lifted the camera to her eye and suddenly, it all became clear to her. She needed a picture of the gardens. The fire was only a detail, one element in the shot. She wanted to capture the quiet of the trees, the low light, the fire just off center, the empty chair that was waiting for someone to sit in it. She noticed the fireflies in the distance again, and adjusted her focus to incorporate them. Then, she moved around the fire until she had just the right angle with the chair, the visual aspects of the composition working like music in her mind—the same way Ben described how it takes all the instruments in harmony to make a song. She had to move, to play her own instrument, until all the elements in view were singing. Then she snapped a shot.

Gavin stepped back over and looked down at her screen. "Wow. That's amazing."

It was as if she'd never understood her camera before. She wanted to spend every minute from here on taking more photos just like that one. In that moment, something changed inside her creatively, and it was as if all the scattered pieces of who she was were sharpening and coming together to give her meaning. Hallie had been right: she wasn't a photographer. Not until this minute. Aunt Clara had just seen her potential before she had.

"Your depth of field is spot on. I love how the trees make a natural frame at the edges. It's almost geometrical. The front lighting you chose with the diffraction of the gardens there is incredible." He tapped the screen. Then he tilted the camera back to her. "Look at the colors now, rather than the actual photo itself. What colors are captured in your shot?"

"Even though the gardens are green, the low natural light causes them to be almost a denim color… And the fire has a gold tone that complements the dark brown of the fire pit and the wooden chair. So, blue, gold, and brown."

"How would you mat and frame blue, gold, and brown?"

"Um… A dark tan-colored mat? Maybe with some texture—like a burlap. The texture would add depth to the simplicity of the shot."

She looked up at him for encouragement, and to see if he agreed with what she said, and he seemed actually interested, as if he didn't have an opinion himself, as if she were the expert, telling him. She continued, "And because the shadows are nearly black, the frame should be black. A simple black frame to balance the texture of the matting. It would be perfect paired with a white canvas sofa with burlap throw pillows in various shades, and maybe a light blue sculpture—something natural like a tree or a vine—on a table nearby..."

He was smiling, a bright happy grin. "You, my dear, are a natural." He laughed out loud. "Come inside. Let's have dinner and then we'll upload your shot to my computer. I'll show you how you can edit it to adjust for crispness and color harmony."

Hallie and Gavin had talked about photography so much over dinner that she'd barely realized when she'd finished her food, the plates sitting empty for hours while they discussed different views and times of day, how their experiences shaped their photography, and the energy that consumed them when they were able to find their shot of the fire pit. She couldn't stop talking about it, asking questions, watching everything he did. They continued their discussions all the way back to Starlight. In her entire life, she'd never felt so artistic. Photography was like this giant open space just waiting for her to figure out how to fill it with colors and furniture and fabrics, and she hadn't grasped until tonight how badly she needed to put herself in that space.

Gavin was an endless stream of knowledge, his ideas blowing her away at every turn. They'd spent the last two hours after dinner tweaking and changing the photo, which she'd never done before and found to be extremely fulfilling artistically. The editing might even have been her favorite part. Gavin told her that he'd help her purchase and install the software if she ever wanted him to, and she told him she planned to buy it as soon as she could.

Hallie waved goodbye to Gavin as he pulled out the drive. She was wired from the excitement. She couldn't possibly shut herself up in her room, and everyone was probably asleep. Really, she was making excuses for why she wanted to share this new exhilaration she was feeling with one person and one person only. She noticed Ben's light was on in the guesthouse. Hallie nearly skipped up to the door and slid her key into the lock.

Ben was on the sofa wearing his oversized headphones, his computer in his lap, concentration etched on his face, with one hand on the keyboard and the other hand resting on Beau. He hadn't heard her come in, and when Ben wasn't concerned, neither was Beau, who only moved his eyes to look at her so he wouldn't disturb Ben's gentle rubbing on his side. With a silly grin, Hallie butted in to Ben's line of vision, making him jump. Beau finally lifted his head.

Ben gave her a crooked smile. "Hey," he said, taking off his headphones. "You look like you had a good night."

Hallie dropped down next to him.

"How much wine did you have?" He chuckled at the sight of her.

"I'm not drunk! Well, I'm drunk on elation."

Ben's face sobered but he was clearly trying to maintain a pleasant look. "Did you have fun with Gavin?"

"I had the time of my life!"

He took in a deep breath and let it out quietly, forcing his smile wider, those ever-present thoughts filling his eyes. "That's great!"

Hallie told him all about what Gavin had taught her, about editing her photo, and how she'd never known that there was anything more than just snapping a shot. She was overwhelmed by the presentation of it, by the excitement of editing and making the image uniquely beautiful. But it didn't stop there. She could envision an entire range of design products to go with it, all of them as unique as the photo itself. She continued on until she realized she'd been talking a mile a minute, but Ben was lost in her explanation, listening to every word.

"I've been telling you for years that this line of work suited you."

"You always like everything I do, so I thought you were just being nice."

His smile contorted to a more serious expression. "I wish you would trust me sometimes." He moved his computer to the coffee table and set his headphones down beside it, facing her. "I like everything you do because I truly believe in you. You don't do things that are mediocre, Hallie. I understand that creative world—I think that's what has drawn me to you since we were kids. I know talent when I see it. I've bet my adult life on that ability."

Once again, she hadn't listened to Ben when she should've.

"But regardless of whether you believed me or not," he said, "you've finally found your passion—I can tell because it's right there in your eyes." He stood up. "We should celebrate. I was saving it, but tonight's important. I have champagne in the fridge."

Hallie's eyes grew round. "You do? Why?"

"I was going to bring it out once you'd completed all the things on your list."

She laughed. "How do you know I'm going to complete the list?"

"Once I saw you trying to make a sandcastle, I knew. You'll get it done." He went around the bar and opened the refrigerator.

"Ben," Hallie said, getting up from the sofa and following him over, his unwavering faith in her abilities troubling her. What if she couldn't live up to his opinion of her? "I'm glad you believe in me, but building a sandcastle and finding excitement in photography doesn't mean I'll finish that list. I've decided to try—for Aunt Clara—but some of her demands are downright impossible."

Ben set two flutes onto the counter and unwound the casing around the bottle. "Nothing's impossible." He pressed against the exposed cork and pointed it away from them into the living area. It wouldn't budge. Ben gritted his teeth and adjusted his thumbs on it. "Nothing's impossible except getting this cork out of the bottle." He laughed, clearly straining against it. He set it down and rested his fingers a minute.

"Let me try." Hallie grabbed the bottle by the neck and pushed against the cork until her fingers were sore, the thing not moving.

Ben wrapped his arms around her, putting his thumbs outside hers. His breath on her neck, he said, "On the count of three, push. Ready?"

She looked back and nodded, succeeding only in taking in the scent of him. It was the smell of home, of everything she'd ever known. She closed her eyes like Gavin had taught her and breathed in as Ben counted, wondering what she was trying to capture in this moment… Her inner voice told her. *Perfection.*

"You didn't push!" he said, his laughter pulling her out of her thoughts.

Hallie looked down, noticing how masculine his arms were, how different they'd become from the years when he'd taught her to fish as kids. That had been the last time he'd had his arms around her like this. She hadn't noticed it at all then, but now they provided security, calm, a sense of overwhelming need for him to never let go. She blinked over and over, wondering if all the romanticizing of the photography shots tonight had made her overly euphoric or something. It was *Ben.*

She couldn't be having these thoughts about Ben… He was off limits in so many ways.

"Try again. Ready? One, two, three!"

She pressed against the cork with him, her thumbs straining, and then *POP!* The cork sailed across the room, landing on the rug. Beau went over and inspected it, the smell of the liquid making him sneeze. But she hardly processed it before champagne erupted from the bottle like a sparkling volcano, angrily fizzing and bubbling down their hands, causing her to squeal. Hallie jumped out of Ben's arms as he moved the bottle to the counter. He grabbed the kitchen towel for her.

"It's all over your arms," he said, smiling.

"It's everywhere."

"Hang on. Here, it's on your neck."

He put the towel against the bare skin of her neck to wipe off the liquid, his hands slowing when his fingertips came in contact with her skin, the laughter sliding off his face. His touch wasn't anything like the Ben she'd known, the boy who'd been a part of her childhood. His light caress was that of a man, and overwhelmingly more than just having his arms around her, she truly felt who he was *now*. She imagined his fingers trailing down her skin, his mouth at her neck… Trying to get the picture out of her mind, she focused on his face, finding his lips as they moved just slightly with his breath, and suddenly all those thoughts she'd seen in his eyes but didn't understand became clear. Her skin prickled with the realization that, not only did she understand his thoughts, but she now felt the same way.

And it terrified her. What was this she was feeling? Their moments of closeness flashed like a slideshow in her mind and she started to wonder if she needed Ben's proximity in her life because she was in love with him. She couldn't live without him. Was that what this was? There were so many reasons this couldn't be happening.

He offered her the towel, their hands touching again as she took it. He gently caressed her fingers with his and his gaze seemed to be asking her if they should move into this new realm. Her breathing was shallow and fast, her pulse racing. Ben had touched her hundreds of times. He'd kissed her cheek, rubbed her shoulders, taken her hand… None of it felt like this. He'd made her feel desirable. She swallowed, the towel woven through her fingers, not wanting to move for fear she'd erase the trail along her skin where Ben had awakened her nerves.

If they allowed themselves to go any further and things went wrong, she stood to lose her best friend. And then if things went right… She'd never be able to offer him a happy life. He deserved more than she could give him. He didn't know… Tears welled up in her eyes, and she didn't have to say anything for him to understand that she wasn't going to do this.

Ben turned away, pulling a paper towel from the roll and wiping down the counter where the champagne had splashed as if nothing had happened, leaving her shocked and confused.

Hallie jumped when he opened the trashcan to throw the paper towel away. He ripped off another and started to wipe the spill on the floor, his strokes hard and fast as if he were upset with himself.

Once he'd taken care of the mess, Ben slipped his hands into his pockets. "All clean," he said, producing a smile. He grabbed the flutes again and handed one to her. "We should drink," he said. He didn't have to say a word for her to know that if she never mentioned this, it would be forever buried in their pasts and he wouldn't put her in that position again.

"To finding the things in life that bring you joy," he said, looking dejected and unlike himself. He lifted his glass. He'd said the words, but there was so much more behind them.

She raised her glass and touched it to his.

Chapter Fourteen

"Good grief, Hallie." Mama's voice meandered through Hallie's consciousness as a streak of light pierced the back of her closed eyelids, making her head ache. "Did you drink all this?" Another vibrating sound rattled in her ears when Mama tugged a second shade to allow the light to filter in. She let it go, the wide vinyl coiling around the roller at the top of the window.

Hallie opened her eyes, the summer sun blinding her. She squinted through it to see a blurry image of Mama holding the empty bottle of champagne from last night. After the first glass, Hallie had told Ben that she was really tired, and he'd corked the bottle and told her to take it with her. She still remembered his eyes when he told her goodnight—they said more than they ever had, or maybe it was just that she could finally read him. She rolled over and put her face in the lump of feathers Aunt Clara had called a pillow when she'd insisted they buy them, because the quality of comfort equaled the design.

"I need to talk to you before we all go down for breakfast," Mama said.

Hallie sat up and stifled a yawn.

"I found Lewis. I asked the police officer who's been helping out with the trespasser if he could find him, and it only took a couple of hours."

"Lewis?"

"From Aunt Clara's letter. Ready for this? He's seventy-eight years old and he lives just outside of town."

Hallie forced herself to focus, this information not making sense. "This Lewis and Uncle Hank share a last name and they're close in age—Uncle Hank *has* to know him." She rubbed her eyes, gaining concentration. "Why do we have family that we don't know about? Could he have been ostracized for some reason? If that's the case, I'm not sure we'd want him coming around."

"But, don't forget that Aunt Clara wanted us to find him. Uncle Hank must know more about this than he's letting on. However, when I told him I'd found Lewis, he closed right up and said that if I brought him here, he wouldn't give him the inheritance. Uncle Hank is the only one with the combination to the safe. So I'm stuck."

"Wow." Hallie rubbed her eyes, still trying to wake up. This was a lot to take in first thing in the morning on a hangover.

"Uncle Hank isn't happy that we've found him, and he's in a rotten mood this morning because of it. I'm hoping being around the family at breakfast will calm him down. It isn't good for him to be so upset."

Hallie's head was now throbbing. "Definitely not. And at some point, he's going to have to give one of us the combination to the family safe. What would we do if something happened to him?" She ran her hands over her face, not comfortable with the conversation. She needed to calm Uncle Hank down as soon as she could.

"Is Ben up yet? He's great with Uncle Hank." Still holding the champagne bottle, Mama went over to the doorway. "Maybe you can go get him, and the two of you can come to breakfast together as a unified front."

Unified. Hallie closed her eyes and remembered the feeling of his arms around her. "Okay. I'll go get him."

She got herself ready for the day and then headed to the guesthouse. The first thing she observed was that Beau's water bowl was gone from the porch, which meant that they hadn't taken their morning walk. She wondered how Ben had gotten away with not walking Beau—his dog loved the water and would pout by the door, making them all feel guilty until Ben took him out. Perhaps he'd stayed up late after she'd left last night, and he was still sleeping.

She knocked twice. When he didn't answer, she let herself in. Only the natural light coming through the windows lit the white space, the gentle slapping of the gulf outside the lone sound around her.

"Ben?" Hallie noticed the perfectly placed throw pillows on the sofa, the absence of Beau's dog bed in the corner of the living room, Ben's computer not wedged onto the side table, the clean kitchen counter… She zeroed in on a single piece of paper lying there and picked it up, running her eyes over her name. She read the note in Ben's handwriting:

I have to go back to Nashville. Sylvan Park just got offered a spot as the opening act in a pretty prominent festival. They want to record a new single and then see if we can squeeze out a few more cuts for the album with what they've got written faster than we'd all planned, although I need to meet with them to find out specifics first. Please tell everyone I'm sorry I had to leave and I love them all. Text me if you need me.

She looked up, disappointment swimming around inside her. She didn't know how to move forward with Ben, but she'd thought she would at least get the chance to figure it out. Now he was gone, and with Uncle Hank not doing well and Aunt Clara's wishes to take care of, Hallie couldn't just run after him. And she probably shouldn't anyway. She pulled her phone from her back pocket, not even sure what she wanted to say.

When she opened the screen, she had a text waiting from Ashley. They'd exchanged numbers the last time they were together, and Hallie had meant to keep in touch but then everything had happened with Jeff… She read the text.

Hi Hallie. Ben isn't answering his phone. Is it all right if I come over to see him? I need to talk to him.

Hallie's mouth was dryer than even the champagne had made it, her stomach feeling like it had a bowling ball sitting in it. The image of Ashley smiling and chatting with her at the Christmas party flooded her mind, and she felt horrible that things hadn't worked out between Ben and Ashley. Even though nothing had happened, Hallie knew how she'd felt in that moment with Ben and the things that had crossed her mind, and it all made her feel responsible for the breakup in some strange way.

But just as concerning was the fact that Ben had left town without even telling them in person. That wasn't like him at all. It was so unlike him that Hallie's heart was pounding. Why hadn't he just come to the main house to say goodbye to everyone? Was there some other reason for him to have left this way? Did it have anything to do with last night?

But then she took in a steadying breath. Ben had set his job on the back-burner to bring Hallie here. She had no idea about the time frame this band had or the amount of work that had been piling up for Ben. He was too considerate to even mention anything like that while she and her family were dealing with so much. Perhaps there was no other reason for leaving the way he had other than the fact that he just needed to get there. It was conceivable that the band had to have things done as quickly as possible, and Ben was just the type of person to give it everything he had.

She called Ashley.

Ashley answered immediately.

"Hi. It's Hallie. I saw your text."

"Hi Hallie! I was just wondering if it would be okay with the family if I stopped by to see Ben. Is he there? I've tried to call him, but I just get his missed-call message. And he isn't answering my texts either."

"He isn't here, but he left a note. I found it this morning. He's gone back to Nashville for work."

The line was silent for a pulse before Ashley said quietly, "May I come over anyway? I really need to talk to someone, and you know him so well…"

Another twinge of guilt snaked through her. But she reminded herself that nothing at all had happened last night, and it wasn't her fault if things hadn't worked out between Ben and Ashley. "Have you eaten? We're making a big breakfast. Why don't you come over and we can talk after."

"I wouldn't want to impose." Her voice sounded vulnerable.

Hallie was certain her family wouldn't mind having Ashley there. If anything, her presence might keep Uncle Hank civil when they brought up the topic of Lewis. "You wouldn't be imposing at all! Please come."

"Okay, I'll be there in ten minutes."

"Great. See you soon." Hallie ended the call and headed back to the main house to help Mama set a place for one more at the table.

Ashley scooted her chair under the table and put her hands in her lap politely. "Thank you, Mrs. Flynn, for having me over this morning,"

she said to Mama. Her blonde hair was tied up into a ponytail, showing off her high cheekbones. She had an innocence to her face that
revealed her honesty and kindness, but she seemed a little hesitant,
not nearly as carefree and happy as when they'd been at the party
together. The circumstances were clearly affecting her.

"It's lovely to have you with us. Pass Ashley the potato casserole,
please, Sydney," Mama said, sitting down beside Uncle Hank.

Robby got onto his knees to reach across the table for the salt.
"Where's Ben?" he asked.

"He had to leave unexpectedly for Nashville to work. Something
with one of his bands…" Hallie told him.

As soon as she said it, Sydney regarded her with unsaid questions.
Her sister's expression made Hallie feel as if she'd done something to
drive him away, but she knew that it was Sydney's desire to protect
Robby that was making her question the situation. It didn't stop the
tingling sensation from crawling up her neck, the responsibility for
Ben's leaving falling upon Hallie's shoulders despite her attempts to
think otherwise.

"I'm so sorry to hear that," Mama said. "I wish he'd had some
breakfast before leaving. I didn't even get to say goodbye."

"Maybe that means he'll be back soon," Robby said, his hopes
showing in his expression.

"Maybe!" Sydney told him, as she passed a bowl of eggs to Uncle
Hank.

Every day that they spent at Firefly Beach, the Flynns had breakfast
together with Aunt Clara and Uncle Hank. It was their time. Aunt
Clara had said that the only way to start the day was with prayer first
and then family. Prayer would guide them and family would ground
them. They had lively conversations around the table; they shared

stories, laughed, and even helped each other through their concerns. But now the atmosphere was empty, just like the old Steinway that sat in the front room. They were present in body, but not present the way Aunt Clara had insisted they be. On the surface, they were still behaving like they had, but things had changed at Starlight Cottage for sure.

"Ashley, how are your grandparents?" Mama asked.

"They're doing well. Mimi and my gramps are getting ready for his seventy-ninth birthday. The house is full of relatives. Mama's throwing them a party and we've all been helping her plan it." She raised her eyebrows and smiled. "Y'all are more than welcome to come!"

"Thank you, Ashley. That's kind of you to ask. We'll see if we can swing by, but we've been busy with things since Clara passed."

Ashley's gaze dropped to her lap out of respect for Aunt Clara. "Yes, ma'am. I understand. It's a difficult time, I'm sure."

"It is," Mama admitted. "And there are a lot of loose ends to tie up. Like finding out about a family friend named Lewis, right Uncle Hank?"

Perhaps Mama thought blurting it out in front of Ashley would be the best way to handle it, but Hallie would've danced around the topic a bit first. Mama wasn't one for beating around the bush, though.

Uncle Hank pursed his lips. "He isn't a friend."

"Who is he then?" Mama asked, urging him with her eyes to tell them.

"He's someone who's been gone from my life for quite some time, and I'd like to keep it that way."

"Even if Aunt Clara saw things differently?"

"Clara got overly sentimental at the end. Or maybe she knew we'd all feel so dreadful she could ask outlandish things of us and we'd feel obliged to appease her." He sent a remorseful look over to Hallie as soon as he said it.

Hallie understood exactly why. Uncle Hank knew that by saying that, he was suggesting Hallie's list could be one of those "outlandish" requests and that Hallie would appease Aunt Clara in her grief. *He'd* encouraged Hallie to finish the list, and he knew that his predicament wasn't so different from hers. She stared at him until he broke eye contact, clearly recognizing what she was thinking.

Ashley quietly piled hash browns onto her plate.

"You always told her you'd do anything for her. I remember hearing you say it over and over growing up," Mama said to him. "Why is this any different?"

"It just is. Case closed."

His eyes began to fill up with tears and he cleared his throat, digging into his eggs, so Mama dropped it. It wasn't like her to make a guest ill at ease, and even in her grief and her struggle to do right by Aunt Clara, she wouldn't start today.

"Do try the breakfast casserole, Ashley," she said, her voice lifting as she handed Ashley the serving spoon. "Feel free to take some home with you. We have more than enough."

Ashley smiled and glanced over at Uncle Hank under her lashes. "Thank you so much."

After breakfast, Hallie and Ashley left their sandals on the porch and took a walk on the beach. Hallie was glad for the sunshine and the squawk of seagulls overhead to lighten the mood. The wind rippled her shirt as they made their way past the sea grass and over the white dunes. They walked until the tinkling of Aunt Clara's glass wind chime on the back porch was but a faint sound under the rush of water around their feet.

"What do you think is going on with Ben?" Ashley said, putting her hands in the pockets of her shorts as she kicked a gurgling wave, the spray spitting out in front of them.

"I don't know," Hallie said honestly. Even if there was something new between them, it wasn't like him to leave Hallie when she needed him. He never did that. "I think he might just be really busy at work."

"No. I don't think so." Ashley's voice was tentative. "I'm sure he told you that we broke up." Her lip wobbled and she turned toward the sea. "When I got to Firefly Beach, I'd asked to meet up with him so I could get some kind of closure. Our breakup seemed so sudden; I don't understand it."

Hallie hated to see Ashley so sad. "Want to talk about it?"

She took in an anxious breath. "I thought things were fine, and then a couple of weeks ago he came by the house and told me he didn't think we should date exclusively, that it wasn't fair to me. I have no idea what he meant by that because I didn't want to date anyone else. How could dating him be unfair to *me* when he's all I want?" She blinked away tears.

"This happened a couple of weeks ago?"

"I remember the very day. I'd just come home from work for my last day before my time off. It was a Friday, and I was hoping he was coming over to make plans for the night because the weather was perfect for drinks outside. We'd talked about going to The Gulch. I'd hoped we could maybe go out and have a nice dinner and a glass of wine or something at one of the rooftop bars."

Two Fridays ago was the day Hallie had called Ben to ask him to come with her to Firefly Beach. And like a flash, she remembered their exchange when Gavin came to pick her up: she'd asked him why it was a natural reaction to make her feel like she had to be afraid of everyone she dated.

He'd returned, "*You* don't have to be afraid of them."

It was all starting to come together… He didn't ever seem to like people she dated because *he* was afraid of them. How long had he felt this way about her? The spot on her chest tingled where his fingers had first been. She rubbed it to make it stop, unable to get a breath.

"I invited him over because I wanted an explanation… I waited, offering him iced tea, letting him chat with Mimi, until the last possible minute, when I could ask him to tell me why, but he didn't give me an answer. He said he had to go, and he wouldn't stay. You know him so well. What should I do?"

Hallie did know Ben well, but this side of him wasn't her expertise. In fact, he was surprising her at every turn. She thought about those blue eyes, the silver flecks in them as he looked at her last night, how easy it had been to know his thoughts when for so long she'd been unable to decipher them.

Hallie didn't know what to say. The truth was, she had no idea what to do.

Chapter Fifteen

Feeling alone, Hallie stood in the open area of the guesthouse, looking around. For what, she wasn't sure. She already missed Ben's little pile of papers on the counter, his headphones resting on the arm of the sofa while he typed on his laptop. She inhaled, wondering if she could catch his scent to decipher what kind of emotion she felt when it hit her, but even that was gone. She still needed Ben to get through this, but she wasn't sure how to be around him now. Perhaps he knew that would happen and that was why he left. There was no "perhaps" about it. That was exactly why he'd left. No matter what, he'd never put work above the people he loved.

There was a knock at the door and Hallie nearly jumped out of her skin, the trespasser still in the forefront of her mind. Without Ben, she was jumpy. The late morning sun was coming in at a slant, casting long shadows through the room, every one of them jabbing her insides with mild apprehension. As open as the little bungalow was, there was no window in the door, probably for privacy since it opened right into the living space. Because she couldn't see who was on the front stoop, she resolved to put a new door in if she was going to spend any length of time there. With everyone else in the main house, no one could hear a thing way out here.

Hallie opened the door slowly with a firm grip on the knob, ready to slam it shut on anyone with less than favorable intentions. She peered through the crack she'd made between the doorframe and the door to find Gavin, to her relief, holding an enormous paper-wrapped parcel. The tension in her shoulders released and she opened the door wider.

"Hi," he said, his face lifted in excitement. "Your sister said you were probably out here. I have something for you. May I come in?"

Hallie stepped back to allow him to enter. He walked over to the kitchen area, stopping momentarily to assess his surroundings, and she had to keep her mind in the present when he stepped over to where Ben had been when they'd opened the champagne.

Gingerly, Gavin set the parcel on the kitchen island. "Unwrap it," he insisted.

Curious, given his enthusiasm, Hallie pulled the twine ribbon loose, the paper slackening around the shape inside. With a tiny tug, she drew the paper from under the heavy object and then lifted it off, revealing what had been covered.

"Oh my goodness!" she said with genuine happiness. She peered down at a larger version of her photograph, matted in burlap and framed in black just the way she'd said she'd have done it. It looked so lovely that she had to remind herself it was her own work.

"Your first piece."

The beauty of it astounded her. It told such a different story in this form than it had on the little screen of her camera.

"I haven't put the paper backing on yet. Would you sign the back of the photograph? I can show you how." He beamed at her, and she wondered how she'd ever worried about his opinion. He was so kind. "I'd like to put it in the gallery. I'll give you one hundred percent of the profit if I sell it. Or should I say *when* I sell it. It's fantastic. Would I have your permission to do that?"

"Yes!" she said, practically bursting. "Gavin, it would be such an honor."

He broke out into an enormous grin. "Glad to hear that. Now, would you trust me if I told you to grab your camera? We have more work to do."

Hallie couldn't help but wonder if Aunt Clara had a hand in all this, and Hallie wanted to make her proud. She thought about Gavin's particular photography style, and as he led her down the stone path to the main house, she considered what her own style would be. What did she want people to think when they looked at her pictures? She remembered Aunt Clara's words: *Life is what you make it.* That was when it hit her. She wanted her photography to be about *life*.

As they walked up the porch steps of Starlight, she lifted her camera to adjust her focus and squatted down to get a new angle of Aunt Clara's rocking chair, leaning just slightly to the left to allow the sunshine to stretch across the surface of it. She took her shot. Just that tiny adjustment was miles better than the last time she'd shot that chair. Now it actually looked like a place someone would sit, the warm orange glow of sunshine giving it life. She was already imagining how to adjust the light and filters when she got back to Gavin's, and she had a million different ways she could display it. Large-weave tan and cream blankets, glass bowls of sand and seashells, blue and white striped throw pillows…

"You read my mind," Gavin said. "I think you might have a natural ability at taking photos of objects in particular." He peered over her shoulder at the image she'd just taken. "You know just how to balance the light and dark in them. Each of your photographs takes on a sort of personality. What would you name this one?"

Hallie pushed the camera away from her to get a focused view of the shot. It was cozy and happy, the way the chair looked in her memory when Aunt Clara was just about to lower herself into it. Her laugh filtered into Hallie's mind, making her feel a wave of jubilation as if Hallie could reach out and touch her. "I think this one could easily be called 'Still There'."

"Perfect."

"What if I did more? What if I took photos of objects that depicted life on the coast? I'm thinking coastal comfort."

"You just named your series." He shook his head, disbelief showing in his grin. "I was going to ask you if you'd do a few prints to put up in the gallery alongside the one I framed."

"My series?"

"Essentially, a series is a grouping of artwork that all fits under one theme. The fire-pit photo in the guesthouse is a perfect piece for Coastal Comfort. And I have a feeling the rocking chair will be as well."

"I'd love to do more," she said, thinking. "What if each piece complemented the others in a color palette?"

"Very branded. I like it."

"So do I," she said, with new perspective about how to give form to this talent she had. Like a tidal wave, ideas were flowing and she was having trouble turning them off. "I'd like to name the framed photo 'Beginnings'," she said. She squared herself at the front door and snapped another photo. "But one series doesn't make a brand. I don't have a real brand yet…"

"You're getting ahead of me," Gavin said with a laugh. "Why don't we take about a hundred shots and then choose the best ones to create your Coastal Comfort series over a bite to eat in town?"

"Okay."

"Great! Then I'd better get to painting the trim before your uncle fires me."

"Let's ask him to go to lunch with us. Maybe that'll make up for my lateness."

"Did the doctor's appointment go okay?" Hallie asked, as she and Gavin helped Uncle Hank sit down at the table at Wes and Maggie's. Mama had taken him for a follow-up to discuss his lab work, but she'd gotten so preoccupied with taking care of things around the house that Hallie hadn't heard the results.

So happy to have Uncle Hank there, Wes had given them the table right by the bar so they could flag him down with their every need. The giant garage doors were open, letting in a delicious breeze that picked up the scent of rum from the mixed drinks Wes was making as it passed over the bar to their table. Soft music played in the background, the sound of steel drums over the light chatter of the tourists like the heartbeat of summer.

"My bill of health was clean as a whistle," Uncle Hank said. "The doctor thinks that it's all in my head. I told him, 'Of course it is! That's where I get dizzy.'"

Gavin grinned at his joke as he set his camera down onto the table.

When Uncle Hank was settled, Maggie placed a cup of black coffee in front of him. No matter how hot it was outside, it was Uncle Hank's first request whenever they visited.

"The doctor wants me to go to grief counseling. He thinks my anxiety over Clara is causing physical problems, and that's why my balance is off."

"It probably isn't a bad idea," Hallie offered. She placed her camera bag onto the floor.

"I don't buy in to all that mumbo jumbo. My wife died. I miss her. I don't need to pay someone by the hour to listen to me tell them that."

Hallie sat down beside him and picked up the plastic menu but didn't look at it. "They have strategies to help you manage your feelings."

"Well, I don't know if there's any good way to manage losing your whole world," Uncle Hank said.

Gavin cleared his throat, his face going white. "Excuse me a second," he said, standing. He walked off toward the bathrooms.

Uncle Hank's sorrow over losing Aunt Clara must have brought back painful memories for Gavin. While he and Uncle Hank had shared a few private moments together, this was out in the open, with Hallie present. Her skin prickled with concern as she leaned forward to see if she could catch sight of him, but the bathroom door had already shut. She turned back to Uncle Hank.

"They're not saying you can't be sad," she said. "But they might help you deal with your sadness… teach you how to be sad without falling down all the time."

"What's the old saying? 'You can't teach an old dog new tricks?'"

"I don't believe that." She watched the surf through the open restaurant doors. It was another red-flag day, the waves impatiently foaming onto the powdery sand. "Aunt Clara wouldn't have wanted to see you this way. She always embraced life, lived it to its fullest. She would be mortified to know that you've quit trying."

Uncle Hank gritted his teeth.

More gently, she suddenly wondered aloud, "What did Aunt Clara say in her letter to you?" She was certain that Aunt Clara would've told him something similar to what Hallie had just said.

"I don't know," Uncle Hank answered quietly.

"You don't know?"

He shook his head. "I haven't opened her letter."

Hallie felt her face crumple with confusion. "Why not?"

"I'm angry with her for leaving." He picked up his mug of coffee and put it to his lips with a shaky hand. "I don't want to know what she has to say."

"She didn't have a choice in the matter." When he didn't respond, she said, "You need to open the letter. It was important enough for her to write it, and she's able to speak to you through it. Don't you want to hear her voice again?"

A tear formed in the corner of his eye as he stared into his coffee.

Hallie wished Ben were here to help her talk to Uncle Hank. He'd know just the right things to say to make Uncle Hank understand. Ben could console him and help him to see her point of view. And what she didn't want to admit to herself was that she wanted Ben to make *her* feel better as well. Uncle Hank's sadness was tearing her apart, and she was working so hard to hold herself together for his benefit.

"How's the coffee?" Maggie said, setting glasses of water down for each of them.

Uncle Hank looked up at her and produced a smile. "It's as delicious as ever," he said.

"Glad to hear it. Where's your friend Mr. Wilson?"

Hallie eyed the bathroom—the door was still closed. But then laughter caught her attention outside. That was when she saw Gavin on the deck, his hands spread on the railing, his face toward the gulf.

"He's outside," she answered. "I'll just go and check on him. Can you give us a few more minutes before we order?"

"Absolutely. I'll come back in a bit."

Hallie excused herself from the table and walked out into the sunshine, squinting through the bright light to focus on Gavin. She came up behind him. "You okay?" she asked.

He turned around. "I'm sorry," he said. "It might be too soon…" He looked weary, uncertain.

"Too soon?"

"Too soon to pretend like I'm not so eaten up with fear that I can't move forward." He looked past her to their table. "I understand your uncle's perspective perfectly. We aren't very different."

"You *are* different," she said. "You're actually trying to move forward."

"I was right where he was for quite a while." He looked back out at the sea, over a family that had set up a ring toss on the beach, their jovial laughter contrasting with the situation between the three of them. "There's a part of me that wants to hold on to that feeling your uncle has right now, because letting it go would allow the possibility that I might forget what we had. But the agony of holding on is exhausting, and sometimes I just want to forget all of it. I'm trying to make a plan for my life. To work to rebuild it. But it feels like I keep mentally falling down whenever I stand up. So I get what your uncle is dealing with."

"I think moving on only means that you're allowing yourself to be okay." She smiled up at this man she barely knew but felt completely comfortable talking to. "You'll never forget," she said, thinking of her love for Aunt Clara. "You'll find more happiness if you allow yourself to look for it." She wasn't sure where that advice had come from. It felt like Aunt Clara was giving her the words to say.

Gavin kept his eyes on the rippling surf.

"There's no rush, though. Right now, we're here to look at photographs. Why don't we focus on that? Let's show Uncle Hank the pictures we took. I'd love to see your shots."

Gavin nodded, took in a steadying breath, and put his hand on Hallie's back to lead her inside. She didn't mind their closeness at all. It felt kind of nice to be the strong one for once.

When they got back to the table, Uncle Hank had nearly finished his cup of coffee. Maggie replaced it with another and took their orders. Hallie lightened the mood by mentioning what she and Gavin had been up to at Starlight Cottage.

She leaned over and turned the screen of her camera toward Uncle Hank. "Tell me the ones you like the best," she said.

Uncle Hank's face lit up when he saw her picture of the front porch rocking chair. But that wasn't all she had. She'd taken pictures of the lighthouse, the shimmering water as it rushed under the dock, the stone path leading to the guesthouse... Hundreds of shots of the house at Firefly Beach. She had an unusual feeling as she clicked through those images of the place that had changed her in so many ways. It had been the house where she'd seen true love for the first time, between her aunt and uncle; it had been the place that had given her security and happiness when her dad left them; and it had been there to watch her grow into a woman. Now it was changing her again. *This* was what was meant for her. The idea had bobbed around in her uncertainty for a while, but the more she leaned in to this talent she'd found, the more right it felt and the bigger it got in her head.

While they talked about her photography, Uncle Hank had life in his eyes, a glimmer of what used to be present all the time. She was glad she'd brought him out today, but one thing had happened that she'd never expected. Hallie had comforted both Gavin and Uncle Hank by herself, without leaning on anyone for support. Hallie was starting to get some of her old strength back.

Chapter Sixteen

Uncle Hank was walking better today. He had a slight spring in his step after their time out yesterday, but Hallie still gave him her arm for support as he headed downstairs at Starlight Cottage. Sydney had gone out with Mama and Robby. They'd taken advantage of Hallie's offer to stay with Uncle Hank and they'd gone to the park to let Robby play, so the house was empty.

After Uncle Hank's nap, having lumbered his way to the first floor on Hallie's arm, he paused in the entryway to catch his breath from the journey downstairs. The early afternoon sunlight filtered in from the glass-paned front door, reaching across the hardwoods.

"Are you hungry?" she asked.

Uncle Hank shook his head, contemplative. "Lunch yesterday was good. I enjoyed it," he said, allowing himself a small smile.

"Me too."

It seemed like he needed a minute, so they loitered there in the hallway, the silence louder to her than their laughter had been over the years. Uncle Hank sent a quick look through the living room doorway, over to the piano that sat in the corner, the top down, like a neglected family member. The old Steinway had been in the center of so many wonderful memories and now it sat unused, abandoned, the keys hidden from view by the dust-covered fallboard.

She gave Uncle Hank a look that she knew, despite her attempt to hide it, told him how much she missed hearing him play. To Hallie's complete surprise, he began to make his way over to it. He sat down slowly on the bench, lifted the fallboard, then lined his fingers up on the keys, resting his right thumb on middle C, which was the only key she remembered from when he'd tried to teach her as a girl.

Hitting each note individually, intentionally giving space for thought between them, he began a slow, sad song that she didn't recognize. She sat down beside him while he continued. His fingers seemed bulkier than they used to, but the sound was still fluid as he picked up the pace. As she tried to decipher the tune, he stopped the song right in the middle and shut the fallboard.

"When I enjoy myself, I forget for a moment that she's gone," he said. "In those instances, I feel like myself again, and I haven't felt like myself since before she got sick. I don't like it when it happens because it seems like she's right in the next room, and when I realize she isn't, it hurts all over again." His voice broke.

Hallie put her head on his shoulder. "I think you should read her letter," she said gently.

"I can't just yet." He leaned on the piano to steady himself and Hallie sat up. "I'm still tired. I'd like to sit down."

"Okay," she said. "Let me help you to a chair."

I hope the music is coming along, Hallie texted Ben.

When he didn't respond, she put her phone in her lap and looked out at the clouds moving in. The air coming off the water was cooler ahead of the storm that was headed their way. Late afternoon rain was one of the things she remembered most about summers at Firefly Beach. Aunt Clara would stay out on the porch until the rain would force her inside. She'd get board games and decks of cards, books and puzzles, spreading them along the floor, the vanilla scent of candles floating through the air as they all giggled and chatted during their games.

Everyone was still gone, and after a few hours in his chair, Uncle Hank had wanted to rest where he could be more comfortable, so she'd assisted him back upstairs. He'd barely made it to his room—it had taken all of Hallie's strength to get him to his bed—so Hallie decided to rest, herself. She'd chosen to sit outside in the gazebo alone. She didn't get much respite, however; scanning the coastline every few minutes to make sure she was actually alone. It was really hard to stay positive without Ben there. And she had so much to tell him about her photography and the design ideas she had to accompany the photos. Not to mention, she'd like to know what was going on with the two of them.

She held her phone up and typed, *I miss you.*

Immediately, this time, the bubbles appeared.

I miss you too, he returned. *I'm just super busy.*

She texted back, *I hope it's productive-busy! Call me when you get a chance.*

Okay.

"The wind is picking up," Sydney said from down the dock, pulling Hallie's attention to her sister, who was walking toward her with Robby. He gripped a piece of paper in his little hand as it waved wildly with every gust.

When they reached Hallie, Robby climbed up onto her lap. "I made this for Ben," he said. "It's the two of us playing football."

A skinny child, Robby wasn't built for football, and he'd gotten hurt the first time he'd tried to play in the recreational league, so Sydney had urged him toward baseball, but he still loved the game. Having been a college quarterback, Ben had the skills to teach Robby how to play, but he was also gentle enough to keep him from getting injured. They spent many Saturdays together watching Robby's favorite teams on television. Ben had taught Robby the names and intricacies of various plays before he'd even learned the entire alphabet. As the team broke from their lineup to execute a play, a player running around the end of the formation, Ben would say, "What's that?"

At four years old, Robby jumped up and called out the name of the play: "Jet Sweep!"

"I was just texting Ben. He's still really busy. I'll bet he'd like to see your drawing when he gets back," Hallie told Robby.

"He said we'd play, but then he had to leave." Robby looked up at her with disappointment in his eyes. "I brought my football and everything."

"I'll tell him you want him to play when I talk to him. I asked him to call me as soon as he gets a chance." She shifted Robby's weight on her legs. "He didn't mean to run off like he did. He just had to go back to work."

When she looked up, Sydney was staring at her, an indecipherable expression on her face. Hallie tried to question it with a look, but Sydney turned her head toward the blowing wind. The waves rushed into the shore, lapping hungrily under the dock, the sky above them a lush shade of gray, billowing in formations that made them appear to be dancing in the wind.

"We should probably get inside before it pours," Sydney said. "*And* we'll want to be inside to soften the mood. When Uncle Hank gets up, Mama's going to try to convince him to let her bring that Lewis guy over. She wants to call Lewis."

Hallie stood up. "Yeah, we should probably get inside."

But they were just a tick too late.

"How dare you suggest calling him?" Uncle Hank bellowed from down the hallway as they arrived at the cottage. He was awake and clearly not very happy at hearing the news that Mama was in possession of Lewis's number. But then, as Hallie, Sydney, and Robby entered the room, he added more quietly under his breath, "He's not coming into this house."

A clap of thunder shook the walls.

Robby ran over to grab the box of colored pencils and more paper. He set Ben's picture down on the table and pulled a clean sheet from the stack.

"At least let us know how Aunt Clara knows him," Mama said, shutting the windows as the rain began sheeting down. The manic tinkling of the wind chime silenced when the last window met the bottom of its frame. Mama twisted the locks on it before searching Uncle Hank for an answer.

He clenched his jaw defiantly.

"We can't just continue to have this stand-off. You're denying Aunt Clara's wishes. I know she'd have wanted you to move forward with this or she wouldn't have given me the letter."

"She's finally gotten me in a position where I can't argue," he said, defeated. His gaze fell to his lap, his lips pursed so tightly they were white with tension and anguish.

Mama's face dropped in sympathy for her aching uncle. "We can leave it for the time being, but we'll have to talk about it later," she told him, her tone gentler than before.

After that, the whole family plunged themselves into a quiet symphony of movement to prepare dinner, the undertaking of a meal at the cottage now a series of trained actions; passing plates and taking one helping before offering the next person the serving dish, whether or not they planned to eat that particular dish.

Just then, Hallie's phone rang. "It's Ben," she said. She felt a new eagerness to hear his voice, but at the same time, she suddenly didn't know what to say or where to begin. It rang again, flustering her. She needed to be in silence to think, but she didn't want to let the call go for fear she wouldn't get another chance to speak to him due to his schedule. "I'll just grab it on the porch."

"You're gonna get soaked," Mama warned as Hallie headed outside onto the porch, closing the door behind her.

"Hello?" Hallie leaned against the house to avoid the rain.

"Hey."

The wind whipped around her furiously, the sky darkening to a solid smoky gray and the choppy turquoise waves looking like static as raindrops pelted them. A single jagged bolt of lightning lit up the sky and then dove down into the sea, another loud clap of thunder chasing it. She pressed the phone firmly against her face, gripping it tightly. "How's the music going?" she asked, unsure of what to say other than, "What the heck is going on with us?"—a subject she didn't want to approach just yet.

"Good." With the phone clamped to her ear, she could hear his light breathing on the other end of the line despite the gusts of wind and the rain. His breaths sounded the way they did when he was worried. "I'm sorry I left so quickly."

"When can you come back?" They had a lot to talk about: what had happened between them, and if Hallie could muster the courage, they needed to discuss why they could never have another moment like that again.

"I'm not sure…" His voice was gentle.

"Robby's upset that you left. He wanted to play football with you. He said you told him you would. I explained about your work."

A frustrated groan came from the other end of the phone. "Damn it," he said in a whisper. "I forgot I'd mentioned that to him. I had no idea when I offered that I'd have to leave."

"I know. I'm sure he'll understand."

He blew air through his lips loudly. And then silence. She could feel his deliberation all the way from Nashville. "Tell him I'm coming back."

An unexpected tightness seized Hallie's chest. Ben was coming back, and while she couldn't wait to see him, she didn't want to have to face telling him the real reason she and Jeff didn't make it. "He'll be so happy," she said instead.

"I'm glad. Hey, I've gotta go…"

"Okay."

"Tell everyone I miss them."

"Will do."

"And Hallie?"

She tipped her head against the house and closed her eyes, afraid to hear what he had to say to her. She didn't know what she wanted him to tell her, but a distress like no other swam through her. Perhaps it was the fear of change, of things being different between them, of having to learn a new normal, a normal where they both found themselves having unexpected feelings but couldn't act on them. "Yeah?" she finally said.

"I miss you the most."

He was changing everything.

"See you soon?" she said, cradling the phone to her face as if it were his hand.

"As soon as I can."

When she got off the call, Sydney's warning screamed at her from inside her head. After Ben had let his feelings show even a little, it had sent him all the way back to Nashville. He was certain to stay far away when she told him her secret. Because once she told him that, any relationship that he wanted other than friendship would be completely out of the question. And she hadn't totally figured out her own, new feelings for Ben. But one thing she did know was that she longed for the feel of his arms around her, to have his eyes on her, his unstill hands caressing her. If she allowed herself to feel what she suddenly wanted to feel for Ben, the only thing that would come of it would be heartbreak. Couldn't things just be simple?

Hallie went back inside, her hair damp. Another clap of thunder pounded them. Robby was drawing a truck. "What did Ben say?" he asked, his pencil moving across the paper as he sketched the road under it.

"You'll be happy to know that he's coming back just to play that football game."

Robby looked up. "Really?"

"Yep. He doesn't know when just yet, but he said as soon as he finishes, he's coming to Firefly Beach."

"I can't wait to see him!"

"Neither can I," Hallie said. And then she locked eyes with Sydney, but turned away quickly, her face burning with the knowledge that everything she felt for Ben was right on the surface for everyone to see.

Chapter Seventeen

It was late. Sydney had piled up Robby's drawings on the table and taken Robby up to get his bath and read stories. Hallie insisted that it was her turn to clean up dinner, and she'd told Mama to relax with her book and put her feet up, so Mama decided to make a cup of tea and head upstairs for a little down time. Uncle Hank had stayed back. He still sat at the clean table, the last one in the kitchen besides Hallie.

"Would you get me a beer from the fridge?" he asked.

Hallie opened the refrigerator door and pulled out a beer for him, and then one for her. "Mind if I have one?" she asked, holding up the other bottle.

"Not at all."

She popped the tops off the bottles and brought them to the table, lowering herself down across from Uncle Hank.

He took a long, quiet drink from his bottle and then peered down at the label, pretending to inspect it, but it was evident that he was gathering his thoughts. "Your aunt is making this very difficult on me." He looked up. "I don't understand why she would leave anything to Lewis."

"Who is he, Uncle Hank?" Hallie held her bottle with both hands, leaning forward in interest.

"He's no one important. He hasn't been in my life for over fifty years, and I'd rather keep it that way… But I think I might need to read her letter. I want to see what Clara says about him. It's tearing me up inside." He reached into his pocket and pulled out a tattered pink envelope. It was creased in half, still sealed, with his name in Aunt Clara's script on the outside. He set it on the table and stared at it, tipping his beer up to his lips for another drink.

"Do you want me to stay, or would you like to be alone?"

"Stay. Please." He pushed it toward her with his fingertips. "In fact, would you read it to me?"

A lump formed in Hallie's throat as she pulled the crumpled envelope toward her. The corners were worn, presumably from being in Uncle Hank's pocket—he must have carried it around just like Hallie had carried hers, unable to let go of the last tangible piece of Aunt Clara. With Hallie's own emotions on the surface, it would be nice to hear her voice, even if only in her mind as she read the writing.

She straightened her shoulders to keep away the pinch that always came whenever she faced life without Aunt Clara head on, and picked at the edge of the envelope flap until she had enough space to slide her finger underneath and free it from the seal. In a split second, she was holding the letter, that familiar script scrawled across the page, beckoning her eyes to decipher it. Uncle Hank took a heavy drink from his bottle as she read.

My Dearest Hank,

I'm praying you'll actually read this. You're as stubborn as anyone I know, and even as I write it, I'm worried that you'll be so annoyed with me for getting to paradise first that you'll grudgingly carry this letter around and never hear the words that I want you to know. So if you're reading this, you've already surprised me…

Hallie looked up at him and smiled.

First of all, I want you to know that if I have the chance at all to be with you in death, I'm there. My chair at the table is full. And I'm looking at you with adoring eyes the same way I did every night, just like those quiet summer evenings after the family had headed home and we were both exhausted from their visit. Remember the bliss we shared, just knowing how, in a small way, we'd helped to raise Hallie and Sydney, and now they were adults who'd gone on to have their own lives? We would just sit in the silence and smile at each other.

Uncle Hank didn't glance over at the chair like Hallie had, his gaze remaining on the letter, but his eyes filled with tears. Her own eyes clouding up, Hallie stood and walked over to the place where Aunt Clara always sat and scooted the chair away from the table a little, as if Aunt Clara had just gotten up and then returned to her own seat. Now, more than ever, Hallie felt her there. She picked up the letter again and began reading the rest of it.

The beautiful thing about life is that we don't have the answers. It's human nature to search for them, and if we're lucky, those burning questions will get answered for us, but even if all of them aren't, when we look back at what we've done, we have so much defining the path of who we are that the little mysteries don't matter. My advice is this: go blindly into the rest of your life. Do the things that scare you the most because if they terrify you, they have worth to you.

Hank, your years are numbered. We won't be apart very long. I know you'll take care of all the business end of this, but you still have work to do, and as I sit here right now, I'm certain that's exactly why you stayed on this earth after I had to leave it. Knowing how stubborn you are about Lewis, I'm giving you a little push. But ultimately, it's up to you to make your family whole. There's nothing holding you back now. I can't get in the way of it anymore. I saw you staring at the empty chair I left for Lewis every holiday.

Hallie stopped reading, the last line hitting a little too close to home. The way they all noticed Aunt Clara's absence at the table was the way Uncle Hank had noticed Lewis's. Who was this man? She probed Uncle Hank with a questioning stare, but he wasn't budging. Since she couldn't get the answers from him, she just kept reading.

Every time we got the family together around the table, you looked at that empty chair. And if it weren't for me, Lewis would have been in it. Go. Fill it. Because my hope for you is that you have not two empty chairs this year at your table but two that are filled—one with Lewis and one with my memory.

Our life together has a breathtaking view from where I sit as I write this. Everyone in your family deserves the kind of love you gave me. I can't wait to see what you do next. I'll be right beside you cheering you on.

I love you.

Forever Yours,

Clara

They both sat in silence, the light tapping of the rain on the roof the only sound around them. The fact that Aunt Clara had already thought of the empty space she would leave before it happened rocked Hallie to the core, and made her believe that Aunt Clara was right there just like she said she'd be.

Uncle Hank drained his beer and gently set the empty bottle on the table. His eyes were still misty, his lips pursed to keep them from wobbling.

"Will you talk to Lewis?" Hallie asked, her voice cutting through the stillness.

With labored movements, he shook his head. "I don't know…"

"You have to. Did you hear what Aunt Clara was saying?"

"I don't know if I want him in my life."

"Aunt Clara thinks he should be."

When he didn't answer, Hallie went over to the window. The heavy rain had lifted, leaving only a gentle sprinkle through the lights that illuminated the property down to the beach. She could make out the turbulent waters, still upset from the storm—as if they were echoing what was going on right now with the letter. Uncle Hank had to do this. Aunt Clara was a brilliant woman and he had to trust her judgment. She had a perspective that was far clearer than theirs, because when she wrote the letter she didn't have any more life in front of her to blur her clarity.

Suddenly, Hallie's thoughts were interrupted by the dark shadow that was walking down the beach away from the property. The figure turned back, staring at the house, unmoving, chilling her to the bone. Could he see her? Her breath caught in her throat.

"Uncle Hank," she whispered, pulling her phone out slowly with shaky hands, her movements minimal in case the person out there was watching her. She held the phone out of view of the window and only moved her eyes to look down at it as she hit the number for the local police, which she'd saved in her contacts after she'd first heard about the trespasser. "Someone's out on the beach," she said quietly, not turning around. "Don't move. I'm calling the police." She hit the speaker icon.

The phone rang twice before someone answered. "This is Hallie Flynn at Starlight Cottage," she said. "There's an intruder on the property."

"Tell us where you saw the intruder, Hallie, and we'll send someone out immediately."

"He's on the beach, just down from the gazebo. He's facing the house right now." She squinted in an attempt to get a description but she could hardly see a thing. He was just an unnerving shadow, a dark form, making the hairs on her arms stand up.

"I've already got two cars headed that way. One has the search dog. The other was patrolling in the area and should be there soon. Lock up and stay put."

"Okay." She ended the call and then turned around to face Uncle Hank, the upsetting presence of the stranger at her back making her nauseous. She sat down, pushing her beer away.

Uncle Hank was looking out the window, with a clear view of the man on the beach. "That's him," he said. "That looks like the person I see every time. He used to come right up to the window, but the problem was that I couldn't get to it quickly enough to catch a good glimpse of him. I was worried I'd fall. He'd be hiding or gone before I could get there. And when he's further away, he's never in a place where I can see more than a shadow. It's so frustrating. He's always deliberate with his movements. He never runs. But even still, I can't get a solid look at him. Ever since you all came, he's stayed further away." Uncle Hank cut his eyes at the image. "You all probably scared him off, since you're young and able to chase him if he gets too close."

She turned to look at the figure and saw him heading away from them down the beach. Hallie silently prayed the police officers would find him. Would they get here in time? "I'm going to check the doors, and let Mama and Sydney know so they aren't alarmed when the police come to the door."

Just as she was leaving the room, she saw the elongated beaming glow from a searchlight stretch across the grass. They were nearly here.

Chapter Eighteen

"Do you want to press charges?" the police officer asked Uncle Hank, as Hallie's uncle sat in one of the two matching dark blue bergère-style chairs that Aunt Clara had delighted in when she'd redone the living room. "We've got him out in the car."

"I think we should bring him in," Mama said from the sofa. "We need to find out what's going on."

Uncle Hank sent a dagger-like look her way.

Sydney wasn't offering any further advice, clearly allowing Mama to handle this. She rubbed her shoulder, rolling her head around. Hallie felt the same way. Things had taken their toll on everyone, but this was something no one had seen coming.

When the police required the trespasser to identify himself, the man gave his name: Lewis Eubanks. It all made sense now. No wonder he was in no hurry to get off the grounds. He was an old man; he couldn't move very fast. And this was his family. But why hadn't he just knocked on the door? What made him cower around, hiding in the bushes? Hallie had never thought of Uncle Hank as a poor judge of character, so if he didn't like this guy, she was starting to wonder if there was a real reason. Was he a bad seed in the family? Should they be wary of him?

"I'll bet he just wants his money," Uncle Hank said. "He probably heard about his inheritance and he's come to get it, but he's too much of a coward to ask me for it."

"All right," Mama said, standing up from the sofa. "I've had about enough of this. If you won't tell me what's going on, then I'll have Lewis do it. Bring him in. We're not pressing charges."

They all looked at Mama with wide eyes.

Uncle Hank didn't speak, but it looked like his face would burst with anger.

"How can you drop all charges? What if he was planning to do something awful to us?" Sydney asked.

"He's family," she said. "And Aunt Clara wanted him with us every single holiday. That tells me that he's good."

"I'll be damned!" Uncle Hank stood with the force of an erupting volcano. He grabbed the arms of the chair to steady himself, his knees barely allowing for the speed at which he rose. "He's a lying, thieving, awful person!"

Mama considered Uncle Hank's words for quite some time. Then, she turned to the officer. "Bring him in."

"Okay," the officer said. "Would you like me to stay?"

"He's seventy-eight years old, and he's family. I think we'll be just fine." She walked the officer to the door and Hallie followed.

"I'll tell you what. I'll stay in the car until you give me the okay that you won't be harmed." He opened the door, mosquitoes buzzing around the porch light as he exited the cottage. He walked to the squad car, opened the back door, and permitted Lewis to climb out.

When Lewis made eye contact, he seemed kind and genuinely mortified by what had transpired. But he had to know that this would happen if he were on the grounds uninvited. He climbed the porch steps with ease, and it was clear that he was younger and in better shape than Uncle Hank, yet he looked so much like him that no one could deny the fact that they were related. He had Uncle Hank's broad, defined features, the same hooded eyes, and silver hair that was so similar Hallie was nearly sure they'd both had the same color growing up.

He greeted Mama. "Nice to meet you," he said, breathless, as she shook his hand. "I'm your uncle," he said. "Hank's brother."

Uncle Hank had never said he had a brother. And from the look on Mama and Sydney's faces, they were just as surprised by it as Hallie was. When Hallie looked over at Uncle Hank, he wasn't in the room anymore, his chair empty.

"Come in, please," Mama said, shutting the door and ushering him inside the living room.

Lewis's gaze swept lovingly over the furnishings, before a loud bang of a door drew their attention down the hallway.

"Here," Uncle Hank barked, marching in and jabbing a check at Lewis. He grabbed Lewis's hand to shove the payment into his grasp, but Lewis drew back, the green and gray personal check from the Eubanks' private account fluttering to the floor. It was made out to Lewis in the amount of one hundred thousand dollars. "What else could you possibly want?"

Lewis didn't flinch at Uncle Hank's anger. In fact, he behaved as if Uncle Hank were acting totally normal, which was very odd since Hallie had never seen him behave like this in her entire life. "I wanted to make sure you were okay," Lewis said, stepping over the check to have a seat on the sofa. He ran his hand along the cushion.

"Get up," Uncle Hank snapped. "You aren't allowed to enjoy Clara's furniture."

Sydney walked over and put a hand on Uncle Hank's arm, her concern for his state clear. He wasn't in great health emotionally already. He didn't need this level of stress.

"I'm so sorry to have worried you all," Lewis said, turning away from Uncle Hank. "When I read that Clara had passed, I had to make sure my brother was okay. I checked on him a lot at first, and I was delighted to see you all come. Once you arrived, I only wanted to make sure someone was here so I'd take my nightly walks onto the property. I live just outside of Firefly Beach, so I'd walk the route to the park in town and cut through the hiking path between the park and the cottage. When you left, I was going to start coming up to see him again."

"Isn't it kind of strange to be peeking into someone's windows?" Mama said, obviously bothered by Uncle Hank's response to him.

"What choice did I have?" Lewis said. "You saw the reception I got when I came in."

"As you should," Uncle Hank said, glaring at him.

"It was so many years ago, Hank; we were all so young. And I've been asking your forgiveness ever since it happened. I had no right to do what I did, but love makes you do crazy things, things you normally wouldn't." He took a step closer to his brother. "She picked you, Hank," he said in almost a whisper. "For fifty years, she picked you, without a waver. I'm nothing but a lonely old man. Forgive me."

Uncle Hank turned away from him.

Lewis addressed Mama. "Thank you for not pressing charges," he said. "If I'd have known I was frightening people, I would've found another way to check on him. I'm so sorry." He walked over to the door and opened it, a warm gust of summer wind blowing the check across the floor like a miniature tumbleweed. "I won't stay. Having me here is obviously upsetting. I only wanted to make sure Hank was all right. There's nothing else I want."

"Wait," Mama said.

Lewis turned around.

"It's late. You live all the way past the park. Why don't you stay?"

"I wouldn't dare intrude," he said, sending a sad look over to Uncle Hank.

"You can't possibly walk home. It's after ten o'clock." Mama brushed past Uncle Hank and shut the door. "I insist. Uncle Hank can pout all he wants, but you're family. Hallie, could you stay in the guesthouse tonight? I'll put some new sheets on your bed upstairs and we'll let Lewis stay here."

Before Hallie could answer, Uncle Hank cut in. "The police officer is still sitting outside. He can drive him home," he said, refusing to acknowledge his brother with anything more than a response to Mama.

"Oh! My goodness," Mama said, rushing to the door. She gave the police officer a thumbs-up and a wave, and sent him on his way. "I can't ask the man to give rides—that's not his job," she said, coming back inside. "Plus, we have to give Lewis Aunt Clara's other letter, remember?"

Uncle Hank was silent, grinding his jaw and remaining defiant. Finally, he said, "Any of you could drive him home, but you won't, will you? Well, you don't know what he did, so you're making a mistake inviting him into Clara's home. If he stays, I'll be upstairs, and I won't come down until he's gone." Then he left the room.

"I'll drive him home," Hallie suggested, feeling as if they were all ganging up on Uncle Hank.

Even if he was wrong, Starlight Cottage was his house and they should be respectful of his wishes. And until she had the entire story, she didn't like the idea of this man, who was a stranger to them, sleeping at their house. They had a child to consider in all this. Was tonight's atmosphere what they'd like Robby to wake up to?

"I'll just grab my keys," she said, without allowing anyone to offer further suggestions.

Lewis lived in an unfussy little bungalow just outside of town, only a few minutes' drive from Starlight Cottage. If it hadn't started to rain again, he definitely could've walked. He was fit for his age. He'd told Hallie on the ride that he spent a lot of time traveling and hiking, and up until a few years ago when his back started giving him problems, he even rock climbed. He was sociable and kindhearted on their drive; nothing like the person Uncle Hank saw when he looked at him. She wanted to know what had happened between the two brothers and Aunt Clara, but she needed to hear it from Uncle Hank first.

Hallie lay in her bed in the sewing room, holding her phone in the dim glow of lamplight. Even though she didn't really know where she and Ben stood, she wanted to talk to him to tell him what had happened tonight. He had this way about him that could always clear the clutter in her mind and make her feel better about the situation. It was nearly midnight, now that she'd had a long bath and gotten ready for bed. There was a missed call and voicemail from Gavin that she'd check later, but right now, she wanted to hear Ben's voice. She texted him to see if he was awake.

He responded right away: *Just locking up the studio. I'll call you in a sec.*

After a few minutes, her phone lit up and she answered it right away.

"You're working late," she said.

"Yeah. I'm trying to move quickly."

She could hear the jingle of his keys as he opened his car door and then the hum when he put her on speakerphone and started the engine.

"I have so much to tell you," she blurted, wishing he were there so she could see his understanding eyes as she told him everything. She started in, talking a mile a minute, beginning with Aunt Clara's letter to Uncle Hank and continuing on with barely a breath until the last moment of her day before she'd climbed into bed and called him.

"So do you believe what Hank says about him?" he asked, his voice clear. The background was quiet now; she must have talked all the way to his house.

"I believe that Uncle Hank believes it. But like any story, there are two sides."

"Right," he said. She heard the rush of water at the sink. Then the sound quieted, and his voice was at her ear again. "I'm coming back tomorrow."

"That's really soon," she said, both thinking he was crazy for making that drive again so quickly, and totally elated at the thought of it.

"We need to talk," he said.

Fear swallowed her. What if he wanted to talk about their exchange over the champagne or all those unsaid thoughts that he always had? And if he was ready to discuss those things, what did she think about them? She tried to decipher the flutter in her stomach when she heard his voice tonight. What she didn't want to admit to herself was that she felt differently about him now. The love she felt was a different kind than the childlike adoration of her youth, and it made her realize that if they did talk about this, she'd have to tell him everything, things she still hadn't had the courage to disclose to anyone. Was he ready to hear what she had to say?

Chapter Nineteen

Hallie headed downstairs for breakfast the next morning with a full day already planned. She was going to spend some time researching editing software.

Gavin's message said that he could help her edit her photos for the series, and he'd show her a few of the programs he liked best. When she'd texted him this morning, he'd told her to come over as soon as she got a chance.

A pensive hush settled over the kitchen as everyone divvied out their breakfast the same way they had all week. Hallie couldn't help but look at the two empty chairs at the end of the table a little differently now. Aunt Clara's seat was still pulled out just a bit. She'd had about enough of this.

They all looked up as Hallie walked in, but something came over her after thinking of Aunt Clara and she couldn't believe she hadn't done it sooner. She waved, giving them a lighthearted look, hoping the mood would brighten. Nothing but utter confusion came from Sydney, a slight interest from Mama and Robby, and definite curiosity from Uncle Hank.

Go time.

Hallie headed right back out of the room, ignoring Sydney's whisper, "Where is she going?"

Swiftly, she entered the living room and sat down at the piano, raising the lid. Then, she played the only song that Uncle Hank had taught her and the only one she knew. She jovially banged out "Happy Birthday" over and over, refusing to stop. When nothing happened, she started playing *and* singing as joyfully as if it were a party. They all needed to just snap out of it for a minute.

"Is it somebody's birthday?" Robby said excitedly from the kitchen.

"Sing with meeee! HAPPY BIRTHDAY TO YOU…" Hallie kept playing loudly. Her fingers moved on the keys, finding the tune as easily as if she were well practiced, and she reminded herself that Aunt Clara was likely there cheering her on just as she promised Uncle Hank she'd be.

After a few minutes more, Hallie moved her fingers across the keys and started again an octave higher. And then lower.

Finally, when she'd hit her grand final note, just before beginning again, she noticed Uncle Hank in the doorway with his hands over his ears. "What in God's name are you doing?" he asked, trying not to laugh.

"You always played before breakfast. You played every single morning while Aunt Clara made her sausage and egg casseroles or her homemade pancakes," she said. "And no one has played before breakfast since I got here. So if you aren't going to do it, then someone else will have to. And this is all I know how to play."

He gave her a wary look.

"You've got more work to do here, Uncle Hank," she whispered. "Aunt Clara said so, and we all know not to mess with Aunt Clara."

He smirked a little.

"Start right here, with your family. Robby doesn't remember that apple tree song you used to play when we were little. He needs to feel what it's like here first thing in the morning—all the laughter, the fun we used to have. In our family, he's the next generation and you are the last of your generation. Teach him what our family is like."

When Hank didn't sit down next to her, she started playing again as the whole family came to see what she was doing.

"All right, all right," Uncle Hank said, stilling her hands, the keys groaning in protest. "I'll play." Hallie stood up, giving Uncle Hank the width of the entire keyboard. When she did, he patted the bench. "Robby, come sit here."

Robby climbed up.

"Any guess where the middle C is?" Uncle Hank asked.

Robby shook his head.

"It's right here." Uncle Hank took Robby's little hand and put his thumb in the same place he'd put Hallie's when she was that age. As Robby pressed the key, the *tink tink tink* of it gave Hallie goosebumps. Sydney and Mama were beaming.

This was what Aunt Clara wanted—Hallie could feel it.

"Can we talk for a minute?" Sydney said, catching Hallie on the stairway as she went up to get her camera before leaving for Gavin's. Sydney never wanted to "talk" in that sense, so clearly there was something bothering her.

"Sure."

Hallie followed her sister downstairs. They settled into two rocking chairs on the back porch. The sun had already burned through the light mist of early morning and the gulf was shimmering in the sunlight. Aunt Clara had always worn turquoise jewelry, and when Hallie was young she used to think that it was the gulf, captured there in the stones of her rings. The water was that same color today, and the storm had left the beaches combed flat by the night's high tide.

Hallie's gaze was still on the water, the warmth just starting to penetrate her skin, when Sydney came right out with what was bothering her. "Do you and Ben have something going on?"

"What?" Hallie whipped her head around to her sister. "No." She couldn't get any more than that out because the burning in her cheeks had derailed any ability to contest Sydney's observation of the situation. But the truth was, they didn't have something going on. They just had the *something*. It wasn't *going* anywhere.

"I've already spoken to Ben about it."

"About what?" Mortification was swimming around in Hallie's eyes, so she looked back out at the water to hide it.

"You know what I think about all this already, and how I feel about having Ben there for Robby, but this conversation isn't about me or my child. It's about you. I see the happiness he gives you when you talk to him, the absolute relief when he texts. Look, it all sounds so perfect right now. He's your best friend. He's an amazing guy. But things like this can ruin friendships—I've experienced it first hand. I don't speak to Christian anymore. Not a word. Anything we had before our relationship has evaporated into thin air, and we've been reduced to court appearances and child support. I can't sit by and watch it happen again."

"Ben wouldn't cheat on me," she said quietly, realizing that this was the first time she'd admitted out loud that there could be something other than friendship between them. She kept her face toward the water, terrified to look at the pain in her sister's face for fear it would scare her to death.

"I know he wouldn't," Sydney said more quietly. "But—and this is what I told him too—it would be terrible if the two of you realized that it wasn't working and you had to pretend because both of you were too kind to admit it to one another. Hold on to this feeling that you have right now and don't do anything to change that. Don't ruin it."

Hallie sat silently. She was aware of her breathing, long, steady breaths going in and out, the way the counselor had told her in the days after... Any dreams she had of finding that fairy tale life had already washed away. Sydney was right, and Hallie knew it. She'd been so swept up in the rush of her feelings that she hadn't taken time to think things through. Being at Starlight Cottage had taken her mind off it all for a little while, and made her feel more like the person she was before everything changed. But now, it was time to face reality.

"You don't have to worry. Ben is a family guy. He needs a family; he's going to want lots of kids when he finds that perfect person—and I'm not her," Hallie said, her words nearly a whisper, tears surfacing the way they always did before she forced the words out. For Jeff. For the counselor. And now for her sister. "Jeff and I found out we were pregnant a few months before the wedding."

Sydney gasped but didn't say anything. Hallie still couldn't look her sister in the eye because the surprise on her face would make Hallie feel even more like a failure. She was broken. Against her will, and through no fault of her own, the guilt she carried over it swarmed her like angry bees. "I lost the baby," she said, her face crumpling. "And they told me that I shouldn't try for more." She closed her eyes, the name of her condition hitting her just as hard today as it had when she'd first heard it. Hallie finally looked at her sister, a tear running down her cheek. "They said I have something called antiphospholipid syndrome."

Sydney, still speechless, shook her head, not understanding what it was, the same way Hallie had been when the doctor had said it to her.

"My immune system mistakenly produces antibodies that make my blood clot irregularly. The doctor prescribed medicine to help. But in my particular case, I doubt I could ever carry a child to term, and even if I managed, my health would be significantly at risk. I had no idea until they did some tests."

"My God, Hallie. I'm so sorry. I'm so, so sorry." Tears welled up in Sydney's eyes as she got out of her chair and threw her arms around Hallie.

The sobs that Hallie had suppressed exploded from her with the force of a rocket, her chest heaving as she buried her face in her sister's shoulder. She'd tried to move forward with things, to act normally, but when it came down to it, this was always at the forefront of her mind now, and she knew that life couldn't be the same ever again.

Hallie gently pushed her sister back to look at her. "Ben deserves more than what I can give him," she said. "So you don't have to worry about me messing things up." As she said it, the despair of never getting a chance to see what might have been descended upon her, stronger than it ever had before.

Chapter Twenty

Hallie pulled up at Gavin's house just a little before lunchtime. He'd promised her homemade pizza and lemonade while they worked on her collection, and she was happy for the diversion. The truth was that her diagnosis was a part of who she was, and while she would still get low about it at times, like today, she had to tell herself to remember Aunt Clara's words about making the most of her life.

It was a scorcher of a day, and Gavin had told Uncle Hank he'd work on painting the trim in the late afternoon, once the sun was behind the trees, and the next two hours or so would be devoted to art. When Hallie saw the counselor after her diagnosis, she found that the artistic expression therapies were the most helpful for her, and she'd definitely felt happier after being immersed in her photography, so she cleared her mind and spent the drive to Gavin's focusing on her ideas for expanding beyond the photography for the Coastal Comfort brand. While she loved taking pictures, a tiny urge was pushing her to do more.

"Pizza's in the oven. I figured we could get straight to work," Gavin said, meeting her on the front porch. Holding open the screened door, he continued, his eyes sparkling with excitement. "Your shots are incredible on the large screen and I've got so many concepts already." He was dressed casually, and she noticed a few specks of paint on his shirt.

"Were you working?" she asked, setting her bag containing her camera and laptop under the hall table, his enthusiasm like a breath of fresh air.

"Yes. I was putting a few final touches on my latest painting just before you came. Would you like to see it?"

"I'd love to."

"Okay. But first, lemonade." He swept through the kitchen, filling two Mason jars with ice and juice, handing her one. His movements were becoming familiar now, and his relaxed demeanor made her feel at home. "Follow me!"

Gavin took Hallie upstairs. She hadn't been upstairs in his home before, and as she ascended the original wooden staircase, she felt the personal nature of where she was going. This was where the bedrooms were and the place where he painted. She felt a little like an intruder, but his smile was contagious and made her curious as to what she would see once they were at the top.

The staircase led to an enormous open space, the entire back of it nothing but windows that allowed light to fill the room and offered extensive views of the gardens, taking her breath away. Against the fresh, white walls the green of outside screamed for attention, but she forced her focus toward the corner where Gavin had placed an easel, the hardwood floors dotted with paint.

Hallie walked over to it.

"Do you like it?" he asked, standing beside her.

She set her lemonade down on one of the tarps next to the wall and returned to the painting, her entire attention on only that. "Oh my goodness," was all she could say. It was acrylic, using big, chunky strokes, but as a whole creating the most gorgeous design. There was a green circle made of budding branches, with varying shades of olive and chocolate, and in the most beautiful cursive script in the center, it said, "Coastal Comfort." But behind the logo, covering the entire canvas, as if the logo were stamped on top of it, was a very lightly painted, translucent version of her photograph of Aunt Clara's white rocker. She couldn't have imagined a better design. It was clean yet feminine, natural and inviting—just like Aunt Clara. She had to blink away her tears of happiness.

"It's only an idea, but if you like it, I can hang it in the gallery by your photos—I've cleared out a room for them—and I can make a digital image of it that you can use for stationery and business cards. Your brand."

She wanted to hug him. "It's perfect."

"I'm glad you like it," he said, smiling at her, clearly elated that he'd impressed her.

"I just feel bad that you're going to all this trouble… What if nothing sells?"

His smile widened. "It isn't about the money," he said. "It's about doing what you love, what you were put on this earth to do. If you get it right, the money will find you. Watch and see."

She believed him. Aunt Clara's business was a perfect example of that.

"Wanna do a little editing?" he asked.

"Absolutely!" Hallie was in her element. Ideas were coming faster than she could get down the stairs. "I'm imagining a movement of muted color as the eye travels around the room in the gallery. So maybe five to six of the white photos, framed in black and charcoal gray, and then add in the burlap-framed print, moving into some of the tan shots like the sand at Firefly Beach and the dock. The color can slowly move to turquoise, so the entire room takes on the feel of the coast."

"You have a very strong grasp of Coastal Comfort already," Gavin said as they reached the kitchen, the timer going off on the oven. He pulled out the pizza and set it on a trivet.

"I feel like it's even bigger than what we've already thought of. I'm wondering if I could pair with local merchants to match furniture and accessories to the prints. Wouldn't it sell more photographs to have coordinating sand-colored throws, white sofas, and seaside-themed candles? Coastal Comfort could be an all-inclusive theme. Designs for the accents have been floating around in my head."

Gavin rolled the cutter through the pizza, his delight clear. "Sounds to me like your aunt wasn't the only designer in the family."

Hallie had been so busy creating in her mind that it wasn't until he said it that it actually occurred to her that this was exactly the kind of thing that Aunt Clara would be a part of. With everything going on in Hallie's life right now, she found these discussions with Gavin to be like oxygen for her deprived soul.

"After we have lunch, let's get that software up and running on your laptop so you can get started. It sounds like you've got big plans for Coastal Comfort."

"Ben!" Robby tore out the front door past Hallie and Sydney, racing down the drive at Starlight Cottage toward Ben's parked jeep. He'd been watching through the window ever since Ben had texted when he'd stopped for lunch to give an approximate arrival time. Beau bolted from the backseat, nearly knocking Robby over with kisses, his tail wagging feverishly.

"Hi Beau." Robby giggled before Ben directed the dog toward a ball in his hand. He chucked it off into the yard and Beau ran after it.

"That's not the only ball I brought," Ben said, reaching into the backseat and holding up a football. "Ready? Go long!" Robby ran at full speed, his head twisted around to watch for the pass, his legs moving as fast as they could go. Ben sent the ball sailing across the yard, spiraling like a bullet straight into Robby's arms. Robby cradled it, changing direction and sprinting full speed over to Ben.

"Did you miss me?" Ben said, picking him up and spinning him in the air.

"Yes!" Robby squealed, clutching the ball as Ben whirled him around.

"Are we going to play football later?" Ben set him down.

"You bet we are! It can be you and Hallie against Mama and me!" With all his might, Robby tossed the ball up into the air. It flew up near the tops of the palm trees that lined the walk.

As it came back down, Ben grabbed it with one hand. Then he pitched it back to Robby. "I can't wait," he said, but his eyes had already found Hallie on the porch.

Seeing him again was like coming home from a long trip, like crawling into her own bed after being away from it. She waved.

"Let's give Ben and Hallie a little time, okay?" Sydney said, putting her arm around Robby's shoulder and guiding him toward the house. She gave Hallie a look of caution on the way inside but Hallie didn't need it. She had enough to restrain herself all on her own.

Ben nodded toward the beach, his gaze not leaving Hallie. She met him in the drive and, together, they started heading toward the water. Beau was already on the shore, his ball tumbling in the light surf as he bounced around it, plunging his snout into the waves and sneezing, clearly pretending he couldn't get it, his tail going a hundred miles an hour.

"Guess what I saw when I passed through town," Ben said. When she didn't answer, he responded to her questioning look. "They're setting up for the Firefly Beach fair." He was making small talk, but those eyes of his devoured her when she smiled.

Hallie had wonderful memories of that fair. "At least we won't get in trouble this time if we walk into town on our own to get Mable's apple fritters."

Ben chuckled at the memory. Mable owned Berkley's Farm on the way into town. While she was known for selling the best produce in town, every year at the fair—only once a year—she made apple fritters, using her family recipe. They were a hit, and everyone wanted her to make them year-round and stock them in the farm shop, but she insisted on only making them for the fair to encourage people to come out and support the community. For days, she prepared for it, and the whole week before the fair, the entire farmhouse at Berkley's smelled like apple fritters, making everyone antsy for the sight of that Ferris wheel on the horizon.

"We should go," he said, leading her to the dock. Beau trotted up to greet them and then ran along the beach, disappearing in the long shadow of the lighthouse. "We could take Robby." Ben sat on the edge of the dock where it met the sand, and patted the space beside him.

"Yeah, he'd like that." Hallie sat down and slipped off her flip-flops, digging her feet into the white sand. She focused on the grand porch that stretched along the back of Starlight Cottage where Aunt Clara used to sit, but she couldn't keep her view off of Ben for long, returning her gaze to his.

"How's everything here?" he asked, clearly trying to work his way up to the looming topic, but she was glad to have a little more time before they had to face it.

Hallie got Ben up to speed on the latest events at the cottage, and she found herself chatting endlessly about the logo Gavin had made for her and the editing software he'd helped her download for her photography. Perhaps it was her own coping strategy to avoid the weighty events in her life, but she just wanted to share her excitement with Ben. It felt so good when he encouraged her.

"Sounds like you and Gavin really hit it off," he said, and she could see that brain of his filling with questions. "You two are becoming fast friends." He smiled, but by the slight hesitancy he showed, Hallie felt the need to clarify their relationship.

"We've really bonded creatively," she said. "But that's all."

Her assessment was right because Ben looked surprised that she'd read his thoughts so easily. "You don't have to try to protect my feelings, Hallie. They've gotten pretty rock solid from seeing you date guys over the years. Just do what makes you happy."

Hallie blew air through her lips in frustration. "I wish it were that easy." The thought came out as a natural reaction to what he'd said, before she'd had a chance to think about how she'd explain.

"What do you mean?"

This would be the right time to tell Ben about what really caused her and Jeff's demise. Without even meaning to, she'd set it up perfectly. But the words got caught in her throat, and she couldn't utter them. She knew exactly why. Ben was the last person she wanted to know about her real troubles because she liked the way he looked at her, as if she were a possibility for his future.

Two expressions of Jeff's were burned in her memory: the elation he had when she'd told him they were going to have a baby, and then the utter disappointment in his eyes when she broke the news that they'd lost it, and not only that, but they would *never* hear the patter of little feet. They hadn't recovered as a couple after that. In their darkest moments, Jeff had made her feel like she'd stolen something from him. When it came to Ben, Hallie wanted him to have everything his heart desired—and she knew he'd eventually want a family with children of his own.

"What's the matter?" Ben's concerned face came into her view. "What happened? Is there something you want to tell me?" He took her hand, his soft caress making the ache in her heart worse.

Blinking away tears, she said, "No. There's nothing I want to tell you." Which was true. She never wanted to tell him.

He was visibly trying to process her huge swing in emotion, attempting to make sense of it and find answers, but she knew he could never guess this. Her secret was safe. Then a realization slid over his face. "We haven't done anything wrong," he said. "You look like you feel guilty of something, but there's nothing to feel guilty about. I'm not with Ashley anymore."

She knew that, but it did raise the question as to why. She considered poor Ashley in all this. *She'd* done nothing wrong. "Why not, Ben? She's wonderful." Hallie wasn't just trying to move the focus off herself. She really believed they were a great couple. "I like her a lot. She listens to the music I do. She has the same sense of humor…"

Ben stood up and ran his hands through his hair. "Yeah, the two of you are very similar. That was what drew me to her. And that's not fair to her."

"But you can like similar qualities in people, right? There has to be some other reason. Why did you leave her?"

He was slowly pacing around, and she could tell that the conversation made him uncomfortable, which was unusual for him. Nothing ruffled him. "Why did you just break up with her out of nowhere?" she pressed him.

"Because she wasn't you," he blurted. His body stilled, his shoulders fallen in defeat. "She wasn't you," he said again more quietly. "I didn't want to tell you that I left her, because it was easier not to act on my feelings for you if you thought we were still together."

"Why didn't you want to act on your feelings for me?"

He sat back down beside her. "It's what I'm used to doing," he said. "I loved you long before I met Ashley. I've always loved you, but I first realized how hard it was to live without you my freshman year in college. While we all piled into the student union on Saturday nights, laughing and carrying on, the truth was that most of those guys were hiding how homesick they were. I wasn't homesick. I was lovesick. I'd lie in bed and struggle to sleep, knowing how far away you were, aching to see you."

"Why didn't you say something then?"

"I didn't want to pull you away from new experiences. We were three states apart. All my admission would've done was cause you to come back to the past, where we were. I wanted you to see what else was out there, to have a chance to follow your dreams."

"And after graduation? You could've told me then." Hallie felt the tears coming. For an instant, she thought that if she'd known this before everything had gone wrong, maybe by some miracle her life would've turned out differently. But if she were honest with herself, she knew that she'd have met the same fate anyway.

"I struggled to find the right time. I wanted to give us both space to figure out who we were, and after a while I got used to holding on to my feelings, waiting until it felt right. When Jeff came along, I thought I'd lost you. I couldn't think straight. I was in my head all the time, my work was suffering… I forced myself to move forward and I started dating Ashley."

Hallie wiped a runaway tear from her cheek, her heart feeling like it would burst. She couldn't believe he'd felt this way for so long…

"When you called to tell me you and Jeff had broken up, it was like I'd been given a second chance. At some point over the summer, I knew I'd have to tell you the truth about how I felt or risk the pain of never knowing what could've been. And I'd learned from your engagement that I can't live with that kind of pain.

"I called things off with Ashley and literally ran to you. But I quickly felt that you had too much on your plate already. And you said yourself that you love being with me because I don't want anything more than what we already have. But that's not completely true..."

Hallie sniffled, trying to get herself together, but she couldn't. Her eyes were filling with tears, blurring her vision.

Ben looked out over the water. Beau was digging a hole down the beach.

She wasn't sure what to say. Her new feelings for Ben were difficult to manage, and she felt unsure of how to move forward because all she wanted to do was wrap her arms around him and tell him how she felt about him, but she couldn't. Her head throbbed and her chest ached with that reality. She was shaking, stunned by her rush of feelings, terrified by the need to feel his touch and to have his lips on hers.

She could tell he was trying to figure out why she'd clammed up before, when she was sure it was so obvious by her reaction now how she felt. If it wasn't guilt over Ashley, then it had to be something else... That's what was going through his mind, she was certain of it. Understanding showed in his face—of what, she wasn't sure.

"Hallie, I get it," he finally said. "I'm not the guy for you."

He'd misinterpreted her emotion. He must have thought she was crying because she *didn't* love him and she knew how much that would hurt him, when things couldn't be further from the truth.

He took in a deep breath and put his hands on his knees, hanging his head as if he needed to get himself together. "It won't change anything between us. It never has before." He sat up and looked into her eyes. "Like I said, I've been in love with you as long as I can remember. And through all your boyfriends and love interests, I'm still here."

He didn't understand at all. But then it occurred to her that she *could* allow him to believe that was the issue. Then she could move on with her life and he could move on with his. Ben would find someone wonderful and have the happily ever after he was destined to have… And she and Ben could go back to being the way they'd always been. It broke her heart, and she didn't know how she would manage if she did let him believe it, but it made the most sense.

"I'm sorry," she said, her voice breaking. She was sorry. Sorry that she couldn't give him what he deserved. Maybe one day she'd have the strength to tell him why. She wiped the tears that had fallen before losing herself in his blue eyes. "I love you," she whispered. "I do."

With incredible composure, Ben leaned over and gently kissed her cheek, only succeeding in tearing her apart, because she knew that he loved her so much that he'd pushed all his feelings down so she wouldn't feel awful about rejecting him. He pressed his forehead to hers. "I love you too." He tipped his head back and let out a little groan of frustration. Then he stood and whistled for Beau while grabbing Hallie's hands and pulling her up. "Time to move forward. No regrets," he said, looking over at the house. "I've got a football game to play." He produced a smile. "And I need a receiver. You up for it?"

Hallie wiped another tear, chasing them away with a chuckle, but it was followed by a sob. Her breath caught as she cleared it. "Yeah."

"Okay," he said, as Beau neared them. "Let's go." With the soft wind at their backs, they headed up to Starlight Cottage together, Ben's hand in hers.

Chapter Twenty-One

"We need music!" Ben said, just before running back inside the cottage.

After Ben and Hallie's discussion, having dinner with the family seemed to lift their mood. Robby's excitement over their upcoming football game had kept the conversation light and happy. They'd spent most of the dinner hour chatting about the game, Robby talking more than he had all week, deciding with Ben where they should set up the field, dividing the teams, and discussing running plays. Ben made a joke about climbing over Hallie's shoulders to catch the ball as one of his secret plays, and even Mama laughed, her amusement causing the whole table to chuckle. Uncle Hank had also asked Hallie to tell everyone about the photographs she'd taken with Gavin, and as she told them all her ideas about Coastal Comfort, she could feel the energy that she'd thought had drained away seeping back in. Uncle Hank hadn't stopped smiling since dinner. The buoyant atmosphere gave Hallie the ability to push her emotions back down, nearly burying them where she wished they'd stay.

Chairs were set up along the edge of the yard for Uncle Hank and Mama, who'd taken their seats for the big game. Mama had her legs crossed, one flip-flop dangling from her toes as her foot bounced with anticipation. She was smiling, contented, reminding Hallie of years past when they used to all sit outside together around the evening fire, toasting marshmallows and telling stories, their faces warm from the fire and too much sun. Today, Mama had popped corn and dished some out for Uncle Hank. Beau was waiting in the wings for any that came his way.

Uncle Hank hadn't protested when Ben asked him if he'd watch the game outside. He was sitting next to Mama, a tall glass of iced tea in his hand, looking toward the lighthouse on the beach, just like he used to do before pointing out the fireflies when Hallie was little.

Hallie realized she hadn't seen the fireflies very much this year. They'd been so busy since they'd arrived that she hadn't gone out to the beach during the slip of time when the sun had yet to completely surrender to night. That was when the fireflies filled the coast. At dusk, when the sky over Starlight Cottage was a brilliant mixture of shades—oranges, pinks, and purples—with all those little white blinking lights from the fireflies dotting the shore, it was an incredible sight. She promised herself she'd spend an evening out there soon. Hallie squinted in the direction of the beach, following Uncle Hank's line of vision, but she didn't see any yet.

One of the living room windows slid open from inside the cottage and a speaker surfaced through the screen, the thump of drums rumbling out and over the makeshift football field that Ben and Robby had set up after dinner, using toy orange cones. The sound of horns came blaring forth over the drums, giving the entire yard the musical atmosphere of a party. Robby, wearing the football jersey Ben had gotten him for Christmas last year, was in the center of the field, knees bending, hips moving, arms flailing around in dance. Sydney joined him, wiggling her shoulders to the beat.

Hallie was glad for the distraction.

Ben jogged back down the front steps with the football under his arm. "So, we're playing to five! Robby, do you have the coin?"

Robby rummaged around in the pocket of his shorts before holding up the quarter that Ben had given him at dinner.

"Heads or tails?" Ben asked him over the music when he met Robby on the field, setting the ball down in front of them. Hallie and Sydney gathered around them. Ben must have noticed Hallie's contemplative mood because he grabbed her hand and gave her a quick spin to the music to make her smile.

"Heads!" Robby nodded excitedly to Sydney. Then he put the coin on his thumb and flipped it into the air. It fell with a small thud onto the ground, Robby jogging over to it. "It's heads!" he called.

Ben plucked it from the grass and tossed it over to Mama. "Okay, then! Your choice: who gets the ball?"

"You start!" Robby picked up the ball and lobbed it over to Ben.

"All right! Take your places!"

Robby ran over beside Sydney and put his hands on his knees, waiting for the play. Hallie lined up behind Ben who had the ball in both hands on the ground, ready to hike it. Ben lifted the ball, and it flew into Hallie's hands. She darted playfully around Robby just as Ben scooped him up and swung him into the air before gently pretending to tackle him, laying him on the grass. Hallie ran to the end of the yard for a touchdown.

"Oooooh!" Ben teased Robby and Sydney, as Hallie spiked the ball. "You're gonna have to answer to *that*!"

Robby grabbed the ball and ran to the center of the field. "We will! You better watch out, Ben! Mama, get ready!" Robby placed the ball on the grass, his little hands barely reaching across the surface of it. Hallie and Ben took their spots on defense. "Hike!" Robby called as he sent the ball sailing toward Sydney, who caught it and started running. Robby dodged Hallie, and Sydney threw the ball over her sister's head right into Robby's arms. Ben was just behind him, but with a wink to Hallie he faked running with all his might, letting Robby reach the end zone.

"One to one!" Robby sang, dancing around in time to the song that was playing.

"It's a close game!" Uncle Hank said from the sidelines. He had his iced tea in one hand and a fistful of popcorn in the other. Mama was clapping beside him. "It's the little ones that surprise you, Ben!" Uncle Hank said with a chuckle. "They're faster than you think!"

"That's right!" Robby said, handing the ball off to Ben to start the next play.

The game continued the same way it started, until Hallie and Ben were one point down to tie it at five to five. Robby had his game face on, the hair at the back of his neck wet with perspiration and a huge smile on his face. "You can't get past me!" he taunted Ben.

At the start of the play, Ben took off with the ball, passing Robby. Like a flash, Robby's little legs working overtime, he threw himself onto Ben's back, wrapping his limbs around Ben. Ben could've easily run to the end of the yard, but instead fell to the ground as if Robby had tackled him, dropping the ball and rolling onto his back. "You got me!"

Robby stood up and cheered, his arms pumping. "We did it, Mama!" he called to Sydney. Then, as Ben sat up, Robby threw his arms around his neck, and as Ben twirled him in the air, the delight was clear on both of their faces. In that moment, Hallie was sure that however difficult it was for her, she was making the right decision letting Ben go.

*

"What're you up to?" Hallie asked Sydney when she came into the living room.

The others were all in bed and Ben had gone to the guesthouse for the night. Hallie curled up on the sofa beside her sister, who was typing on her laptop. Sydney closed it and exhaled an anxious breath.

"You've been so concerned with having to complete Aunt Clara's list, but I'm kind of envious of it."

"What?" Hallie folded her legs under her and grabbed the afghan that Aunt Clara had always kept on the arm of the sofa, draping it over her legs. In the summer, that room was always chilly at night from the air conditioning, and Hallie's thin T-shirt and pajama shorts weren't enough to keep her warm.

"In her letter to me, Aunt Clara gave me money and told me to quit my job and do something I loved. She knew I *hated* being a paralegal."

"We all knew you hated it." Hallie grinned.

When Christian left, Sydney had to have her own income, and with her degree she landed a position at a small law firm. At the time, she'd been so relieved to be able to pay the bills, but the more she got into it, the more she realized it wasn't what she should be doing with her life. To make matters worse, she had an awful boss who barely ever let her take time off for Robby, and always seemed put out when she'd have to take a sick day.

"And when I blabbered on about how much I hated it, you'd say, 'You need to find something else.'" She picked at a piece of fringe on the afghan and then pulled a corner of the blanket over her own legs, sharing it with Hallie. "I didn't find something else because I don't know what I'm supposed to do. Aunt Clara didn't give me any ideas like she gave you. The two of you were so close that I feel like she worked a little harder on what to give you than she did the rest of us. Look at how your photography is coming along; it's leading you where you want to go. You're extremely talented and I can't wait to see what happens when you put Coastal Comfort out there."

Hallie had thought the exact opposite about Aunt Clara's instructions, but now her sister's point of view seemed just as valid.

"Too bad I didn't write a list when I was twelve," she said. "I wrote letters to boy bands instead, trying to get them to do events near me." Sydney laughed at her own comment.

"You could be a publicist," Hallie said with a giggle.

"Very funny." Sydney shook her head, amused. She opened her laptop again. "I was looking at jobs…" She paused. "Here at Firefly Beach." She met Hallie's gaze.

"Are you thinking about staying?"

"Maybe. Uncle Hank could use someone to take care of the cottage and Robby's already comfortable here. It just seems like the perfect place to be right now."

Hallie couldn't imagine not having her sister just down the road in Nashville, or seeing her popping into Mama's house when Hallie and Mama were having coffee, like they did on the weekdays when Hallie was out running errands for the agency. She always made a sneaky stop by Mama's and had a little chat before heading back to work. But then again, everything else seemed to be unrecognizable about her life. Hallie tried not to let her unease about it show.

"I wondered if Uncle Hank would let me pay rent so Robby and I could live in the guesthouse."

"I doubt he'd charge you a thing." Hallie shifted closer to her sister. "What jobs were you looking at?" she asked, nodding toward the laptop.

"There are a few office jobs, but none that really hit me," she said. "I'll keep looking though." Her face brightened. "But guess what I did see! The Firefly Beach fair is opening tomorrow night."

"Ben told me! I want to go."

Sydney's face dropped in concern at the mention of Ben's name. "You two okay? You both were putting on a brave front at dinner but I could tell something was going on between you two."

Hallie felt the ache inching its way back in. "We're okay." She abruptly stood up and folded the afghan. "It's late," she said. "Mama will have us all up bright and early for breakfast, so we'd better head to bed."

Sydney could obviously read between the lines because she set her laptop on the table, stood up in front of Hallie, and gave her a hug. "Everything has a way of working out."

While she wanted to believe that, Hallie wasn't so sure. But what she needed to do was hold on to the idea that she could still make the best of what life had given her. Standing there in a room that was filled with glorious memories, she thought about Aunt Clara. She hadn't had any children and her life had been amazing. Aunt Clara had made an impact on everyone she met; most importantly, her family. Hallie vowed to give it everything she had and do the same.

Chapter Twenty-Two

An eight-year-old Hallie was in her favorite yellow sundress and brand-new tap shoes that Aunt Clara had bought her. She was dancing, her new shoes pattering against the hardwoods, the dress fanning out around her, while Uncle Hank played the piano. Aunt Clara took her hands and spun her around, and Hallie wondered if the potatoes were going to burn on the stove, their sizzling coming through during the pauses in the music.

"You are really something, my dear," Aunt Clara said, beaming. "Don't ever be afraid of anything. Just jump in…"

Knock. Knock.

Hallie was aware of crisp sheets under her.

Knock. Knock.

The sun shone through her eyelids and she realized she'd been dreaming.

"Hallie?" Mama's voice came from her door, which was cracked open. "I've got potatoes and eggs on the stove so I have to hurry, but I wanted to get you up. Breakfast is almost ready. I had Robby run out and tell Ben in the guesthouse. Come on down, okay?"

"Okay," she said, her voice groggy.

After Mama left, Hallie squeezed her eyes shut and tried to see Aunt Clara's face again. She wanted to drift off, back to that place and that time when everything was all right, when the music played. And for a second, Hallie thought she had fallen back asleep until, with a jolt, she realized that she wasn't dreaming. Someone was downstairs playing piano, and the only one who knew how to play like that was Uncle Hank.

Hallie sat upright in bed, threw the covers off her legs and ran downstairs, stopping at the bottom to find Uncle Hank in the living room, his back to her, his fingers moving fluently on the keys, the glorious music of her childhood flooding the room. Just the sight of it brought tears to her eyes. That was the Uncle Hank she knew. She ran over to him and threw her arms around him.

His fingers stilled and he looked at her. "I dreamed of Clara last night," he said. "She told me I'd better get in here and play."

Hallie choked back her tears, finding it more than a coincidence that she, too, had dreamed of Aunt Clara. She racked her brain to try to remember what Aunt Clara had said, and then it came to her: *Don't ever be afraid of anything. Just jump in.* It didn't make any sense to her. But that didn't matter because Uncle Hank's dream did mean something to him.

"Lookin' good, Miss Flynn." Ben's voice came from the hallway.

It took her a minute to realize that his crooked smile was at her expense. Hallie had been so excited to hear Uncle Hank playing that she'd run downstairs without even a peek in the mirror. With a quick glance into the kitchen, she realized that everyone else seemed to be ready for the day. She ran her hands through her tangled hair and went over to him as Uncle Hank began playing again, this time more softly.

He looked down at her affectionately. "No, I mean it. You're lookin' good." He broke out into a huge smile, and kissed her cheek.

Hallie rolled her eyes, but she liked his playfulness this morning. "Oh, now that the cat's out of the bag, you're going to be openly flirty with me?"

"I'm not flirting," he said with mock offense. "I'd say that to anyone." He stepped down the hallway. "Morning, Syd! Lookin' good!"

"What?" Sydney leaned over the table to see what he was up to. When he didn't say anything more, she shrugged it off and went back to talking to Robby.

"Why are you so spunky today?" Hallie asked, soaking it in.

He hung back from the kitchen for a minute to answer her. "I shouldn't have dropped all that on you—I'm sorry. Sorry for leaving without a word and sorry for putting you in the position I put you in yesterday. But it felt good to get it off my chest. Remember what I told you when we were kids? I said that whenever you're upset, I'll make you feel better. That's my job. I just forgot for a second."

Hallie gave him a hug, a big squeeze, an indescribable fondness for him bubbling inside her chest. Then she pulled back, an idea coming to her. "Know what I want you to do with me today?"

"What's that?"

"I need you to go shopping."

He stared at her. "Shopping?"

"Yes! For Coastal Comfort. I want to get ideas and bounce things off you. Then maybe you can help me contact some local merchants once I have a sense of what I want."

His eagerness to help was clear, and she could tell that he enjoyed seeing her move forward with building this idea. "I'd love to."

Mama peeked her head into the hallway, a scrambled egg-covered spatula in her hand. "Y'all grab Uncle Hank and come on in before this food gets cold. And don't tell him but I made blueberry biscuits with Aunt Clara's recipe."

"Did I hear you say blueberry biscuits?" Uncle Hank said, coming up behind them, his face pensive. "I didn't have to hear it though—the smell gave it away." He closed his eyes and inhaled. They all waited on pins and needles to see if Mama's gesture might be too much for him. "That, right there, is the smell of heaven."

He looked up as if he could see right through the pearly gates. And then he smiled. It was as if a gray cloud had lifted. There was a buzz around the table. Robby was talking to Sydney about yesterday's game. Uncle Hank pointed out the two biscuits he wanted, asking Mama if she'd used the buttermilk or the whole milk. Ben was dishing out the eggs, and suddenly, Hallie felt it: the feeling she'd had for all those years around this table at breakfast. *This* was Starlight Cottage. But there was one thing that had always been there that she just couldn't shake: that empty chair. She wasn't going to ruin the mood by bringing up Lewis now, but later she'd ask Uncle Hank to tell her the whole story.

"I can't wait to show you my photos!" Hallie said when she rounded Ben's jeep. She grabbed his arm as they headed toward the gallery. "Gavin cleared out an entire room for them. I'm so eager to see them all framed and ready to go."

Ben opened the gallery door and allowed her to enter first.

There were a few people mulling around, chatting amongst themselves.

"Hey there." Gavin greeted them as he walked up from the counter at the back of the old house-turned-shop.

"Hi! I stopped by to see the room you made for me," she said, barely able to contain herself. She felt whole for the first time in a very long time. "I brought my friend Ben with me—you remember him, right?"

"Nice to see you again." Ben offered a friendly handshake. "Hallie's really excited to see what you've done with her work, if you can't tell." Gavin and Ben shared a moment of unity in their amusement.

"I can't help it—it's exciting! Once we see the photos, Ben's going to help me shop for ideas. I plan to design a few pieces to go with the photographs to make a one-of-a-kind look, so people can buy a full design without having to hunt for things to match the photographs themselves. Then I'll see if I can find some local merchants who are interested in pairing with me on the Coastal Comfort line."

"You're always one step ahead," Gavin said, walking them down the short hallway to one of the rooms. "Have a look." He gestured inside.

Outside the space, on an easel made of driftwood, was the Coastal Comfort logo. It was absolutely stunning. But what floored her was what she saw in the room. Hallie walked inside with Ben and she was overcome by the sight of her photographs. They were all matted and framed just like she and Gavin had talked about, and he'd hung them in color order from lightest to darkest and in clusters of complementing shades, exactly the way she'd wanted. Aunt Clara's chair, the seashore, the lighthouse, the back porch with the paddle fans, the stone walk—they were all there on display. Hallie stood there in disbelief that she'd created this, because all the shots looked like works of art, like someone else had done them.

"You've done an amazing job with the display, Gavin," Ben said, his eyes darting around as he took in all the pieces.

Gavin nodded in appreciation.

"I'm completely blown away by these." Ben walked over to the stone path image and gazed at it. "Every one of them is going to sell. I can guarantee it."

"He's right," Gavin agreed. "I finished the display this morning before we opened, and I've sold two already and had orders for prints."

Hallie clapped her hand over her mouth. "Oh my gosh," she said through her fingers. "I haven't even gotten the home décor in here yet."

"You can if you'd like, but you don't need it," Gavin said. "The photographs speak for themselves. People are looking! And the weekend is just getting started. But email me photos of some of your décor ideas and I'll share them with the people who buy your pieces, until you can secure a partnership with a local craftsman."

"Okay, I will."

Hallie spent the next few minutes telling Ben about each of the photos; what she'd done with their perspective, and her editing techniques. Like he was so great at doing, he listened, smiling, clearly thrilled for her.

"You might need a bigger space," he said once they were back outside. "Maybe you could have your own showroom." He opened the jeep's passenger door and Hallie climbed in.

"I've only sold two!" she said, before he shut her door and got in on his side.

"Two in about four hours. And Gavin said he'd also sold prints. Do you know how much he's selling them for?"

"We chatted a bit about that last time we were together. He's priced it all using the same pricing he does for his own."

Ben nodded. "It's definitely working. I'm glad he's helping you." He turned onto the main road that paralleled the beach. "You'll want to keep a firm grip on sales and make sure you're staying competitive but also getting the most that you can for your work. I'm sure Gavin has dealt with it all before, though."

"It's a lot to think about."

Ben gave her a quick glance and a crooked grin. "It's all good stuff. I've been there. You've got Gavin to consult, I'll help you with what

I can, and we'll research the heck out of what we don't know. But eventually, if this all takes off, you're going to need people to help you manage things. You'll need a salesperson, a receptionist—have you thought of consulting on decorating so that people will know where to put this furniture if they buy it?"

"I've thought of all of it—it's so enormous that it scares me sometimes. I'm also envisioning a design *team* that will help me get it all off the ground, but I don't know if I'll have the means to start so grand. I didn't believe that anything would come of it, and especially so quickly."

"That's just it, Hallie. You have to believe. Don't let it scare you too much. Just breathe and follow your instincts."

Hallie couldn't help but think about that dream she'd had of Aunt Clara. *Just jump in.*

Chapter Twenty-Three

By the time Ben and Hallie got back to Starlight Cottage, she had a phone full of furniture images to use as a springboard for her designs, and ideas from some local merchants. She'd been madly emailing them to Gavin to pass along to any potential buyers. When she looked up from her phone, she noticed that Lewis was sitting alone in one of the rockers on the front porch.

"Who's that?" Ben asked, bringing the jeep to a stop.

She sent a wide-eyed look over to Ben and answered, "Uncle Hank's brother." Hallie got out of the car and shut the door behind her. "Mind if I talk to him a minute?" she asked as Ben came around to her side.

"Not at all. I'll check on Beau in the guesthouse. Come get me if you need me."

"Okay."

Lewis offered a friendly wave to Hallie as she approached. He seemed relaxed, tipping lightly back and then rocking forward as if he had all day to sit there, although his forehead glistened with perspiration from the thick humidity. For an instant, Hallie was filled with the hope that Lewis and Uncle Hank had put aside their differences, but recalling Uncle Hank's face the night Lewis had come inside, she doubted that was the case.

"Hi Lewis," Hallie said when she reached him.

"Hello, Miss Hallie. It's so nice to see you again." He pulled a folded handkerchief from his shirt pocket and dabbed at the dampness on his face.

"May I?" She gestured toward Aunt Clara's chair, beside the one he was in.

"Of course." Lewis returned the handkerchief to his pocket and put his hands on his knees, rocking again.

"Mind if I ask why you're on the porch?" she ventured.

"Well, I ran into the police officer in town today. The one from the other night. He and I had a good chuckle over the mix-up with thinking I was some sort of prowler, and I bought him a coffee." He stopped rocking. "While we were making conversation, he asked what my letter said. I didn't understand. That was when he told me that your mother had mentioned that she had a letter for me from Clara, and they'd helped her track me down. They'd located me before I'd even shown up here."

"That's true," Hallie said. "The check that Uncle Hank was trying to give you was your inheritance from Aunt Clara. She wanted you to have it."

"I don't want her money." Emotion seemed to fill his throat, because he coughed as if he needed to clear it. "I just want her letter. I want to know what she has to tell me after all these years. I came to the cottage today to ask Hank for it, but he wouldn't give it to me, so I told him I'd sit out here until he was ready to hand it over."

"You realize that you could be out here a very long time?"

"Yep." He started rocking again.

"I'll see if I can talk to him." Hallie got up. "I can't guarantee I can change his mind, though."

"I've got the rest of my days to sit here until he does."

"Wish me luck." Hallie opened the front door.

"Good luck," he said. "You're going to need it."

Hallie walked into the house, past the living room. The piano fallboard sat open from this morning. She looked for Mama and Sydney but they weren't there. They must have gone out somewhere. "Uncle Hank?" she called into the silence, peering into the kitchen, but the lights were off, the table empty.

"In here," he called gruffly from Aunt Clara's office.

When she got there the door was open and he was sitting in Aunt Clara's office chair, running his hands along the edge of her desk, lost in contemplation. "What are you thinking about?" she asked gently, coming over to him and putting her hand on his shoulder.

"Do you know why your aunt gave Lewis a hundred thousand dollars?"

Hallie shook her head. "I don't. That's a lot of money."

"Yes." He lifted a framed picture of Aunt Clara and him off her desk and peered down at it. "When Clara wanted to expand her design company, we were young—still getting on our feet financially; we were considering buying a home together with our savings. She'd sat on the idea for quite a while, but it was eating her up and she finally told me. Clara and her business partner Sasha Morgan saw a real opportunity to expand abroad. However, it takes money to make money. She faced two possibilities: one, marry me and buy a house, or two, use all her savings to invest in her business."

He set the frame back down, staring at it as if it held the rest of the story. Perhaps it did.

"Lewis had already made a fortune by his twenties in real estate up in New York, and he had offices both in Nashville and up north. He was just young enough with no obligations to still be dangerous with his investments. He and Clara used to have lively conversations about their businesses; she really enjoyed talking to him about it. He gave Clara ten thousand dollars to expand, and we were thrilled by his offer, but felt like we couldn't take it. That was more than we could repay him back then, and we didn't want to be indebted to family. He insisted, telling her that he knew what it was like to start from nothing. Sasha Morgan said she could offer her savings, and if they took Lewis's gift they'd have enough to really get things going worldwide. Clara and I could buy our home and she could still build her company. Against my better judgment, Clara took Lewis's money and promised him that one day she'd pay him back tenfold. But I never let her. Not after what he did."

Hallie sat down on the office floor, her legs crossed, looking up at him. "What did he do that was so bad, Uncle Hank?"

"He started showing up wherever we were, to see how the business was going. Flashy. Dressed well, new cologne..." Uncle Hank cut his eyes at the hallway, and Hallie remembered that Lewis was probably still sitting out there. "It wasn't the way my brother usually presented himself, or the way he usually behaved. I knew him when he was scared of the dark and didn't give a hoot what kind of haircut he had." Uncle Hank clenched his fists as if he had pain in his fingers. "He smiled a lot, laughed at Clara's jokes, leaned in to her when she spoke. I didn't like it, but Clara told me it was nothing. One day Clara showed me a bouquet of flowers he'd brought her. She told me that Lewis had asked her to go away with him. He'd told her he was in love with her."

Hallie's mouth dropped open. "Oh my God."

"Clara was beside herself with guilt. She'd spent all those moments with him and taken his money, and she felt like she'd led him on somehow. She said she had to talk to him, but I told her not to. I wasn't ever going to speak to him again, and she didn't have to either."

"Did she ever talk to him?"

Uncle Hank took in a long, steadying breath. "A few days later, she told me that she'd gone to see him to tell him how much she loved me. She tried to talk about their meeting with me, but I refused to listen. I didn't want to know. I was still too angry about it to waste a minute of my time on him. I just asked her to tell me if she had any sort of closure, and she said she did, so we left it at that."

Lewis didn't seem like the sort of person Uncle Hank was describing at all. He lived in a modest home; his clothes, from what Hallie had seen, were average at best. He appeared kind and humble. "What if he's changed?" she offered.

Uncle Hank's eyes landed on Hallie. "Clara was the best thing that ever came into my life. She was the sun in my day. And he tried to steal that—it blindsided me. Lewis wanted to rob me of my greatest happiness for his own gain. To me, that's unforgiveable. And if he's changed, then great. But he won't be a part of my life."

Hallie sat up on her knees to get closer to his eye level. "Uncle Hank, Aunt Clara had things to say, but she knew she had limited time to say them. She left her own words for Lewis. You need to give him the letter. It's between him and Aunt Clara—you don't have to be a part of it if you don't want to. But Aunt Clara has trusted you with this. You have to give him the message. For her."

Uncle Hank drummed his fingers angrily on the desk, clearly considering her words.

"If he's still on the front porch, I'll take it out to him. You won't even have to see him if you don't want to."

With a huff, Uncle Hank walked over to the safe and turned the dial several times to line up the combination. The door swung open and he snatched an envelope that sat in front of the rest of their family documents, leaving a second envelope that was underneath it in the safe—Hallie's. He shut the door and spun the dial to lock it again. His lips pursed in disapproval, he held it out to her.

Hallie stood up to take it from him.

"My hope is that this will make him go away for good," he said before leaving the room. "Ask him if he wants his check," he called over his shoulder. "And then tell him not to come back."

On her way through the house to the front porch, Hallie tried to reconcile what Uncle Hank was telling her about Lewis with what she'd observed of him. If he and Aunt Clara hadn't come to some sort of understanding, she wouldn't have saved an empty seat for him at the table every holiday. Nor would she have left him the money she'd promised to pay him back *or* have written him a letter. There was a gaping hole in this story, and without Aunt Clara there to tell it, the only way Hallie could get answers was to ask Lewis. She was going to have to find out what had happened if she was ever going to convince Uncle Hank to include him in the family. It was obvious by Aunt Clara's actions that that was exactly what she wanted. But finding a resolution between the two brothers seemed a long way off at this point.

She was relieved to find him still on the porch. He sat up, his back pulling away from the chair, when he saw what was in her hand.

"I'll give you this," she said, "but if you want it, I'm going to need some answers first."

"Anything you'd like to know."

Hallie lowered herself down into Aunt Clara's chair.

"Did you try to get Aunt Clara to leave Uncle Hank and run off with you somewhere?"

He stopped rocking, his face sobering. "Yes. But that was a very long time ago."

Hallie gripped the envelope with both hands. "Wanna tell me the story?"

"If you'd like."

"I would."

He looked out over the yard, pensive. "When Hank said he wanted to introduce me to his girlfriend, I had no idea how serious they were. When I met Clara, she was the most beautiful woman I'd ever laid eyes on," he said without changing his gaze. "She had a smile that could turn my stomach inside out. Hank told me that she wanted to buy her first house—she was looking for a very small fixer-upper. I found a few to show her, and the truth was that, despite my attempts to avoid it, I was smitten." His face lit up with the memory. "I'd only just moved back to the Nashville area to help take care of our mother, who wasn't well. I had found success very early in my career in New York and was already selling large estates. I was so good at real estate that I even surprised myself. A house the size Clara was looking for wasn't a lot of money to me at that point in my career, but I didn't care. I spent days searching for her; I toured areas myself to make sure they'd be safe. I wanted Clara to have the very best I could find her.

"I was drawn to the way she truly cared about people. It didn't matter if they were strangers. People she met on the street, shopkeepers, taxi drivers... me. She treated everyone as if she'd known them forever. I wanted to be around that kind of empathy for others. I fell fast and hard for her—I couldn't turn it off."

"Did you find her a house?" Hallie asked, this new piece of Aunt Clara's life like a rare treasure.

"I did." He smiled, his eyes returning to the letter briefly, and then there was sadness in them, before meeting Hallie's gaze. "She loved the house. But she didn't buy it. She and Hank had been discussing the purchase. He'd planned to live there with her, but after getting engaged to him she refused to buy a house that Hank hadn't helped her choose, so they ended up buying something else after they got married."

Hallie barely noticed the heat of the setting sun. She was completely drawn to Lewis and his story. The decision to buy a house with Uncle Hank so he could be an equal part of it was so very Aunt Clara. She was always true to herself and her feelings, while still being wonderful to everyone who knew her.

"She came by my office downtown and told me she was going to wait a bit, that the engagement had changed her plans. While their relationship had been more serious than I understood, Hank's proposal had surprised her—she hadn't seen it coming. She was positively glowing about it. What had been a surprise to her had been a bombshell for the whole family. Hank had never so much as brought a girl to dinner, and yet he'd proposed without telling a soul. But I knew why, because I'd have done the same thing if Clara had loved me. Everyone was thrilled, and I had to be just as excited for them.

"For the entire engagement, I split my time between New York and Nashville to help with my mother. Clara was at all our family gatherings. We had too much wine, stayed up late… I got to see her when she tiptoed downstairs to get a glass of water first thing in the morning. I tried not to let my feelings grow, but they did. With every breath, I fell harder. She had no idea."

"How heartbreaking." Hallie was captivated. She couldn't look away from this man. "But you had to know that she loved Uncle Hank."

He nodded. "But it became even more difficult. She was around me all the time. With our mother's health in steep decline, Clara was always there. She started asking me questions about growing her design business because I had done the same with real estate, and we connected on that, spending tons of time talking about ideas and how to manage the affairs of growth. I couldn't escape her, and I also couldn't make myself stop loving her.

"She made me want to be better. I started taking care of myself, worrying about how she perceived me. I'd close my eyes at night and relish the memory of her laughter, the smile she'd given only me when I'd said something amusing. I was torturing myself. I knew I shouldn't feel this way, but I couldn't make it stop."

Hallie closed her eyes and thought of Ben. What would it be like for her if he were to get engaged to someone? She couldn't help but think how her feelings would be quite similar. Now she knew that kind of love.

"Then my mother passed away. Something clicked, and the finality of her life ending made me impulsive. In my grief for my mother, an intense fear took over me, and at that time I just thought that if I didn't at least try to tell Clara, I'd never know what was meant to be."

Tears filled his eyes and he cleared his throat, the rest of his story still noticeably difficult to tell.

"I bought her flowers. Buttercups and hydrangeas, her favorites. I still remember how the cellophane around them rattled with my trembling hands. I knew what I was doing was wrong, but I was too young to understand that I could forever alter the course of all our lives by giving in to my feelings like I did. I should've considered how what

I was about to do would affect everyone, but my mind was filled to the brim with Clara—there was no room to think about anyone else. I hadn't gotten where I had in life by not taking risks, and at that time I felt this was a gamble worth taking. My future happiness depended on it. So I went to find her and ask her to choose me. I promised her that I'd spend my entire life making her happy."

His head dropped in defeat.

"I was young and irresponsible. Clara basically told me that later, in her own kind way. And I see that now. But it was difficult to understand through the anguish and misery of hearing that she loved only my brother. I can still see the sympathetic smile she gave me as she told me, and it haunted me the rest of my life. I'd never failed before that moment. But not only had I failed with Clara, I'd completely ruined things with my brother. When it all finally came down on me in the days after, I realized I'd lost big time and I wasn't sure how to recover."

"Did you try to talk to Uncle Hank?"

"Once I'd made it through the haze of heartbreak, I tried to tell him how sorry I was, but he wouldn't listen."

"So what happened after that? Did you ever get married or settle down with anyone?"

He shook his head, but despite his answer he seemed content. "It was a moment that changed how I looked at life. While I wasn't the one for Clara, I took hold of her compassion for others and the humanity in her interactions with people. It made me realize how empty my life was. I sold the business in New York and donated half of my fortune to charities that I felt strongly about. I invested the rest, sold my penthouse, and moved to Mexico, where I could fish and read on the sand for hours until the sun went down around me, and I could go to sleep and not have to think about what I'd done. I worked with kids, teaching them English, and I used some of my money to build a school there.

"But about eight months ago, I heard from a friend that Clara was ill. That was when I came to Firefly Beach. I kept a low profile, spending most of my time in the neighboring towns. I didn't want to upset her. I just wanted to be near her, hoping by some miracle she'd feel my presence, and the admiration I had for her would keep her strong. It made no sense, but I wanted to support her and Hank, even if I wasn't there with them. When she died, I moved here permanently, trying to find the peace that Clara found here. And I have.

"When I first came back though, just once, I saw her in town—it was early on in her illness and she looked tired and weak, but she was still beautiful Clara. I told her how she'd changed my perspective on life. I also told her how sorry I was for putting her and Hank in that position, and how my hope was that one day I could be forgiven. I asked her to tell Hank that I was here, that I'd stay out of his life until he wanted me back in it, but as soon as he asked I'd come sprinting. I'm still waiting for that day."

"I wish I could help him to see," Hallie said, the story making her feel a little overwhelmed.

"So do I."

She handed Lewis the letter.

Lewis pressed it against his heart. "Mind if I read this in private?"

"Of course I don't mind." Hallie stood up and walked down the front steps, headed for the guesthouse. And at that moment, she realized she needed Ben.

Chapter Twenty-Four

When Hallie opened the door of the guesthouse, she found Ben sprawled on the sofa, his eyes closed, wearing those big headphones of his. She'd have thought he was asleep were it not for the tapping of his foot against the sofa arm. He was probably listening to the latest track for one of his new bands. The sight of him filled her with the calm she needed. He sensed her presence and opened his eyes, sitting up. Beau stirred in his spot on his dog bed in the corner.

"Hey," he said, taking off his headphones and setting them on the side table.

Hallie plopped down beside him. "I just had a very long talk with Lewis, and I can't believe what he told me." She was still digesting it all. "Before I go into it though, I need a glass of wine. Do we have any in the fridge?"

"I brought you a new bottle of the blackberry you like." He got up to get her some.

"You did?" Hallie followed him into the kitchen area. "You were slam busy every day, closing up late that one night we talked, and you still had time to go out and get my wine?"

He gave her a loving look. "Always."

Affection for him swelled in her chest. She felt the urge to give in to it, to tell him exactly how she felt about him, but it wouldn't help anything. Lewis was living proof of the havoc that being honest could cause. Ben was honorable. He'd stick by her even though she couldn't give him a family, and she feared she'd cause him regret. So instead of hugging him like she wanted to do, she hung back from him, walking around to the other side of the counter.

"I'll pour us each some," he said, turning his attention to the wine cabinet. He grabbed two glasses and filled them, handing one to her. "So what did Lewis have to say?"

"A whole lot. But just the thought of it all has made me tired. I'll need some time before I can tell you everything."

"You need to have fun. Drink that down."

They sat across from each other and talked about nothing important, to clear her mind. They chatted about Ben's latest work with his new band, how one of the songs was giving them all fits, and how he'd managed to secure a backup track with three of his favorite artists. Hallie had told him that she wanted to spruce the house up for Uncle Hank, get the bushes trimmed, make sure the irrigation system was up and running—he needed to feel like it was home again. Ben had made a joke about her using the hedge clippers, recalling when she'd nearly chopped an entire bush down to the ground while trying to wrestle the electric trimmers, making her laugh so hard she had tears in her eyes.

The entire time, she was filling up her glass. They hadn't talked like this in so long and she'd missed it. She leaned heavily on her hand, settling in to a slightly numb state of euphoria.

Ben noticed her happiness and grinned at her. "I haven't seen you this relaxed since your college roommate's wedding." He laughed at the memory. "What was her name? Beth?"

Hallie folded her arms and let her head fall onto them, her back heaving with her laughter. "I'm not that bad right now!" She remembered all the dancing she and Ben had done. She'd kicked off her shoes and dragged him onto the dance floor, insisting she lead. And he'd let her. They were such a funny pair together that the guests formed a circle around them, rooting them on. She lost her balance and started to fall, but Ben swung around in a flash, catching her and lifting her up, making it look like a move from the movie *Dirty Dancing*, which sent the crowd into cheers.

"Hang on." Ben went over to the stereo, set his wine on the living room table, and started tapping on his computer. "I know what you need. Listen to this."

He hit a few more keys and music filled the room. It had a beat that was as fluid as the waves outside, mentally rocking her mind back and forth before she could even get up to move her feet. It was fast and happy, rhythmic. Ben moved the coffee table to the side of the room, making Beau shift from his bed to the sofa. Then Ben took Hallie's hands and pulled her to the middle of the floor.

"You can lead," he said. "Just don't dip me."

Hallie started laughing again, but caught her breath for a moment when Ben spun her around. They were dancing, his hands moving along her body, her head tipping back, the moment like nourishment for her soul. No one else could make her feel like this.

After a few songs, the music slowed down, the sound of acoustic guitar filtering in around them—slow and soft like the wind. Her shoulders relaxed. She let go of Ben and leaned over to the table, grabbing her glass, drinking her wine, swaying to the sound of the band. She danced for a few beats before she noticed Ben looking at her with a soft grin on his face.

Gently, he took her glass and set it back on the table next to his. Then he reached for her hands, pulling her toward him, wrapping his arm around her waist and moving with her until they were slow-dancing together. She put her head on his chest, allowing herself to take in the scent that was so uniquely Ben. His lips hovered around the top of her head, and she could feel his breath.

"Do you like it?" he whispered into her ear.

She nodded, not knowing if he meant the dancing or the song, but she didn't care. In that moment it felt like he could save her from everything going on around her. With this one dance, he could make it all fade into black.

His movement slowed further and she opened her eyes to see why. Ben held her gaze. "It's more difficult now," he said quietly. "Now that you know how I feel, I can't hold it back anymore." He pulled her closer. "I knew that would happen, which was why I left. I don't know how you want me to be with you now."

She reached up and put her arms around his neck. "Just be yourself," she said honestly. She loved the way he held her, and she wondered if he could sense it.

With a tender grin, he said, "That's the problem. If I'm myself, I want to do this." Gently, he touched his lips to hers, and it was as if every nerve in her body had been asleep her entire life, waking with a vengeance in that second.

She pulled back and she could see the trepidation on his face, but something occurred to her. "Number four," she said, before laughing quietly.

"What?" he asked, disoriented by her response.

She pulled him closer. "Number four on my list: kiss a boy I love." Then she shrugged. "I have to. Aunt Clara said."

Ben tipped his head back and laughed. Then his smile faded to that intoxicating fondness he had when he looked at her. He held her face in his hands and pressed his lips to hers again. It was soft at first, their movements in perfect sync with one another, building, years of longing for this moment exploding in his response to her. She felt lightheaded and exhilarated, like anything was possible if they could just do it together. His lips were tender and gentle, and she devoured the summery salty taste of them mixed with the blackberry wine.

When they finally slowed to a more respectable level, Ben kissed her cheek and then said into her ear, giving her goosebumps down her arm, "We'll have to do that again."

Hallie couldn't get her thoughts straight. All she could think about was how she wanted to throw caution to the wind and blurt out that she was completely in love with him. She understood now why he'd had to leave, because if she didn't get out of there she'd lose her resolve. Their kiss had made it all too real and she didn't know where to go from there. "We can't," was all she could get out, her emotions coming faster than she could decipher them.

He got closer to her face, with a love-struck grin. "We really do have to. You know how much of a perfectionist your aunt was with her work, and if this is going to count for number four on the list, it had better be perfect." Ben pulled back, pleased with himself. "So that was just practice."

"It was pretty perfect already," she said, totally in the moment.

"Nah. We can do better!" Without warning, he picked Hallie up, running to the sofa, nearly falling over the coffee table, making her shriek and giggle at the same time despite her muddle of feelings. He laid her down, lowering himself over her, and brushed her hair out of her face sweetly. "Let's practice some more right now," he said, consuming her with his eyes, her past and present and future all there in his gaze.

This was the person she'd been born to love, the person she couldn't live without. The way Uncle Hank had described his adoration for Aunt Clara—this was it! For the rest of her life, she'd compare everyone to Ben, and they'd lose because there was no one in this world more perfect for her. How had she not seen it? Suddenly, all her choices before this one seemed trivial. She'd never find another man who would even come close to making her feel like she felt right now.

Kiss a boy I love.

I love you, she thought as she looked into his eyes. *I do*. She wanted to tell him. She wanted him to know that everything he'd done for her, all the things he'd ever said to her—they'd all been so perfect. He'd done everything right. But they couldn't… She felt the prick of tears, panic and fear rushing in, and she pushed him off her.

"What are you afraid of?" he asked, sitting up next to her. "You meant that kiss as much as I did. What's stopping you from giving in to your feelings?"

She wished by some miracle that they could move past her own issues, but if they couldn't she had Robby to think about. She'd let her feelings make her choices for her, and if she continued to do that, she could ruin everything. Hallie knew what it was like to grow up with only her mother, and while her mother was wonderful, Hallie always felt the absence of a male figure in her life. She'd savored her time with Uncle Hank, and in Robby's case, Uncle Hank's health didn't allow him to do the things he used to do with Hallie. Robby needed Ben for that. And the rest of her family needed Ben in other ways too.

Hallie didn't have an answer to his question without giving away Sydney's fears or disclosing her own, and she didn't know if telling him any of it would change things anyway.

"Look. I know you pretty darn well," he said, taking in a long breath and letting it out, clearly attempting to regain focus. "Something is eating you alive, and for whatever reason you won't tell me what it is. I wish you would."

He took her hand and rubbed the back of it with his thumb, causing a lump in her throat.

"But I'm not going to put any pressure on you. Tell me in your own time." He intertwined his fingers in hers. "Let's get ourselves together, and later we'll see if Robby's back and take him to the fair. We'll go on the rides until our tummies ache and our cheeks hurt from laughing, and I'll win you an obnoxiously large teddy bear that you'll have to drag around all night."

Hallie laughed despite herself, her anxiety lifting. "Can we get one of Mable's apple fritters?"

Ben grabbed her other hand and pulled her up as he got off the sofa. "We'll need to get in line first thing," he said with mock seriousness. Then a sweet solemnity washed over him. "Let's have some fun tonight."

Still feeling light with intoxication, Hallie agreed. This was exactly what she needed.

"You're goin' down!" Ben said to Hallie from inside his cobalt blue bumper car, with Robby giggling from the passenger seat as the cars began to move.

Mama, Sydney, and Robby had been at the aquarium all afternoon. When they got home and Ben mentioned the fair, Robby had been thrilled to go, so Hallie and Ben offered to give Sydney a break and take him. Robby had wanted to leave right away, so they did. They'd been on nearly every ride there.

"You'll have to catch me first!" Hallie turned her steering wheel with all her might, Ben and Robby coming straight for her. Trying to maneuver the car while laughing was no easy feat, but she managed to dart out of the way, swinging around and bumping the side of Ben's car before heading in the other direction.

"You're gonna pay for that!" Robby giggled. "Get her, Ben!"

"We're coming for you, Miss Flynn!" Ben dodged two cars before clearing everyone else and coming over to Hallie's side.

Laughing uncontrollably at the goofy faces he was making for Robby's benefit, she could hardly make her little yellow car move. Ben was headed straight for her. Then, *whack*, he got her, right on the back corner, only making her laugh harder.

"I'm hungry," Robby said when the ride was over, and they'd climbed out of their cars. "And my feet hurt from walking."

Ben lifted him up piggyback style. "Well, you've got a few dinner choices: you can have that big bag of cotton candy over there, a slice of pizza the size of my jeep, or the Firefly Fair special, which is a world-famous apple fritter and ice cream. *Or!* We could get everything and nibble all evening."

"Sydney would never speak to us again," Hallie said, her cheeks hurting from smiling so much.

The sun was setting, the lights of the rides and the stalls all flashing in neon colors, the air filled with bells, chatter, an occasional scream of excitement from someone on a ride, and the coastal sounds that were always present at Firefly Beach. Hallie's face was warm from the sun, the breeze finding her every now and again to cool her.

Robby slid off of Ben's back and ran around in front of him. "I want cotton candy!" He was hopping up and down, heading over to a stand covered in bags of pink and blue.

"You have to at least have a corn dog or something," Hallie said.

Ben was already at the stand, buying him the biggest bag they had.

Hallie joined them. "That's enormous!" she said, digging around in her wallet for some cash to get him a corn dog too.

"It's about fun tonight, right?" Ben said, handing Robby the bag. Then he pulled Robby back up onto his shoulders, the bag dangling precariously from Robby's fingers by Ben's ear. Before Robby could answer, Ben took Hallie's hand. "What's next?"

"Play that, Ben!" Robby said with excitement, pointing to a game with two basketball hoops that seemed to be placed miles from the shooting line. It would take a rocket launcher to get a basketball that far.

"Think I can win it?" Ben asked, twisting to look up at him.

"Yes!" Robby squealed.

"I did promise Hallie a great big bear. She wants one really bad." He winked at her.

Ben walked over to the stand and then squatted down to let Robby climb off his shoulders. Then he took out his wallet and grabbed a few bills from it. "I'll play five games, please," he told the attendant, handing him the money.

"Five?" Hallie said, surprised. "You really only have to play one, or none for that matter."

"And let you go home empty-handed? Never."

Robby leaned on the counter, pulling wads of pink cotton candy from his bag and stuffing them in his mouth, his eyes glued on Ben as Ben took the first basketball from the attendant and bounced it once in front of him. Ben lifted the ball up with both hands and sent it flying into the air. The ball sailed toward the basket in a straight line, hitting the rim and rolling around it before bouncing out.

"Ooooohhh!" Robby cried. "That was close, Ben!"

Ben shot another one with the same precision. It hung in the air, and the three of them stood silently, watching it go. The ball went in, bounced back and forth, and then popped back out.

"No!" Robby said, a mass of cotton candy in his fingers. "That should've gone in!" He started jumping up and down. "Shoot another one! You'll get it in."

"Third time's a charm," Ben said, making the shot. This time, the ball went in and slid all the way down the net, a victory bell sounding. Robby and Hallie both screamed with glee.

"What prize would you like, sir?" the attendant asked.

Ben turned to Hallie. "Take your pick." He waved his hand across the line of gigantic stuffed animals in every color of the rainbow.

"What color should I get, Robby?" she asked, but she was still smiling at Ben.

Robby finished his bite of cotton candy and said, "Get the green one."

"The big frog?"

"Yes!"

The attendant pulled down a frog that was so huge Hallie wasn't sure how she'd maneuver it around through the rides. He awkwardly handed it over the counter to her. "Thank you," she said with her face full of green fur, and then she set it down on the ground, leaning on it.

"You still have two more shots," Robby told Ben.

Ben ruffled his hair and then stole a bite of cotton candy, popping it into his mouth. "I do! Think I can win you one too?"

Robby's eyes grew round. "Oh, I hope so!"

"If not, Robby, I'll give you mine."

"Oh no, Hallie," Robby said with worry on his face, "I know how much you really wanted it. Ben said so."

Ben laughed. "You won't have to worry about that. I'm going to win you one. Or at least go down trying."

He took the ball from the attendant and threw it toward the basket. It looked like a perfect shot, and the ball went in but it bounced out. Robby's face collapsed in disappointment. But with a deep breath, he regained his composure. "You can do it, Ben."

"Last shot, buddy." He bounced the ball a few times, lining up his angle visually. Then, slowly, Ben put the ball into position, both hands on it. He heaved the ball at the basket. Just like before, it went in, and Hallie held her breath until she heard the victory bell, the ball dropping down to the end of the net.

"You won, Ben!" Robby said, dropping his bag of cotton candy and wrapping his arms around Ben's waist.

Ben squatted down to be at Robby's eye level. "Which one do you want?"

Robby walked back and forth, assessing his options while Hallie picked up his cotton candy, twisting the bag shut. Then she went over to Ben and kissed him on the cheek. "He'll remember this for his whole life," she said. "I'm sure of it."

Ben put his arm around her and gave her a cuddle, kissing the top of her head. It was quite possibly the best feeling in the world.

Chapter Twenty-Five

Hallie grinned to herself when she woke to the gigantic green frog sitting in the corner of the sewing room. Last night was amazing. They'd ridden nearly every ride there. Robby had fallen asleep in the jeep on the way home, and Ben had carried him inside and upstairs to his room. When he met Hallie in the hallway, Ben gave her a kiss on the cheek and told her goodnight before heading out to the guesthouse. Hallie had been nearly as exhausted as Robby, falling into bed and losing consciousness almost immediately.

Her phone had a text waiting from Gavin, but she'd get it in just a bit. Instead, she inhaled the smells of morning at Starlight Cottage: bacon, eggs, potato casserole with cheese, homemade buttermilk biscuits... She got up, washed her face, pulled her hair back, and headed downstairs to her family.

The piano was silent this morning. Hallie had hoped to hear music as she padded down the stairs, but instead all she heard was the clinking of dishes and the sizzle of food on the stove, silent the way it had been since they'd arrived. As she entered the kitchen, she found out why. She immediately zoned in on the two empty chairs at the table: Aunt Clara's, which she'd expected, but the other chair was Uncle Hank's. There was a new face in their circle this morning.

Lewis.

"Good morning," he said with a cautious smile.

"Hi." Hallie walked over and sat in her chair across from him, her eyes questioning.

"I was invited," Lewis said, holding Aunt Clara's letter into the air. Mama and Sydney exchanged glances.

"Has Uncle Hank been down to breakfast yet?" Hallie asked.

"Yes," Mama said, that one word filled with countless contemplations. "He's decided not to eat this morning. He's back in his room."

"Hey there!" Ben said, coming in and nuzzling up to Hallie playfully. "Hey, buddy." He walked over to Robby and gave him a friendly pat on the back. "How's that belly feeling after all the cotton candy?"

Robby giggled.

Then he reached a hand across the table. "You're Lewis, right?" As if it were totally normal for Lewis to be there.

"I am." Lewis shook his hand.

"Ben. I'm a family friend." He sat down next to Hallie. "They feed me occasionally."

Lewis smirked, obviously trying to figure Ben out.

"Where's Hank?" Ben asked, only then observing the tense silence. He pushed back from the table. "I'll go get him." Before anyone could respond, Ben was gone again. While Ben probably didn't know what he was getting into by going to find Uncle Hank with Lewis at his table, if anyone could calm him down, it was Ben.

Hallie leaned closer to Lewis. "What did the letter say? Can you tell us?" she asked.

Lewis held the letter in his fist as a smile spread across his face. "She said she wasn't angry with me. And I knew that already. She also said that I was welcome to come for a visit and that she insisted I do at least once. She suggested breakfast, since that was the time everyone always got together before the day pulled the family in different directions. I brought some muffins." He gestured toward a basket on the table.

"That was very kind of you," Mama said.

Hallie realized that the others didn't know the whole story behind why Uncle Hank was so upset with him, or how sorry Lewis was for interfering in Uncle Hank's life. And Uncle Hank didn't know Lewis's side. Everyone needed to hear it all. "I'll check on Ben," Hallie said, getting up.

After looking in a few rooms, she finally found Ben and Uncle Hank upstairs in his bedroom. Ben was sitting on the edge of the bed nodding at Uncle Hank. She'd expected to see Uncle Hank in a fury, but he wasn't. He was speaking calmly with Ben. They both stopped talking when Hallie entered.

"I'm guessing you're here to bring me downstairs," Uncle Hank said. He was civil, composed.

"What do you think about that?" Hallie asked, curious as to his change in demeanor when Lewis was the subject of conversation.

"When I got upstairs, I kept remembering Clara's letter," he said in almost a whisper, "the part where she said everyone deserves the kind of love I showed her. That's Clara. She loved everyone with all her heart. And if she taught me anything, it was that. Years ago, when she had a choice, she chose my love. She had faith in *my* love. I have to show her that her choice was right, that my love for her was bigger than anything else in her life. It's so incredibly difficult to bring myself to love my brother after what he did. But by trying, I'm honoring Clara."

Hallie took his hands and squeezed them. "That's the Uncle Hank I know," she said, emotion welling up. "I missed you. Where have you been?"

He blinked as his eyes got misty.

"I know you're still really angry with Lewis. But he told me what happened after Aunt Clara chose you, and I truly believe that if you hear him out, you'll have it in your heart to forgive him."

His jaw clenched, and Hallie knew how difficult it still was for him.

"You don't have to be his best friend. Just let him tell you. Let him sit at our table." She tugged on his hands. "Let's all go down together. The whole family."

Ben, who'd been sitting quietly on the edge of the bed, stood up. "I'll just grab a muffin and head out. You all need your family time."

"Nonsense," Uncle Hank said. "You're family too."

The three of them went downstairs together. When they came in, Uncle Hank nodded at Lewis, which was miles above how he felt for him, Hallie was nearly sure. Uncle Hank was giving it everything he had—all for Aunt Clara.

"I'm just finishing up the grits and hash browns now," Mama said guardedly over her shoulder, as she stirred the potatoes on the stove.

Uncle Hank kept his hand on the back of his chair but didn't sit. "That means I have time to play piano, then."

"Yay!" Robby hopped out of his chair. "Can I play too?"

"Of course you can." His gaze fluttered over to Lewis. "Shall we show them?"

A smile crawled across Lewis's face. "It's been a long time."

Uncle Hank nodded.

Lewis and Uncle Hank walked out of the room with Robby trailing behind. Sydney and Mama followed, the sight so intriguing that Mama left the potatoes on the stove. Uncle Hank and Lewis went into the living room and sat down next to one another at the piano.

Hallie hovered in the doorway and Ben came up behind her, placing his hands on her shoulders like he always did.

Lewis put his fingers on the keys, pausing for a second as if he had to get his emotions in check. Uncle Hank placed his hands on the notes where he was going to start, and then the two began playing in unison. Their fingers moved together effortlessly as if God himself were choreographing them, as if they'd always been meant to be a whole. The melody was sweet and fluid, the most beautiful music Hallie had ever heard come from that piano. Tears fell down Mama's cheeks and she wiped them away. Sydney stood beside Robby, motionless and transfixed. Ben's hands slid down from their position on Hallie's shoulders, finding her waist where he wrapped his arms around her, holding her as emotion welled up in her throat. This was the start of something wonderful. Hallie could feel it.

Ben's phone rang as he leaned against the white brick of the lighthouse. He peered down at the screen, his brows pulling together.

"Everything okay?" Hallie asked. She sat down in the shaded grass next to where Ben stood, her flip-flops lying beside her bare feet as she leaned her head against the lighthouse, and closed her eyes to take in the salty air and the pure joy that she felt after breakfast this morning.

"It's Ashley." He didn't answer and the ringing finally stopped. He put his phone back in his pocket. "I'll call her later."

Hallie looked up at him and he lowered himself down next to her. "I'm worried, Ben."

"What are you worried about?"

"I'd hate to see you lose out on someone wonderful. You wouldn't have started dating Ashley if you didn't see a future with her. I know you. You aren't a short-term dating kind of guy. So why did you *start* dating her?"

"I told you. Because I thought I'd lost you."

"And now?"

"I'm willing to take my chances." He gave Hallie a warm look that knotted her stomach.

"That's not fair to me," she said.

"What do you mean by that?"

Hallie swallowed and tried to get the words to come out, when everything inside her was screaming to say something different. "I just don't want you to think that there's a chance for something more between us when I've never told you there would be."

Ben propped his knees up and rested his arms on them as he looked out at the ocean, his expression frustrated. "You're not making sense to me, Hallie." He turned back to her. "I'm getting mixed signals from you. But even if there's no chance for you and me at all, in the end, I can't date Ashley." He put his face right in her line of sight. "I'm in love with you. Completely and totally in love with you. I don't know what more to say than that."

The lump had found its way back into her throat and her chest ached with his admission. He was right. She was sending him mixed signals. She had to give it everything she had, and not let her feelings for him show. "What if I told you that I don't ever plan to get married? I don't want to."

He huffed out a sigh of disbelief. "I'd say that's weird, since I know how long you've thought about your wedding, but okay. It doesn't matter. What matters to me is being with you."

"And I don't ever plan to have children," she said, the last word stinging on its way out. A sob rose in her throat but she suppressed it.

Ben stared at her, his thoughts unreadable. The tide ebbed and flowed on the shore, constantly calling out its song, a stark contrast to the silence that rested between her and Ben. "You? You don't want a family?"

She shook her head, unable to say anything more. She wanted to hide in his chest, to feel his embrace, to hear the sweet sound of his voice as he told her he could fix this. But she knew that wasn't a possibility.

"Ever?"

"No," she croaked, before the tears came like a tidal wave. She brushed them away angrily, one after another. A picture of Ben last night at the fair with Robby on his shoulders, laughing with him, getting him the cotton candy—like snapshots in her mind, banging together and creating a piercing noise in her head. She knew how great Ben was with children, and after last night she also knew that not only did she have to protect Robby and Ben's relationship, but she could never take fatherhood from Ben. That would be selfish.

Ben looked down at the grass, fiddling with a piece of it, those ever-present thoughts in his eyes turning to questions, and then, there it was: the disappointment she feared. That look wrapped around her soul, strangling her.

"I'm sorry," she said, her breath shallow, feeling like the world was crashing down around her.

"We'll figure it out," he said.

Hallie stood up. "There's nothing to figure out at all. You deserve to have a family if you want one." She faced the gulf, the turquoise water doing nothing to calm her.

"We can talk about this later," he said.

"No. This is done." She waggled her finger between them. "I love you, Ben. You're my best friend. But that's all we can be."

For the first time in her life, Ben looked vulnerable. She'd hurt him. But if they became anything more than friends, even greater pain would be inevitable. Best to get the disappointment out of the way before anything began. She was saving them both a lot of heartache and regret.

"I'm going into town to see Gavin," she said, attempting to get herself together. "He said he has something to tell me." Before she turned away, she said, "Please think it through properly before you talk to Ashley again. She's really great."

Ben didn't look at her. He just sat, stunned, shaking his head, and she wondered if he believed her. He had to. It was as simple as that.

Chapter Twenty-Six

Hallie pushed the gallery door open and stepped into the icy air-conditioned entryway. Gavin was talking to a couple about one of his paintings when he waved to her, and motioned for her to give him just a minute to finish up with the customers. She wandered over to the room that held her photography, and immediately noticed three blank spots where her pictures had been. It looked like Gavin might have sold another one.

"Hi there!" Gavin said, walking in like a ray of sunshine.

"Did you sell my lighthouse door photo?"

His smile widened. "Yep."

"Oh my goodness! That's three!"

"Well, I have better news than that."

"What is it?"

Another few people walked past them, telling Gavin goodbye as they headed out. The bells on the door jingled to signal their exit.

"There's this new magazine called *Southern Rush*—have you heard of it?"

She had. It was the latest up-and-coming national home decorating publication. Aunt Clara had bought a subscription to it last year. Even through her struggles, she wanted to be on the cutting edge of her profession. She'd told Hallie that this magazine was so good because she thought it was right on the cusp of the next big thing in design. "I know it," she'd said.

"I hope you don't mind, but I spoke to an editor for the magazine—she'd done an article about me so I had her contact information. I told her you were a photographer but also a designer, preparing for the launch of your Coastal Comfort brand, and I emailed her your photographs and the furniture you found to go with them. She loved the sort of one-stop-southern-shop concept you've created, and she wants to do a piece on you for their December issue."

Hallie gasped. "You're kidding." She couldn't believe it. And then a warm rush of happiness filled her. Gavin had called her a "designer." Until that moment, there had only been one designer in the family. Could there really be design in Hallie's future? She tried the title on in her mind. *Designer*. Could she eventually move past her Coastal Comfort series and do more? Aunt Clara had an eye for art, and she could choose beautiful pieces for her clients, but Hallie planned to build on Aunt Clara's design strategy, commissioning entire lines of furniture to go along with her art. Instead of just designing a room for a client, she could give them a one-of-a-kind ensemble that she'd created using the client's specific tastes and ideas. She could fill their room with photographs of the client's family and items they treasured, match furniture colors to the colors of *their* lives that were displayed on the wall…

"She'd like to give you a call, just for an interview."

"Of course."

This new identity Hallie pondered was thrilling but terrifying all at the same time. She knew her plans were bigger than any of her projects at the agency. She'd done full-scale advertising displays at major venues, but that was nothing compared to running an ongoing business like she was thinking about. Aunt Clara's were big shoes to fill, if Hallie were going to survive in the home design world. She had the Flynn family name, so once people knew who she was they would undoubtedly compare her to Aunt Clara. Was she ready for that type of scrutiny? And even if she were, she'd need funds to build her business. Her ideas were grand already and she felt like she'd barely scratched the surface. Aunt Clara had started small, but Hallie's initial ideas would require more money than she had. She didn't even know if she was going to get an inheritance, but if she did, would it be enough to get something this big off the ground? Hallie felt the overwhelming need to use the platform of *Southern Rush* to bring her ideas to life, but the timing wasn't good. Her business was still in its infancy.

Despite her concerns, she could hear her aunt's dreamlike voice: *Don't ever be afraid of anything. Just jump in…*

It seemed too vast to get her head around, but she struggled to think of it in smaller terms. The notion of it felt so natural to Hallie that she couldn't go back to just photography. It didn't feel whole to her anymore without the other pieces of the design process. But she'd have so much to learn. Hallie couldn't possibly be a designer… Could she?

"I was wondering if you wanted to go into town and take a few shots. You brought your camera, right?" Gavin said, interrupting her inner deliberations.

"I did bring it," she said, feeling an overwhelming need to get started and create. She wanted to turn her Coastal Comfort series into a Coastal Comfort line, with all the décor options anyone could possibly want. While she had no idea how she'd manage it, the only way to find out was to get started. "I'd love to." She'd found that the world seemed nearly perfect through the lens of her camera. And right now she wanted to shut out all the things she had on her mind and focus on her Coastal Comfort line, starting with the photography.

"Hop in the truck," he said with a conspirator's grin. Hallie understood it perfectly. There was no one else who knew what it felt like to be under the spell of a camera, other than Gavin. She jumped in.

He pulled out of the drive and headed toward Firefly Beach. The empty road stretched before them, a single gray slip of surface hugging the coast. Hallie's window was down, her elbow propped up on the opening, the wind pushing against her face as she took in colors and textures, storing them away for later.

"Where are we headed?" she asked, wondering what he'd meant by "town." Would she find a line of white picket fences or a shop door covered in seashells? Or would they go to the public beach? She imagined tiny feet in the sand, seagulls perched on buoys...

"I'd planned this a while ago and I was going to go by myself, but then I thought of you, and it occurred to me that I don't have to do things alone anymore when I have friends in the area." He looked over at Hallie, happy. "I've scheduled a charter. There's a boat docked off the public landing with our names on it. Wanna take a quick boat ride?"

"Oh, I'd love to!"

"We're going to an island off the coast. It's full of sea life and panoramic views. I've been there twice before on my own, but it would be nice to have another photographer's perspective. We could get some really great shots."

When Hallie had first met Gavin, she'd been intimidated by his talent, yet here he was treating her like an equal in his profession. Maybe she wasn't supposed to have a family or find that perfect person, but this she was sure about. Aunt Clara had seen it way before Hallie had, and now it was so clear. Perhaps it was because she and Aunt Clara were so similar. And just like her aunt, Hallie found happiness in this work. She just hoped that she, too, would find it enough to fulfill her completely. Maybe one day she wouldn't think about the family she'd never have; maybe she would stop feeling the void at some point. She wondered if Aunt Clara ever felt like she'd missed out by not having children. Had her work been enough? In Hallie's case, it would have to be.

She wasn't sure how to make it all happen, but she knew that there was no way she could go back to her old job now and be happy. Perhaps she should live off her savings for a while like Sydney was doing. The only problem was that she didn't have enough, and if Aunt Clara had left her an inheritance, she couldn't access it until she'd completed the list. How would she ever finish it?

Gavin parked the truck and grabbed his camera from behind the seat. Hallie got out and immediately lined up a shot. Bobbing in the water was a gleaming white sport cruiser. She shielded her view with her hand to temper the champagne sunlight that glistened off the waves and the boat's silver surfaces. Hallie twisted her lens, lining up the water in balance with the sky, the boat just off center, like a pearl against the indigo horizon. She snapped a photo just as two seagulls soared together overhead, their shadows like perfect arches.

"I can't even get you onto the boat," Gavin said with a laugh.

He hopped aboard and held out his hand to guide her. She stepped onto the dock and then over the side of the boat, hanging on to Gavin for support as her weight rocked the vessel slightly.

"That's why I enjoy being with you," he said. "I find your enthusiasm inspiring. You see everything as if it were a shot. How have you not become a photographer before now?" He shook his head.

"I suppose I just needed to meet the right person to get me started," she said, making him smile.

Gavin tossed her a life vest and cranked the engine. The gulf waves sloshed against the side of the boat, and a gust of wind blew Hallie's hair behind her shoulders as he backed it away from the dock. Hallie sat on the vinyl cushion at the back and faced the sun. She tilted her head up to feel its warmth on her skin along with the spray of the sea as the boat picked up speed, the engine purring under her. With nothing but a vast sea ahead and a horizon as shiny as a sapphire, it was easy to forget what troubled her. Even if she tried, the thoughts got hung up on their way into her mind as they attempted to filter through the summer heat, the earthy scent of the hissing ocean waves, and the coastal breeze pushing her against the seat of the boat. Hallie took in a big gulp of air, letting it saturate her with summertime. These were the smells and sounds of her childhood, and every wonderful memory she had was wrapped up in this atmosphere.

Gavin pointed off toward their left at a small island floating in the midst of the enormous gulf, the lush green of its center contrasting with the white sand beaches that lined its edge. Hallie held on to the boat handle to keep herself steady as Gavin changed directions and headed toward it. As they got closer, Hallie braced herself against the back of the seat and snapped a shot. She cupped her hands over the screen in an attempt to view it, but all she could see was the meandering coastline snaking along the bottom of the picture. It looked like it could be a keeper though, by the shape of the shore and its positioning. She couldn't wait to see it once they got back to Gavin's.

They dropped anchor after Gavin pulled the nose of the boat onto the beach, bringing them to a soft slide of a stop. With every breath, she felt more like herself in the coastal rhythm of sea and wind, her camera strap around her neck, the mass of thick metal in her hands. The feel of the focus under her fingers was what she imagined the keys to feel like for Uncle Hank when he played piano: natural and fluent. Hallie zeroed in on a starfish that was half buried in the powdery white sand, waiting to get her shot until a bundle of dried kelp floated by.

Gavin walked up next to her, his camera at his face, shooting one of the palm trees. "It's exquisite here, isn't it?" he said, lowering his camera. He let it hang around his neck and walked over to the water, stepping into it with his bare feet and dipping his hand in. He scooped up a sand dollar. "Look at this beautiful creature."

Hallie ran her finger over the five-point star in its center, having never seen one this deep brown color, only to jump back when the spines started to move around the edge of it.

"It's still alive," Gavin said. "Did you know that you aren't supposed to keep it if it's alive?" He set it back in the water and took a photo of it through the clear surf. "They turn white once they die, when the sun bleaches them. I find them oddly comforting because their beauty comes in death." He looked back down at it. "I like to think that there's some good in death, some cosmic purpose in it."

"I think there is," Hallie said. "I feel my Aunt Clara everywhere. I think they're still with us, just no longer among us."

"I battle with that idea, because if Gwen is with me then it's difficult to move on."

"But I think she'd want you to. You can't stop your life forever because hers was cut short. That would be two tragedies."

"I had this idea to move down here where no one knew me, find a purpose that could make the days more bearable, and then settle into that life until it started to feel normal. Eventually maybe I could even learn to love again." He walked out of the water onto the sand and sat down. Hallie plopped down next to him. "I rebuilt the house because that was always our plan, and if I didn't just continue on, I'd fall apart. Then I decided to move into it, to leave my job and see where life took me, all the while forcing myself to move forward. But sometimes I still falter."

"That's understandable. It's hard to lose someone like that."

"I'm so glad for your friendship. You make me feel like I'm not crazy, like there's more ahead for me."

"Ditto," she said, holding up her camera.

That made him smile.

When Hallie pulled up, Ben was throwing a ball to Beau in the drive-way. "I've been waiting for you," he said, with an intensity to his words, as she got out of the car. He chucked the ball across the yard and Beau ran to retrieve it. "We need to talk."

Hallie shut the car door and stepped up beside him as he led the way to the guesthouse. Something was different about him, but she couldn't decide what it was, and that made her uneasy. She'd always recognized his emotions the instant he had them, but this was something dissimilar to his usual demeanor.

Ben opened the door and let her go in first. Beau caught up and trotted behind them, dropping the ball at Ben's feet and lapping up his water from the bowl by the kitchen island.

"Why didn't you feel like you could talk to me?" he asked, his eyes so penetrating that she had to sit down on the sofa. He joined her.

"About what?" she asked, already fearful of what he'd found out. The shame and guilt she felt for losing the baby rushed back in. It didn't make sense to feel blame—her therapist had tried to tell her that, and they'd had lengthy conversations about visualizing different feelings in relation to this—but her feeling of brokenness always surfaced, and with it came shame.

"Sydney told me what happened. With your pregnancy."

Now she felt betrayed. It was *her* story to tell. "How dare she tell you," Hallie started, but Ben cut her off.

"No. Don't misplace your anger on Sydney. She told me because I confided in her. I fell apart on her. I told her that I don't know how to live without you and it's killing me." He ran his hands across his face, making it red. "I pleaded with her to help me understand you because I didn't all of a sudden. You weren't making any sense. You've always wanted to get married and have a family, and one loser of a guy wouldn't change that inside you. You're the most optimistic person I know. And you'd bounce back from that. I needed answers and I pressed her for them."

"So now you see," Hallie said quietly, tears surfacing.

"Why didn't you just tell me you couldn't have children? That's way down the line. And when we did have to face it, we could figure it out together."

"I don't want you to have to figure it out. I saw the disappointment in your eyes when I said I wasn't going to have a family, Ben," she said.

"My disappointment was that I thought I knew you better than anyone and I'd misread something. I was disappointed in myself for not catching it. But the more I thought about it, the more I believed there was something else going on because I *do* know you, Hallie. I know you better than I know myself." He reached over and wiped her tear. "You never disappoint me."

"You say that now, but years down the road, if we're together, I don't want you to have regrets. You've told me before that you want a family—your own children, a little boy who looks like you." She brushed another tear away. "You've said it since we were kids. And I can't give that to you. We're at an impasse because I won't let you settle for less than what you ought to have."

"Tell me you don't love me, and I'll stop trying," he demanded. "Tell me that you wouldn't like to wake up next to each other every morning, to spend the rest of our lives together, to know that no matter what our day was like, we would always come home to one another. Tell me, Hallie."

Hallie couldn't lie to him. She could never say she didn't love him or want those things because that wasn't true. Her vision blurred with her tears.

"Why can't we just take it day by day? Do we have to have our whole lives planned out?"

She took in a calming breath. "No, we don't. But every time I look at you, I'll be reminded of what I know you want and what I can't give you. And I don't want to live like that because the guilt would ruin me. It's not healthy. If I'm ever going to get over this, I have to move forward with no ties to the past."

Hallie had never seen such unhappiness in Ben's face before. And nothing had made her heart ache like his sorrow did right then, because she knew that kind of sadness. He felt loss. Just like she'd felt when she lost the baby, and when she'd lost Aunt Clara. She could see it in his eyes. And she couldn't do anything about it. She needed a reprieve before she completely broke down.

"I need to take a walk," she said.

Ben didn't answer.

"I'm going out on the beach. I'd like some time to be alone for a while."

He finally met her eyes. "Okay."

*

"I'm so sorry," Sydney said, joining Hallie in the gazebo. She sat down and put her hand on Hallie's thigh as remorse poured from her face.

Hallie had been crying out there so long that she'd lost track of time. The evening sky had put on a glorious show of oranges, pinks, and purples as the sun set, but it did nothing to soothe her. Hallie had barely noticed. Her eyes swollen and stinging, she looked out at the beach for the fireflies, but they weren't there. She'd probably missed them.

"I went by the guesthouse to check on Ben and he told me you two had talked." Sydney leaned in, demanding Hallie's attention. "It wasn't my place to tell him, Hallie," she said, welling up. "I know that. But he looked completely shattered. I felt an overwhelming need to make him understand that *he* wasn't the issue. I could guess what was keeping you from being with Ben just by listening to his side, and I had to tell him."

Hallie squeezed her eyes shut, feeling hollow. It didn't matter now who told whom, or any of it. The reality of the situation had settled upon her, and Hallie didn't know where to go from here.

"What I said about Robby, I didn't understand what was going on with you and Ben. I'm sorry I said anything at all. Please know that I'd never stand in the way of the two of you, knowing how strongly you feel for each other."

"I know," was all she could get out. She didn't want to say there wasn't anything going on between her and Ben because she wasn't really sure if that was true. All she knew was that she was heartbroken.

Sydney put her arm around her and Hallie leaned on her shoulder.

"Do you think you two will get past this?" Sydney asked.

Hallie shook her head and shrugged, lost.

"It's a tough thing…" Sydney pulled her closer. "But no matter what, it's okay for the two of you to still be friends. You know he'll always be there for you."

"Yeah." Hallie traced the grain of wood along the bench where they sat, considering the idea of being just friends. If they could go back to the way they were, she could still have Ben just like she always had, and while she would forever want more, maybe they could get past it in time and just exist in that notion that they couldn't have it all. And Ben would eventually move on and find that perfect person who could give him a family.

With no other possible answers, Hallie had no choice but to move on, even if it was killing her. She resolved to put her effort in what fulfilled her as a person. She would sink herself into Coastal Comfort and work on her plans for an eventual line. She had given Gavin her number and she was expecting a call from the magazine tomorrow. It was time to push all her sorrows aside and get herself ready for that call.

Chapter Twenty-Seven

Hallie was up the next morning even before Mama had started making breakfast. Her computer sat on the kitchen table, its screen full of Hallie's images, multiple internet tabs open to local furniture makers as well as candle and linen companies. She'd sent emails to various businesses, introducing herself and her new business, and asking them if they'd be interested in collaborating on décor to complement the color scheme in her Coastal Comfort series. She'd even asked the locally known Ridley Furniture Company if they'd like to enter into a partnership to produce some of her designs if she sent them over. She'd drawn dressers with inlays of the five points on the sand dollar engraved in a pattern over the surface of each drawer, chairs with legs the color of the gulf sand, lamps with teal and azure blown glass… She had quite a few ideas, and they were coming to her faster than she could draw them, her sketches spread over the table.

Hallie's computer pinged with an email and she opened it immediately, a flutter of excitement rippling through her. Ridley Furniture Company had come back to her before business hours began. Knowing her aunt, they were very interested and wanted to meet with her.

It was important that Hallie distinguish her own talents from the dynasty set forth by Aunt Clara. With all her ideas in a muddle, she opened a new document on her laptop and began to devise a business plan. She needed organization and she needed it fast. She began to type. *Overview: Hallie Flynn Design provides luxury, one-of-a-kind home concepts for upscale beachgoers. We aim to be the leading brand in home décor by putting people first at all costs. At Hallie Flynn Design, the customer is not just a fellow beach lover—she is family.*

Then she started planning the logistics, scribbling notes onto paper and madly clicking through search results on her computer. She started to jot down ideas on her strategies and how she'd get the business going, goals, timelines…

Then she replied to the email, saying she could stop by today and to let her know a good time.

"Good morning," Mama said, breaking Hallie's concentration.

"Morning," she said, as Mama peered over the chair to view all the papers spread over the table. "You know those photos I've been taking? Look," she said, turning her computer around.

Mama gasped and came closer. "Oh, honey, they're gorgeous!"

"I've been thinking about following in Aunt Clara's footsteps, but I'd do it a little differently, add my own twist." Hallie showed her what she'd typed and the different ideas she had for home furnishings. "I thought about contacting Sasha Morgan to see if she had any pointers for me. She might be able to look over my business model, since she has so much experience."

"Maybe you could work for her until you get on your feet," Mama suggested.

"Maybe… But I really feel the need to do this my way."

Mama smiled. "You have always had your own view of things. Uncle Hank went on and on about your photographs after you all had lunch the other day, and I was going to ask you to show me once everything calmed down." Mama cinched the belt of her housecoat tighter and then took a seat at the table, dragging one of Hallie's drawings toward her with a finger. "You're so talented," she said, looking up at her, but Hallie could tell she had more to say.

She waited for Mama to tell her.

"I see the sparkle in your eye when you're doing something creative. It's always been there. But lately that sparkle has been absent quite a bit. Something is bothering you. I'm worried about you *and* Sydney," Mama said. "Your sister was beside herself yesterday but she wouldn't tell me what was wrong, except it had something to do with you. I wondered if you'd explain it to me."

Hallie hadn't told her mother about the baby for two reasons: one, it was too difficult for Hallie emotionally to tell anyone but the counselor, and two, Aunt Clara had just passed away and Mama was so grief-stricken that Hallie just couldn't add to it. While she didn't want to relive the tragedy of losing her first child or to think about her health concerns right now, Starlight Cottage was about family and being there for one another. Her mother needed to understand what had happened. "Let's make a cup of coffee," Hallie said, "and then I'll tell you everything."

Hallie and her mother were still at the table talking an hour later. Mama was supportive and loving. She'd even moved to the chair beside Hallie so that she could put her arms around her. It felt good to tell Mama everything. Hallie realized that it was so much better when people knew because she didn't feel like she was facing it all alone. And to her surprise, no one had looked at her differently. Hallie felt protected by her family and she knew that, while her future plans were still uncertain, they'd be with her along the way.

"Why don't you ask Ben to breakfast, honey," Mama said. "I'm sure he'll wander in at some point, but it might be good for you to be the one to get him. I'll bet he feels pretty uncertain at the moment. He needs to know that he's family no matter what happens with the two of you. And he also needs to feel that you, too, are there for him."

"Okay," Hallie said, piling up her papers and closing her laptop. "When should I tell him breakfast will be ready?"

"I'm making sausage, egg, and cheese casserole, so it should be done in about forty-five minutes."

Hallie slipped her flip-flops on, and gathered the items into her arms to drop off in the sewing room before heading over to the guesthouse. There was a small part of her that worried about seeing Ben, because she wasn't sure if she could keep her feelings for him from showing and she didn't want another round of yes-we-can-no-we-can't. But she missed him. There was something inside her that came alive whenever he was with her. No one else could do that.

The morning was warm, but the breeze sliding off the gulf was still cool, washing over her on her way down the path to the guesthouse. The familiar song of the sea sang to her like it had so many days of her life. It was always there for her, whispering as if to say, "Shh. It's okay." Hallie knocked on the door, and when no one answered the first thing she did was check Beau's water bowl, to make sure Ben hadn't left again. The stainless steel bowl was still there, half full. Hallie got the hide-a-key and opened the door.

"Ben?" she called, stepping inside.

Beau trotted up to her, his tail wagging furiously, and put his forehead on her leg.

"Where's Ben?" she asked, stroking Beau's back.

Beau went over to his bed and curled up on it just as Hallie saw a piece of paper on the counter.

Gone to see Ashley.

Hallie turned the paper over to check the other side. No explanation, no further details. But then she remembered that she'd told him he should give things a chance with Ashley. Perhaps that was what he was doing. A twinge of unease snaked through her at the thought, but it was the right thing for everyone. Ashley was a wonderful person, and she was good to Ben. With a mixture of hope for Ben and sadness and disappointment over her own circumstances, Hallie said goodbye to Beau and left the guesthouse.

Uncle Hank played piano this morning, and at breakfast Hallie brought up her most recent ideas—Hallie Flynn Design and her Coastal Comfort décor line, which would branch off from her Coastal Comfort series of photographs. Everyone was thrilled to hear it and the conversation lasted nearly the whole meal, which was fine with Hallie because she didn't have to think about Ben. After, to keep her spirits up, Hallie threw herself into work. She researched possible website designs, domain names, and online content options. She mapped out more of her business plan, polishing it up to take with her when she met with Chase Blythe at Ridley Furniture later today. She'd gone back and forth a bit more with him on email, and he seemed very interested in her ideas.

She was so deep in thought that she almost didn't notice Uncle Hank smiling from the doorway of the kitchen, where she sat with her computer.

"Do you know what I love most about this view?" he asked.

She closed her laptop and gave him her full attention.

Uncle Hank came over and sat down across from her. "The complete concentration I see on your face when you're working. It's the same expression Clara used to get when I'd pop into her office. Sometimes she'd work a few minutes before she realized I was at the door. But I never minded, because she was doing exactly what she was put on earth to do. I think you're the same."

"A furniture maker and a magazine reporter want to talk to me about Coastal Comfort, but I worry because they know I'm Aunt Clara's niece. I'm sort of using her name…"

"No you're not." He crossed his forearms on the table. "You've created the start of your own identity with Hallie Flynn Design; you just happen to be related to Clara. You're allowed to tell people that. What Clara was worried about was you kids using her name to get ahead yourselves. You aren't doing any such thing. You've done this all on your own."

Hallie was relieved to have Uncle Hank's blessing. It made her feel like somehow it was Aunt Clara saying it was all okay. "I'm starting to see Aunt Clara's purpose in making me complete the list. It's like she knew what I needed."

"Of course she did," Uncle Hank said, a wistful smile on his face.

"Although I don't know what making a sandcastle has to do with anything."

Uncle Hank laughed and then looked out the window briefly before saying, "Maybe that one was for me. I enjoyed it."

"You've come a long way too."

He nodded.

"Think you'll see Lewis again?"

"I don't know. It's difficult to reverse decades of feelings in a day or two. It's not easy. But I think I can manage if he fills his seat at the table."

"That's a good place to start."

Once she'd driven into town, Hallie had a few minutes to burn before her meeting with Mr. Blythe of Ridley Furniture, which was helpful because Ashley was standing outside of Sally Ann's Bakery. She waved at Hallie to get her attention as Hallie parked. With her laptop and bag of sketches in the front seat of her car, she locked up and crossed the street.

"I thought you were with Ben," Hallie said. "He left a note…"

Ashley's face was freshly powdered, her lips a dewy coral color, but when she looked closely, Hallie noticed the rims of her eyes were pink. Ashley produced a million-dollar smile and fiddled with her handbag. "He came to see me, but he left already, and I decided that I needed a slice of Sally Ann's peach cobbler with vanilla ice cream."

"That sounds amazing."

"Yeah," she said, "peach cobbler solves anything." She sniffled, but tried to cover it up by taking in a deep breath and pushing the air out with a smile.

"Did something happen between you and Ben?"

Ashley put her sunglasses on with a shaky hand. "He told me how he feels about you," she said. "And now I understand why it isn't fair for him to be with me. And I can't blame him for ending things if he's in love. While it still hurts, I'm coming to terms with it, and if I had to lose him to someone, I'd want it to be someone like you."

"Oh, Ashley, I'm so sorry things didn't work out. I tried to tell him how wonderful you are…"

"If his feelings aren't there, there's nothing I can do. He's a great guy and he was kind in telling me, and sweet for listening. It just wasn't right for us. It hurts, but it's okay."

Hallie gave her a hug. "If you ever want to talk, I'm here."

"Thank you, Hallie. I hope things work out with you two." With a wobbly smile, Ashley opened the door of Sally Ann's Bakery. "I'll see you later," she said.

Hallie said goodbye and headed across the street to meet with Mr. Blythe.

She only waited a few minutes before he greeted her in the lobby of the showroom. "Chase," he said, shaking her hand. "So you're the niece of the infamous Clara Flynn." Hallie would have to get used to being referenced as such. It was only natural, given Aunt Clara's reputation, but one day, Hallie hoped that her name might come first in conversation.

"Yes. My design ideas are a bit different from hers, but we both shared the same passion for sure."

"Well, let's see what you've got and how we can help," Chase said.

Hallie pulled out her laptop and opened it on the counter with the register. "I have a specific color palette in mind, and I'm looking to design patterns on the furniture that would mimic those in the photographs—not matchy-matchy but more subtle…"

Hallie continued to review her concepts with Chase, and she was so inspired that she stopped twice to jot down more thoughts on her way home after speaking to him. He told her his ideas and they discussed the terms of their partnership. She couldn't have been more thrilled. Not only would she be able to showcase the furniture on her website, but he'd carry the pieces in-store as well. They were starting small, with the idea that they could build as her company and clients grew.

She couldn't wait to tell Gavin all about it and see what he'd be willing to put in the room with her artwork, so she stopped by the gallery on her way out of town.

"That's amazing," he said when she told him. "And we'll have a little more space without the easel that held your sunset shot. You'll be happy to know that I sold it."

"You did?" The idea that strangers would have her photographs on their walls was nearly unbelievable. Hallie peeked into the room with her photos, and every blank space gave her more courage to move forward with her plans.

"Yep. I'm so happy for you! How's your website coming?"

"I quickly looked into it this morning, but it might be a good idea to get your take on a few things," she said, still reeling from it all. Truthfully, she'd love nothing more than to spend her time collaborating with Gavin. She wondered if perhaps working with her helped Gavin avoid his dark thoughts the same way it did for her. In a way, they needed each other to get through the hard times.

"You should get it up and running as quickly as possible. If I were you, I'd work on designing that first. I can help if you need me to. When's your call with the magazine?"

"In two hours."

"What are you doing right now?" he asked. "The gallery's quiet this afternoon. We could work on it over a couple of sandwiches from Wes and Maggie's. You can take the call here if you'd like."

"I'd love to."

"Wonderful. I'll call us in an order."

"While you do that, I'm going to step outside and make another quick call," she told him. She felt hope now when she looked toward the future. This was more natural than any job she'd ever done. As she closed the gallery door behind her, she dialed the number at the advertising agency where she worked and gave her notice. *Don't be afraid. Just jump in.*

Chapter Twenty-Eight

Ben's jeep was still gone when Hallie pulled into the drive at Starlight Cottage that evening. After the call, she'd gone to Gavin's house and spent all afternoon there, planning and creating her business.

Wondering where Ben was, since he wasn't with Ashley, she pulled her phone out to text him, but then thought better of it and slipped it back into her pocket. Hallie went in to find her family and tell them all about her day.

Sydney was playing checkers with Robby on the living room floor when Hallie came in. Mama was in the chair by the window reading a book, and Uncle Hank had dozed off on the sofa. He stirred and sat up when Hallie went over to Sydney.

"How'd it go?" her sister asked, moving a checker piece. Robby jumped over it, taking her checker and giggling. "You got me," she said to him, and then turned her attention back to Hallie.

"I got Ridley on board, and the call was super fast but really positive. The editor wants to do a piece on me for the December issue of *Southern Rush.*"

"That's wonderful!" Mama said from her chair, her finger holding her place in the book. "Oh Hallie, I'm so excited for you."

"Mama, may I go outside and swing?" Robby asked.

"Of course you can. I'll be out in bit."

"You've far exceeded your task of becoming a photographer. You're building an empire instead," Uncle Hank said as Robby left the room. "Aunt Clara wouldn't believe it."

Sydney repositioned herself near the window so she could watch Robby. He ran across the yard, toward the tire swing Ben had hung for him, a little shadow against the waning sunlight of evening.

"I'd like to rent out a small showroom and jump right in, but I'll have to wait," Hallie said. "I need to build up some funds to invest. And of course I need to complete the list to find out what else Aunt Clara has in mind for me…" She offered Uncle Hank a questioning look, but he just shrugged.

"What's left on your list?" Sydney asked, picking up the checkers game and putting it back into the box.

"A bunch of things that'll take years to accomplish," Hallie said. "Uncle Hank, the letter's right there in the safe. Can't I just have it? I did the most important one."

Uncle Hank gave a sympathetic pout. "I can't do that. If Clara wanted you to do those things, as unconventional as they seem, I have to trust that she had some reasoning behind it."

"But come on," Hallie said, frustrated. "Have a wish come true? Live somewhere else? Kiss a boy…" A surge of something she'd never quite felt before slid through her veins when she uttered those last words. She tried to label it: fear. Like something was wrong but she couldn't understand what. "I kissed Jeff—that should count," she said, ignoring the feeling. After Aunt Clara passed, I was still with Jeff and I kissed him."

"But you didn't have Clara's letter yet, so I don't think that will work, I'm afraid," Uncle Hank said. "If you'd still been with Jeff and kissed him after getting the letter, it might count."

"I kissed Ben," she blurted. "In the guesthouse."

Her words came out hurried and quiet, distressed. She was desperate to get them out, to unload them, to read the faces of her loved ones when she told them, in the hopes that their reactions would dilute the fear that was still with her. But as they all stared at her with wide eyes, she finally placed what the fear was. It was the dread that she would go through life and never be truly happy, because Ben was the only person who could do that for her. If only she could be everything to Ben that he wanted from his future too.

"And what happened after?" Sydney asked slowly, as if the question had come out while she was still digesting Hallie's original declaration. Ben must not have told her sister that part, and Hallie hadn't let Mama in on her little secret during their talk either.

"I told him about my diagnosis," she said.

Uncle Hank leaned forward. "Diagnosis?"

Hallie filled Uncle Hank in, but the whole time she was thinking about Ben, wondering where he was, why he hadn't returned yet, how he was feeling, if he was all right…

"My God," Uncle Hank said. He looked up at the ceiling as if he needed help from Aunt Clara. But then his focus returned to Hallie. "She never shared this with anyone, but the reason Aunt Clara and I don't have any children is because she was plagued with the same thing."

While her similarities to Aunt Clara had always been apparent, they were now uncanny. Nearly every aspect of Hallie's life mirrored her favorite aunt's. The resemblance was stunning, and Hallie couldn't speak for a few seconds. Instead, she pleaded with Aunt Clara inside her head to guide her from here. She needed Aunt Clara's words of wisdom more than ever.

"What was Ben's reaction?" Uncle Hank asked.

"He wants to take it day by day, but I told him that I didn't think I could do that." Emotion rose in her throat. "He's a family man. He needs kids—little boys with his humor and kind smile, or a girl with the same sparkle in her eyes—and I can't give that to him." She wiped a runaway tear. And then she looked at Uncle Hank and saw him through new eyes. He was every bit a family man, just like Ben—they were so much alike, which was why they'd always gotten along so well. How had Aunt Clara managed?

But before she could ponder her question, the front door flew open and Ben rushed in, ignoring them all, a laser focus on Hallie. He came over to her and grabbed her hands. "Come with me," he said, pulling her up. Robby ran through the door to see what was going on, and Ben gave him a smirk and kissed the top of his head. "I'll be back, bud. I've got to do something with Hallie."

Sydney called Robby over to her, everyone in the room watching Ben with interest.

Ben took Hallie by the hand and nearly ran out into the yard, down the path, over the walkway that led to the beach, her bare feet moving as quickly as possible, until they reached the sand. Hallie gasped. The entire shore was full of fireflies, just the way she remembered it. She'd waited this whole trip to see them and only now had she gotten her chance. She watched the bobbing lights, like a downpour of diamonds floating above the sand. Ben stood behind her and put his arms around her as if nothing had happened between them, and it felt like none of it had been real. And for right now, she wanted to pretend it hadn't.

It was as if he wanted to take his time after that rush to get her out there. They hadn't moved for quite a while, and her pattering heart had slowed to a more regular beat. And then, he leaned forward. "Follow me," he whispered tenderly into her ear, giving her a shiver despite the heat. She walked with him over to a blanket and a little pile of three gifts. *Gifts?* They were all wrapped in solid pale blue paper, with silver and white ribbons trailing from the bows on top of each one.

Ben kneeled and lowered her by her hands onto the blanket, the fireflies dancing in the distance. Hallie sat down and stretched her legs out in front of her. "What is this?" she asked.

That affection in his eyes had returned in full force. "What did I promise you when we were kids?" he asked.

Hallie was having trouble coming up with an answer, her head so full of questions.

"I said that we wouldn't have the problems that other people have because when you're upset, I'll always make you feel better." He grabbed one of the boxes and held it out to her. "Open it."

Hallie untied the ribbon and ripped the paper off, revealing a white rectangular box that fit in her hand. She took off the lid and peered inside. "A key?" It was unmarked, completely average.

Ben grinned and handed her the second box, a little larger than before. "Open this one and then I'll explain."

She tore at the paper and ribbon, eager to find out what was going on. When she removed the lid, she found a folded stack of papers. Confused, Hallie took them out and straightened them. Her hands began to shake, but her mind hadn't caught up with her subconscious. "Life's Promise Adoption Agency?"

Ben, still kneeling in front of her, took her hands, those blue eyes swallowing her like they always had. "At the beginning of this trip, you made a wish, and I don't even think you knew it. We were standing in your mother's driveway, the car packed for Firefly Beach. You might not remember, but I do, because it was my wish too. You said, 'I wish we could spend time together with nothing hanging over us.'" He let go of one of her hands and grabbed the key from its box. "I told you that when I thought you loved someone else, I could live with that, knowing you were happy. But I don't think you're happy like this, and it's killing me. Because I can make you happy if you'll let me." He held up the key. "This is my house key. I want you to move in with me."

She opened her mouth to say something but he stopped her with a loving look, and she knew that she needed to let him get all of this out first.

"And if you want a family, we can still make our own. Things like hair color and height don't make a child yours. It's the love you share with them that matters. Our family is out there. There's a baby on its way to us right now, waiting for his parents. Or her parents." Ben's eyes glistened with emotion. "We can't let them down."

Hallie could hardly manage the emotion she was feeling, but she couldn't say anything yet. It was clear that Ben had more to tell her.

"Your list is now complete, Hallie. But there's something still on my list."

Ben pulled her up to a standing position and gave her the last gift. She could barely see through her tears to unwrap it, the paper and ribbon falling like feathers onto the sand. In her shaky hand, she held a small box with a single hinge on one side. She lifted the lid and in one moment, all her fears melted away. Nestled in white satin was the most amazing emerald-cut solitaire diamond she'd ever seen in real life. When her eyes found Ben, he was on his knee in front of her.

"Marry me. Grow old with me. I can't guarantee that everything will always be perfect, but what I can promise you is that whenever we face the hard stuff, I will *always* do everything in my power to make you feel better."

Hallie couldn't stop the tears from falling. Ben's love and the lengths to which he would go for her were overwhelming. She couldn't get the answer to move from her throat to her lips. "Yes," she said, a tidal wave of relief engulfing her, knowing without a doubt that everything was going to be okay as long as she and Ben did it together.

Ben stood up, took the ring from the box, and slid it onto her finger. Then he put his hands on her face, and in the midst of a storm of fireflies against the lavender sky, he kissed her.

Chapter Twenty-Nine

"You're gonna be my uncle?" Robby said, throwing his arms around Ben's neck as they all sat at the kitchen table.

"Yep." Ben laughed and then gave Hallie a look. This time she could read every single thought in those eyes of his, and they all pointed toward their future.

"I still can't believe it. I'm so happy," Mama said, dabbing her eyes with a wadded up tissue. She'd been crying tears of joy since Hallie and Ben had come in to tell them all everything. They'd asked them to gather in the kitchen, and before they'd announced their news, Hallie had called to invite Lewis over. He'd come right away. Then, she pulled Aunt Clara's chair out from the table just enough to give her room in case she was there with them. Hallie liked to think she was.

Uncle Hank walked in and handed Hallie the envelope from the safe, then took his seat. Hallie drew it to her slowly, her name scrawled across the outside with the message "Open once you've finished what's in your first letter" in parenthesis.

"Will you all stay with me while I read it to you?" Hallie asked.

No one moved a muscle. They were all there for her. Ben put his hand on hers and kissed her cheek, nuzzling over to her ear for a second, making her smile. Not wanting to wait a minute more, Hallie ripped open the envelope and pulled from it the pink lacy paper that matched the first letter.

Dear Hallie,

If you're reading this, then you've finished the list. Congratulations! But do know the list wasn't important. What meant something to me was the knowledge that you were moving forward, changing up your life. I watched you sinking into the monotony of a nine-to-five job, settling for the first man who offered you security, and I saw you losing your purpose, your God-given talent; it was being chipped away with every punch of your work clock. I don't know if you got married, but if you did, I pray it was for love. I pray that you know the kind of heart-stopping, intoxicating, mind-altering love that I found with your uncle.

Hallie, you are strong. You are capable of everything your heart desires. You deserve to have it all…

Hallie started to read the rest of Aunt Clara's message but then she stopped, her eyes scanning the next sentence, and looked at everyone around the table.

"What does it say?" Sydney asked.

Her inheritance would not be like everyone else's. She read the remainder aloud.

I'm not leaving you money. Instead, I'm giving you another task. I'd like you to call the phone number at the bottom of this letter and introduce yourself. What you do with your life is entirely your choice, Hallie. I hope that I've done my part in helping you realize what you're capable of. I can't wait to hear all about it when we meet again on the other side. I'll be waiting.

All my love,
Aunt Clara

"Uncle Hank, do you know this number?"

Uncle Hank squinted down at Aunt Clara's writing and shook his head. "No idea." Lewis leaned over and then shook his head, baffled.

"Call it!" Sydney urged her, excited.

Ben encouraged her with a nod, so she pulled out her phone, and with everyone around her for support, she tapped out the numbers and hit the call button. Then she put it on speaker and set the phone in the middle of the table, her hands trembling.

The phone pulsed, everyone waiting on pins and needles to find out what Aunt Clara was up to in the final request of her life. Everything about Hallie's inheritance had been unique, and this was no exception. For an instant, she thought about how Aunt Clara's money would have helped her get her business up and running, and how her savings weren't big enough to support the grand plans in her head, but with every ring, she trusted Aunt Clara's judgment, now more than ever.

"Hello?" a woman's voice said from the other end of the line.

"Hello. This is Hallie Flynn." Hallie didn't know what else to say, but she didn't have to say anything more because the woman clapped and laughed on the other side.

"I'm delighted to hear from you, Hallie. I'm assuming you've read your second letter then?"

"Yes." Hallie's curiosity was killing her. She squeezed Ben's hand and he affectionately rubbed hers with his thumb, calming her racing heart. "With whom am I speaking?" she asked.

"This is Sasha Morgan, your aunt's business partner. We've met a few times when you were visiting, remember?"

"Oh, yes. I do. It's nice to talk to you."

"Nice to talk to you too. You see, your aunt has something she wants me to give you."

"Oh?" Hallie looked around the table at the happy faces of her family.

"It seems that you're now the proud owner of fifty percent of Morgan and Flynn Design. And since I'm nearing retirement, if you're interested in maintaining the company, once you have enough capital I'd be willing to offer a full buy-out. The company will be entirely yours one day if you want it, and you have my blessing to run it your way—Clara said you'd almost certainly have some ideas of your own. Is that something you're interested in?"

Hallie clapped her hand over her mouth, tears surfacing yet again. Hallie owned half of the business. That was half of every showroom across the world, all their eighteen offices worldwide, the Morgan and Flynn branded lines, half of Aunt Clara's multimillion-dollar company. It was hers. She would have a team of people supporting every idea she had. She could employ multiple companies to produce her designs. Morgan and Flynn had a client list as big as a phone book…

"Hallie?" Sasha said through the phone, her voice amused. "Clara said it would probably be a shock to you. What do you think?"

"I couldn't be more thrilled," she said, as she took in the adoring faces of all her loved ones together. Aunt Clara had helped Hallie to see how her aunt had viewed her own life, how vivid and full of possibility it could be. Hallie had absolutely no idea what the future would hold for her, and she didn't mind a bit. As she sat among her family, she could hear Aunt Clara's words: *Your life is a blank slate. Dream it up just the way you want it, and then go get it.*

Hallie couldn't wait to do just that.

Epilogue

"Ben!" Hallie called, rushing into their house, dropping her handbag on the floor and nearly knocking into him, her copy of *Southern Rush* wedged between their bodies.

Ben chuckled at her excitement and held Hallie steady, before leaning down and kissing her lips. "What do you have?" he asked, but his doting eyes didn't leave hers until she pulled back.

"The article is published," she said, waving the issue of *Southern Rush* in front of him before taking off toward the living room. Ben chased her, making her giggle as he scooped her up and they collapsed onto the sofa. She and Ben had been waiting to read it for months since her phone interview. Hallie had asked Ben to check the newsstands every day this week, and she'd done the same.

She'd used the *Southern Rush* article to break the news of her transition to Morgan and Flynn, and to unveil her plans for moving the company forward. With an entire staff of creatives, she'd found her first board meeting incredibly inspiring, and she was blown away by the possibilities. Sasha loved her ideas and was open to allowing her to move in the direction that she felt was right.

Ben tossed the magazine on the floor and took her hands, kissing her neck. "Is it good?" he asked.

"Yes!" She squirmed to get free, but his lips found hers.

"We'll read it later," he said, his hands moving along her waist.

She wrapped her arms around him, as Ben simultaneously kissed her and shooed a curious Beau over to his pillow in the corner.

Hallie tipped her head back. "You sure you don't want to read it now?" she asked. "It's really great."

"Hmm…" Ben said, deliberating. Then he started nibbling at her neck. "I can think of something greater than that article."

Hallie laughed and twisted out of his grasp.

Ben sat up with a lighthearted huff. "No, really," he said. "I do have some amazing news that definitely requires celebration."

"What is it?"

She picked up the magazine and tossed it onto the coffee table, on top of a pile of bridal books she'd been perusing over the last few months. Once Gavin had finished the trim, Hallie had reassembled the staff at Starlight Cottage and hired a painting company to refresh the entire estate, including the dock and gazebo where she and Ben planned to say their vows. She'd also redesigned Mama's wedding dress, creating a contemporary slip of satin with beading at the edges, which would also be woven into the dainty band that would encircle a pile of loose curls at the base of her neck.

"I'll tell you when we get to Starlight Cottage," he said.

"At the wedding?"

"Mm-hm."

"But that's months away!"

"You'll have to wait."

"That's not fair. You can't put something like that right in front of me and then not tell me. I'm going to have to convince you…" she said, pressing her lips to his and pushing him back down onto the sofa.

She hovered over him, grinning, holding his wrists as if she could keep him from getting loose.

"I'm proof that waiting is possible. You made me wait a *ridiculous* amount of time…" He broke out of her hold, rolled around until he'd pinned her down, and tickled her, making her shriek with laughter, writhing under him and pawing at his hands to stop.

When he'd slowed, Ben planted a tiny kiss on her lips. "Don't bat your eyelashes at me. You know I can't handle it. It makes me *crazy*." He kissed her again and then pretended to gobble her up.

"Be serious," she said, stopping him. "What is it?"

"The home study is finished. We've been cleared for adoption."

Hallie sat up and threw her hands to her mouth in elation. "We are?" she squeaked.

"Yep. I've already secured Sylvan Park for the *enormous* party we're going to throw to celebrate!"

Hallie laughed, her heart full.

Ben put his hands on her face and looked into her eyes. "We're gonna be amazing parents," he said.

With a grin, she knew he was right, and *this* time, she listened to him.

In Aunt Clara's final letter, she'd told Hallie that she deserved to have it all. She hadn't understood the meaning of that little word "all" until she'd found it. Her entire future had been waiting for her in the house at Firefly Beach. Her destiny had been right there all along; she just had to jump in and grab it.

"What are you thinking about?" Ben asked.

"Grabbing my future." She took hold of his hands and pulled him toward her for another kiss.

A Letter from Jenny

Thank you so much for reading *Summer at Firefly Beach*. I hope it got you longing for those endless summer days, feeling the warm sand on your feet, and the coconut smell of beach cocktails!

If you'd like me to drop you an email when my next book is out, you can **sign up here**:

www.bookouture.com/jenny-hale

I won't share your email with anyone else, and I'll only email you when a new book is released.

If you did enjoy *Summer at Firefly Beach*, I'd love it if you'd write a review. Getting feedback from readers is amazing, and it also helps to persuade other readers to pick up one of my books for the first time.

If you enjoyed this story, and would like a little more summer time on the beach, do check out my other summer novels—*The Summer House*, *Summer at Oyster Bay*, *The Summer Hideaway*, *Summer by the Sea*, and *A Barefoot Summer*.

Until next time!
Jenny x

Acknowledgments

I am eternally grateful to my husband Justin, who has provided unwavering support, weathered the ups and downs of my journey by my side, and allowed me to follow my heart.

To my friends and family, I thank you from the bottom of my heart for all your positivity and encouragement. Another thank you goes to Megan Liesinger for the useful conversation about adoption.

I am so appreciative of the creative community here in Nashville, and delighted that I was welcomed with open arms. I am continually inspired by this new city I call home.

Huge kudos to the folks at Bookouture, the most fantastic publisher around. An enormous thank you to my editor Natasha Harding, who keeps it all running smoothly, even when I throw bumps in her path. To Oliver Rhodes, I couldn't do this without him. I am so thankful for his vision, patience, and leadership.

9 781786 817341